Boss

CEE BOWERMAN

BOOK ONE

COPYRIGHT 2020

This is a work of fiction. Names, characters, places, brands, media, and incidents are either the product of the author's imagination or are used fictitiously. Any resemblance to similarly named places or to persons living or deceased is unintentional.

This is a work of fiction. Names, characters, places, brands, media, and incidents are either the product of the author's imagination or are used fictitiously. Any resemblance to similarly named places or to persons living or deceased is unintentional.

All rights reserved as this is the property of CLBooks, LLC and Jessica Johnson Photography.

Professionally edited by Chrissy Riesenberg

CEE BOWERMAN BOOK LIST

Texas Knights MC

Home Forever

Forever Family

Lucky Forever

Love Forever

Texas Kings MC

Kale

Sonny

Bird

Grunt

Lout

Smokey

Tucker

Kale & Terra (Novella)

John & Mattie

Bear

Daughtry

Hank

Fain

Grady

Conner Brothers Construction

Finn

Angus

Mace

Ronan

Royal - COMING APRIL 2021!

Rojo, TX

Rason & Eliza

Atlas & Addie

Time Served

Boss

Please follow Cee on Facebook, Instagram, and Twitter.

Also, for information on new releases and to catch up with Cee, go to www.ceebowermanbooks.com

A NOTE FROM THE AUTHOR

Dear Reader,

I hope you enjoy getting to know the people of Tenillo, Texas. In this book, I'll introduce the members of the Time Served MC and share a little bit of their histories as you get to know Boss and Jenn while they find their way to each other.

Of course, this series goes hand-in-hand with the Ciara St. James series that is also set in Tenillo. You can get to know her people in the Ares Infidels MC series written by her. She and I are working together with the characters, locations, and timelines so that if you read this book, then the first in her series, then my second, and her second (and so on and so on), you'll see both sides of the stories about the residents of Tenillo and the adventures they have while they work together to clean up their town.

I've been very lucky to get to work with Ciara, and she and I have formed a friendship that I believe will last beyond our writing collaboration.

Another friend I've made in this process is Jennifer - the woman who catches Boss's eye and then his heart. I based quite a bit of Jenn on my friend, right down to how much she loves animals, collects tin signs in her kitchen, and absolutely loves s'mores in any form. Jennifer has become a good friend and I value her input while I'm writing, and enjoy her funny personality every single time we talk. I was so happy to give her a story, and even if it's fiction, let her live out a few things she's always dreamed of.

I hope you enjoy this book and all the ones to come, and I'd like to thank you for giving me a chance to entertain you with the people who run around in my imagination. I enjoy bringing them to life in the hopes that you, as a reader, will enjoy getting to know them.

Love and laughter,

Cee

PROLOGUE

ONE YEAR AGO

BOSS

"Did you guys hear about that home invasion that happened a few blocks from here last night?" Tom asked as he sat down across from me at the table.

I glanced up from my phone at the other men sitting around me. I smiled when they started grumbling things like 'What's this world coming to?', 'Damn thieves need to get a job!', and my personal favorite, 'Back in my day someone broke into your house, they got shot!'.

The violent comment was grumbled by Pop, the oldest of our coffee group and my mentor, employer, and good friend. He was 79, but still spry and feisty. The man kept me on my toes, and he enjoyed every minute of it.

Pop's group of friends who met for coffee somewhere in town almost every morning were other businessmen and members of our community. Harvey Korbyn owned Harvey's Garage. Jack Bentley owned a real estate company and was getting ready to retire and leave it all to his two sons. Hal Markham owned a hardware store but was mostly retired while his son handled the day-to-day operations. Pop's friend David Tenillo was a farmer whose family started our town. Tom Dolby, the owner of the donut place where we were gathered today, usually joined us between customers to gossip with his friends.

On most days, unless one of David Tenillo's kids, Harvey's nephew, or Jack's oldest son Ben showed up, I was the youngest guy in the room. At 49, that was an oddity, but when the old guys started saying things like "Back in my day . . .", I felt like a youngster again. Then I'd do something like turn my head wrong and wrench my neck and remember how 'back in my day', I could do things like that without pain. That was when I turned into the old guy grumbling about shit.

As if that simple thought was a reminder, I realized it had been a few weeks since I hit up the chiropractor. I needed to make an appointment soon.

"Did you hear me, son?" Harvey asked as he rapped his knuckles on the table to get my attention.

"Sorry, I was wool-gathering. What did I miss?"

"You should run for chief of police so you can get this town back in order and take the bad element out," Jack explained. "I'd vote for you."

"What are we voting on?" Kye Korbyn, Harvey's nephew, asked as he pulled up a chair to join us. Kye was ex-military and the president of a local motorcycle club, the Ares Infidels. He went by the name Sin, but the old men at this table still referred to him as Kye since they'd known him his entire life.

"Boss should run for office," Harvey reiterated. "We think he could get a handle on all this crime that's getting out of hand. Jimmy Don was a great cop, but he's getting up there in years. He's decided to retire before he's too old to do all the fishing he has planned. Boss was a cop back in the day.

He could definitely be the new chief of police."

"Well, there ya go." Sin gave a firm nod, but I could tell that he was holding back a smile. "The elders have spoken, and that's how it's going to be. Howdy, Chief."

"Spoken or not, I don't know that the town would elect an ex-con to be in charge of their police department. Is that even legal?"

"*Can* an ex-con be elected to office?" Jack asked the table in general. There were shrugs all around, and he reached for his phone. "Let's find out then."

"Wouldn't Sin be a better bet as chief? He's a veteran, a law abiding citizen, and it's not illegal for him to carry a gun. It would make more sense to nominate him, wouldn't it?" I threw Sin under the bus as I asked the group at large. That got a low growl from Sin, but it made me smile.

I could tell that all the men at the table wanted to reply, but they were holding back, probably to spare my tender feelings. Pop, on the other hand, didn't give a shit. "He's an honorable man and would stick to the letter of the law. You'd just stuff some half-dead drug dealer in a dumpster and let him bleed out while he made peace with his maker."

Sin had just taken a sip of his coffee and started sputtering and coughing violently. He was just as likely to stuff a drug dealer in a dumpster, but if the old guys wanted to believe otherwise, we'd let them.

"Google says that he can get elected, but he can't take office unless his record's been expunged," Jack explained. "We'd have to get a judge to do that before he could take office."

"See? I can't do it. There isn't a judge that's going to wipe my record clean."

"You still golfing buddies with Judge McAlister?" Pop asked Tom. When Tom nodded, Pop said, "Give him a call, and get him down here. See what he can do."

"You guys are serious?" Sin chuckled as he looked at the men around the table. When they all agreed, he smiled over at me. "It might not be a bad idea, you know."

"Shit. It's never going to happen."

"If they do figure out how to get you elected, will you take it? They have a point about your methods. That might be just what we need around here to turn the tide."

"We can get him elected," Harvey assured us.

Hal agreed, "Yeah, we can!"

"If by some miracle you old geezers make it happen and figure out how to get me into the chief's position, I'll take office and do things right," I assured the group, knowing it would never happen. I'd served 10 years for second-degree murder. They didn't have enough evidence to prosecute me for the other three murders they'd accused me of back in the small town where I was a cop, or I'd still be in prison to this day. "Now, I've got to get on the road. My boss is a dick, and he'll dock my pay if I don't get my shit done today."

"Asshole," Pop hissed at me. "I'm a damn good boss. Anyone else would fire your ass for that smart mouth of yours."

"Good day, Chief," Sin called out with a nod as I stood up from the table.

"Don't encourage them."

"You just threw down the gauntlet with some of the stubbornest men in the state, and you don't think they're going to figure out a way to prove you wrong? You're sadly mistaken, Boss. You're going to be wearing a badge come January 1st."

"If that happens, I'll be sure and deputize you," I warned him. "If I'm going down, I'm taking you with me."

JENNIFER

"Your next applicant is here," Connie, my assistant, said from the doorway of my office.

"Who is it?"

"Her name is Farrah Anderson. She's the one with four years of experience at Andersen Imaging."

"Hmm. Go ahead and bring her back. Will you get us some coffee, please?"

"Of course."

I hit a sequence of buttons on my keyboard, and the monitors in my office blinked once. A picture of a beautiful white sand beach with clear blue water appeared on all six screens. I'd taken the picture on my vacation with Ethan a few years ago. Every time I saw it, I could hear the waves coming in and feel the ocean breeze in my hair.

Connie pushed the door open and led in a petite blonde woman with red-rimmed eyes. I stood up and held my hand out to her as I introduced myself and then I asked, "Have we met before? You look familiar."

"I met you in the spa at a Cabo San Lucas resort a few years ago."

"That's it!" I recalled with a smile. I'd bumped into her as I turned a corner and had been taken aback at how freaked out she was when I helped her pick up the things she'd dropped. She'd been a timid mouse of a thing and had stared at me the entire time. "What a crazy twist of fate that you ended up here today! We're a million miles from that beautiful resort, aren't we?"

"Yes, ma'am."

"Well, Connie will be bringing us some coffee in just a minute, but let's go ahead and get started. Tell me about yourself, Farrah."

"I lied," Farrah blurted out. "I'm not looking for a job. I just needed to talk to you, and I didn't know what else to say to get you to see me."

"You could have just made an appointment," I suggested as I studied the young woman. She had tears in her eyes now, and I noticed her hands were shaking as they hovered over her stomach. "What do you need to talk to me about?"

"I'm pregnant!"

"Congratulations?"

"Ethan is the father, but he refused to tell you about the baby because you'd divorce him."

"What?" My voice was deadly calm now, and I felt every muscle in my body start to tense while I waited for her to repeat herself. I must be having one of those silent strokes or something because I could almost swear she'd just said my husband knocked her up.

"I met him five years ago when he was a guest lecturer in my computer technology class at UW. He took me to dinner that night, and we've been together ever since."

"Together? You and my husband?"

Farrah wailed, "I'm sorry! He said that you were sick and he couldn't divorce you. You'd just had surgery!"

Ethan and I had tried to have children for years. Five years ago, I'd had one final procedure to remove the blockage in my fallopian tubes and attempt to retrieve some of my eggs in the hopes that I'd be able to have a viable pregnancy. When that didn't work, the already tense atmosphere between my husband and I was just exacerbated.

When I didn't respond to her, Farrah continued, "He said you were depressed, and he was afraid you'd kill yourself if he left. I thought it was all going to be okay. I thought that I could deal with having to share him with you. But now that I'm having his baby, I just can't do it anymore."

"Share him with me?" Even though I was freaking out on the inside, I was oddly proud that my voice sounded so calm. I didn't sound nearly as crazy as I felt right now. "You thought you'd share *my* husband with me."

"I thought it was the only way. He swore he'd tell you about us as soon as you were better, but then I saw your Ted Talk about women in business on YouTube, and you seemed just fine!"

"Ethan's been having an affair with you for five years?"

"It will be five years in three months."

"Oh, three months makes all the difference," I said sarcastically. "It's not entirely horrible that you've been fucking my husband until you hit that five-year mark. It's just standard bullshit before five years, but after you hit that milestone, they give you a medal. I guess you actually get a baby to go along with it."

"Jennifer?" Connie whispered as she set the tray I'd requested on the corner of my desk.

"Connie, Farrah's not applying for a job with the company; she's here for the trophy wife position. She can't have any coffee because she's pregnant with Ethan's baby."

"Oh, shit."

"I'll make you a deal, Farrah," I said as I sat down behind my desk. I folded my hands in front of me and watched the young woman glance around the room before her eyes finally lit on mine. "If you'll keep the fact that you came to see me between us for the next few days, I'll give you Ethan on a silver platter. He'll be all yours, and you'll never even have to think of me again - let alone, fucking show up in my office."

"You'll give him a divorce?"

"Of course! And I'll even make sure he gets everything he deserves."

SIX MONTHS AGO

JENNIFER

"I'm going to miss you too," I told Connie before I pulled her into a tight hug. "We'll talk all the time, and after a few weeks in charge, you'll be so pissed off at me for leaving this shitshow in your hands that you'll be cursing me instead of missing me."

"We both know I've secretly been running the place for years," Connie whispered before she let me go. "I hit the jackpot when I found you. It was the only place I'd ever worked where my boss cussed as much as I did."

"You have been running the place, but now you've got the title to go with the power. And if someone doesn't like your mouth, fire their ass. Seriously, though, I'm just a phone call away if you have any questions, and I can fly back if you need me."

"I can't believe you're still not sure where you're going."

"I haven't decided yet, but when I do, you'll be the first and only person I'll tell."

"Fresh start. I know. I'll keep my lips sealed even if someone tortures me."

"You're the only one I want to keep in contact with, and if Ethan finds out where I am, he'll figure out a way to harass me."

"He's like a woman scorned."

"I think he was angrier about what I did to his clothes than he was when they told him he lost all of his shares in the company."

"I don't understand how you stayed married to that dick for so long."

"He broke me down until I thought no one else would want me," I admitted. "I *almost* feel sorry for Homewrecker Barbie now that he's her problem and not mine. But I don't have time for anything to do with Ethan, his girlfriend, or his upcoming fatherhood. Instead, I'm going off into the wilds of America to find myself again."

"Maybe you can find a real man while you're out there in those wide open spaces."

"I don't need a real man. I've got something better. It has batteries and only makes noise when I push a button. I don't need anything more than that."

"You have to leave now? Stay and let me take you to lunch."

"My new truck is packed and ready to go. I'm excited, and so is Moe."

"Moe gets excited when a bird flies past the window."

I glanced down at my dog and smiled. I was holding the leash loosely in my hand, and he didn't even care. I'd been standing in one place for too long, and he'd decided it was nap time. He was on his back, spread-eagled with his junk out there for the world to see with his tongue hanging out of the side of his mouth.

"As much as I hate to interrupt his nap time, I'm going to load him up and hit the road. I'll get in touch after a while and check in, but for now, I'm just going to work toward relaxing and letting the stress of the last 20 years roll off of me. Once I find the new me, I might show up at a board meeting or something just to keep everyone on their toes."

"Be safe, Jennifer."

"You, too, Connie. You'll find that there are just as many bad guys in corporate America as there are out on the streets. Watch yourself."

"I will."

"Come on, Moe. It's time to hit the road." Moe opened one eye and then slowly rolled from his back to his side before he sighed heavily and got back to his feet. "You can sleep in the truck, lazy ass."

With one final wave, I glanced at Connie and the building behind her where I'd spent most of the last two decades. After a while, I'd miss her, but I'd never miss this building or what it represented - a sham of a marriage and my lost chance at motherhood. As far as I was concerned, the whole place could burn to the ground.

THREE MONTHS AGO

BOSS

"Mr. Barnes, it is the ruling of the court that because of your excellent standing as a member of the Tenillo community,that your conviction and subsequent time served in prison be expunged from your record. I'll be happy to welcome you as chief of police when you take office."

I turned and glanced at the men in the row behind my chair in the courtroom and saw that every single one was smiling. For months, they'd been harping about making me the top cop and had even gone so far as to start campaigning on my behalf. Last month, I'd nearly wrecked my motorcycle when I glanced up and saw my face on a billboard with the caption, "Elect Tyger Barnes for Tenillo Chief of Police." It was then that I realized the old geezers were serious about this shit.

Last week, I'd been greeted at the gas pump outside a local convenience store by a man who said, "Good morning, Chief Barnes!"

Without lifting a finger, giving a single speech or doing a damn thing to help, I'd won the election the day before. People expected me to take office at the beginning of next year, but that couldn't happen with my record.

When I'd been contacted yesterday afternoon by one of my friends and club brothers, Captain, regarding today's court proceedings, I'd gone along with it, thinking no judge in his right mind would expunge the record of a convicted murderer. I'd get out of taking office on a technical default and then I'd be free and clear.

Even my lawyer was an ex-con, for Christ's sake. Captain, or Auggie Brass as the rest of the world called him, earned his law degree while he served 20 years for murder, but that didn't seem to bother any of the people he represented or the court we were standing in now.

Pop and his cronies had taken care of my felony record right along with my election. I'd almost bet that they enjoyed the irony of having another murderer represent me today.

The row of men behind me weren't the only crazies in the room. The old judge in front of me was just as fucking nuts as they were, and I realized that he was in league with them. All of a sudden, I was no longer just some ex-con. I was an elected official who'd be sworn into office on January 1st.

What the fuck sort of wormhole had I entered? Up was down, and left was right. Nothing made sense anymore. I fought the urge to glance around for hidden cameras. I was being Punk'd. There was no other explanation for the shit that was going on around me.

"Court is adjourned."

When I stood up and turned around to face the crazy men, I ignored the other people in the courtroom who were calling out their congratulations. Pop, Harvey, Hal, Jack, and Tom were seated shoulder to shoulder, and all five of them were grinning like loons.

I glanced at the men seated in the row behind the geezers and saw Sin Korbyn and a few members of his MC. They were just as stunned as I was, but they were also just as amused as the old guys sitting in front of them.

"It's time to celebrate," Pop told everyone. "Lunch is on me. Maddy's expecting us, and she even made your favorite dessert."

"Since he's a cop now, shouldn't we have donuts?" Saint, another man from the Ares Infidels MC, asked the group.

"We'll have bacon at Maddy's as an homage to his law enforcement title," Captain told the men with a bark of laughter. "He's got the next four years to eat donuts."

BOSS

"Would you like a cup of coffee, Chief?" I heard a woman ask from the doorway behind me. It took me a second to realize she was talking to me even though I was the only person in the room. I'd been the Tenillo police chief for two hours now and had just managed to get away from the press conference and my first official speech less than 20 minutes ago.

And now, after such an exciting morning, I was staring out of my office window wondering what size U-Haul truck I'd need to rent to pack up all my shit and leave town.

I glanced back at the door and saw Julia, the office manager, leaning against the door frame. Julia and I had quite a history, but we also had an unspoken agreement that we'd never mention our former 'relationship' that mostly consisted of quickies up against the side of her car in the bar parking lot or stuffed into one of the stalls of the bar bathroom. Julia was, I assume, happily married to one of the town council members, and from what I'd gathered during our conversation, today was her first day back after having her first child a month or so ago.

"Sure, Julia. That would be great."

"Cream and sugar?"

"Is it that powdered shit?"

Julia let out a laugh and then nodded. "Yeah, it's the powdered kind. Want me to go to the store and grab some cream?"

"Is that part of your job description?"

"I'm the office manager, Chief Barnes. Ordering supplies is one of my duties, so, yes, buying you some real cream for your coffee actually is in my job description."

"Anything but hazelnut creamer. That stuff tastes like shit."

"I'll remember that. Anything else?"

"Is there a file somewhere with names, job descriptions, and the like?"

"You have access to the HR files. There's a link on the desktop screen that says HR, and you'll be required to put in your password for access."

"Okay, I guess I should do some homework while you're gone."

"I'll hurry back. Myrna is in her office. She can get the phones and the door. She'll come get you if she needs you."

"Thanks, Julia," I told her with a smile. "It's nice to have a friendly face here in the office."

"Of course, Chief Barnes. It was a pleasure to meet you this morning, and I look forward to working with you."

I was right. Julia and I *did* have an unspoken agreement, and apparently I needed to develop amnesia just like she had. I'd wait to do that until after I'd looked through the personnel files and figured out if there were any other landmines I needed to avoid. I hadn't exactly been celibate since I got out. Since I came directly to Tenillo after 10 years in prison, I'd fucked my way through a good part of the 30 and above female population of town during the first few months I was here.

It was really going to suck if I knew any more of my employees in the biblical sense. I didn't know how working with a one-night stand or a weekend fling would play out in the long run, but I was sure that if there were more around here, our encounters wouldn't be nearly as seamless as the one I'd had just now.

"Have you heard through the grapevine if there might be any employees I've *met* before?"

"As far as females, there's only Myrna Chavez, Chelsea Robbins, Lorene Powell, Rhonda Goodwin, and me. We're all happily married women, and each for more than 10 years. I sincerely doubt that you *met* any of them before today."

"When I talked to the former chief a few weeks ago, he said you were worth more than ocean front property. I think he was right."

"I'll be back soon. My number's programmed into your phone if you think of something else you need." Julia turned around and walked back into the main area of the police department, and I heard her call out to the women who were working before the bell over the front door announced her exit.

I'd just sat down at my desk when the door chimed

again. A few seconds later, I heard my friend and club brother's voice talking to Myrna.

"Let him back, Myrna," I said loudly before she had a chance to walk back to ask. The inner office area was surrounded by a chest high desk and bulletproof safety glass with gaps here and there for people to slide items and paperwork through as needed. A person entering from outside either had to have a badge to scan, or they had to be buzzed in by one of the office employees. I'd need to give the ladies in the office a list of the men who could always come straight back. That included my brothers from my motorcycle club and the old geezers who put me in this office in the first place. I waited just a second and then saw Hook's smiling face when he walked through my door. "What are you smiling about, fucker?"

"Chief, is that any way to talk to a member of the community you vowed to protect and serve? I voted for you after all."

"Fuck you, Hook. You're not even allowed to vote. Don't you have a goat to romance or something?"

"That was below the belt even for you, man," Hook grumbled as he sat down in the chair across the desk from me. "Just because I'm a vet doesn't mean you guys should make so many animal jokes. It's just fucking gross."

"But it shuts you up every time."

"How's life in elected office?"

"I've been here for an hour. I haven't even met with my officers yet. I'll see all of them at shift change this afternoon."

"Old guy didn't introduce you while the two of you had tea and crumpets last week?"

"Do I look like the kind of man who eats crumpets? What the fuck is a crumpet anyway?"

"We'll have to ask Stamp. I've got no idea."

"How's his online shit going anyway? Last I heard, he was traveling to hole in the wall restaurants and dive bars, eating their food, and getting paid to do it."

"He's still doing that and making a mint at it. He does his virtual cooking lessons from the road while he's in their kitchens, so it mixes the two things. He's a hit, just like Preacher."

"I can't believe that Preacher found a job where he gets paid to share his crazy shit with the world."

"Not all conspiracy theories are crazy," Hook argued. "Some of the shit he says makes a lot of sense."

"Aliens? Really?"

"I didn't say all of it, just some of it, but people eat that shit up."

"It probably helps that Preacher looks the way he does. Same with Stamp."

Both Preacher and Stamp were handsome men who caught almost every woman's eye. We were all members of the same motorcycle club which was ironically named Time Served. I'd been appointed president when the last one passed away suddenly from a massive coronary. Hook was also a member of our MC along with quite a few other men who didn't live in Tenillo. Kitty, Chef, Bug, and Santa all lived in other places, and we got together a few times a year to catch up, usually around the holidays.

All of us who belonged to the MC were convicted felons who'd been chosen by Pop to live at his compound outside of town when we were released. Pop's son had been in trouble with the law years ago and served more than 10 years in prison. When he got out, he couldn't find a place to live, and no one would hire him. His only support system was Pop and the other employees of the companies Pop owned. Pop's son ended up falling back in with the same crowd and situations that had put him behind bars in the first place and died running from the cops while he was transporting a car full of drugs and guns

Pop had never gotten over losing his son but took his grief and started a club of sorts. A club that welcomed men like me and my brothers who had served time and didn't have a support system to fall back on when we were released.

Somehow Pop had become acquainted with a chaplain who traveled through the prison system. The chaplain would occasionally encounter an inmate he thought would do well under Pop's supervision once he was out. I was one of those inmates.

I'd been in prison for more than a decade before I got released and had no family, no home, and no job. If I hadn't settled in and started working for Pop at his scrap yard, I would most likely be behind bars right now. The same could be said for the other men in the club.

Pop had started the Time Served MC years ago to help give the men he saved a sense of brotherhood and family.

He'd work with each newly released man to get a motorcycle up and running and give them so much more than a bike. He was actually giving them a hobby that they could use to help release their aggression and worry, the skill to take care of it, and a vehicle to let them find freedom that they craved.

As time went on, most of the inmates found their path in life and with help from Pop, figured out how to support themselves before they moved out into the free world. Pop would have one who fell down and ended up back in prison every now and then, but for the most part, the men he helped became successful, productive citizens. And sometimes, as in my unique case, they became an elected official licensed to carry a gun.

Our MC was loosely based in Tenillo with men all over the US, since they'd moved on after adjusting to life on the free side of the razor wire. I knew all of the members since I was the prez, but there was a core group of men I knew better than the others. We'd clicked and formed an inner club of our own. We kept in touch even when we didn't have club business to discuss.

Hook was one of that group. He'd moved off of Pop's property after a year or two but stuck close by and started working with another veterinarian in the area. Just last year, he'd purchased a huge plot of land outside of town along with the animal sanctuary that stood right in the middle of it. The old veterinarian he'd worked for retired and let Hook have everything for a song because he knew how dedicated he was to the animals.

And since we were all a little twisted, we liked to tease Hook about how much he *loved* the animals.

"Did you just come to fuck with me, or did you need something?"

"I was in town for supplies and thought I'd drop by to laugh at you for a few," Hook admitted.

"I'm glad you did. I've been tossing something around my head for a few days, and I'd like your opinion."

"Yes, you need a haircut and a face lift. And you look fat today. You should lay off the donuts," Hook quipped.

"Fuck you." I glanced up at Hook's face and for some reason a spot on the wall behind him caught my eye. It was a small hole, not even as big around as a pencil eraser, but with technology these days, there could be a camera in there complete with audio and night vision. I stood up and said, "I've got one of the office ladies getting creamer, but I feel like a walk down to the coffee shop. I think you owe me a cup, don't you?"

"You *are* my illustrious new elected official. I guess I should buy," Hook answered as he stood. It looked like he was staring at me but then I realized he was looking at the bookshelf over my shoulder. "I've got an hour or so before my first appointment. Let's head out."

I followed Hook out and glanced down at the doorknob as I walked past it. It had a shitty little lock, and I'd need to fix that issue immediately. If my gut was right, someone had bugged my office, and I didn't want to give them an opportunity to reconfigure after I'd tracked their equipment down and shut it off.

"Myrna, I'm going to Jitters for a cup of coffee with my friend here," I told the dispatcher when I stopped in her office. "If you need me, I've got my cell."

"Yes, sir, Chief Barnes."

Hook waited until we were down the front steps before he said anything else. "I think there's a camera or some sort of microphone stuck in the space between the third shelf and the side of that bookcase."

"And there's a hole in the wall behind the chair where you were sitting that probably has a camera in it. I'm out of my element here. Sixteen years ago, I knew about all the newest gadgets and shit. Now I've seen enough television to know they can hear you from farther away and record everything you're doing if they've got the right equipment."

"They can do that with doorbells now, Boss."

"Yeah, yeah," I grumbled. "I was already thinking I'd like to ask Sin to come sit in on the shift change meeting this afternoon when I meet the majority of the officers. Now I think I might need him to determine if I'm under surveillance too."

"Shit. That old man that was chief must have been on the take for years. I wonder who was paying him and what they wanted him to ignore."

"No fucking telling. Give me a second, and I'll call Sin to see if he can help me out."

"Why do you want him at the meeting?"

"I don't know what branch he was in, but I can tell by looking at him he was in charge of something hardcore. He's got that air about him. I'd imagine that the government taught him or one of his guys how to read people for their tells and tics. I can do that to an extent, but it's just my gut. There's no science involved."

"Like Criminal Minds."

"Exactly." I held up my finger. Sin answered on the first ring. I told him what I suspected and asked if he could meet me soon to talk about a few things. Once I hung up, I looked over at Hook and chuckled. "He's at Jitters with a couple of his guys."

"Great minds think alike. Want me to take off?"

"Nah, come in with me. You might think of something from a different angle. Great minds and all, remember?"

"Both of you were right. There were three cameras at different angles in your office, all wired for sound. We found eight more cameras throughout the building along with a tracking device on your fancy new ride," Sin told me just minutes after I sat down across from him inside The Hangout, a restaurant/bar that his club owned and operated.

"Fuck." When we met this morning, I'd asked him to sit in on the meeting and have his men search the rest of the building while I had everyone occupied. Now I was in his club's hangout getting a status report on what they'd found.

"My guys shut down all transmissions while you were talking and took everything offline so whoever is monitoring the office couldn't see who was inspecting their equipment.

Everyone else in the building was inside that conference room, and I doubt they were looking at their phones to notice that not a single one of them had a signal for about 20 minutes."

I was shocked that he could shut down all signals at one time, but I wasn't surprised such a thing was possible. "Did you install the new cameras?"

Phantom, another Ares Infidel, laughed for a second and then said, "We did a much better job of hiding our work than they did. That's for damn sure."

"So I'll be able to see who goes to figure out why their equipment isn't working."

"Exactly," Sin assured me as he slid two keyrings across the table. "I'm sure you noticed your shiny new lock on the doorknob. We also installed a deadbolt. Here are the keys."

"I left the note just like you asked," Phantom told me with a smile. "I thought that was pretty funny. When the guy sees it, you'll have to screenshot the look on his face so I can hang it up in my office."

"I'll do that. By now, they know their shit is offline, and my office door is unlocked. I bet they go in some time tonight or early tomorrow morning."

"We sent your guy the links and logins for the equipment we installed, and he said he won't have a problem getting a handle on the system," Phantom told me with a smile. "If he needs anything, just have him call me."

"Preacher should be able to take care of it," I assured

the men. "He's a techie, and by now, he's probably researched and gone on a rant about the equipment you guys installed. We'll see it on YouTube tomorrow, I'm sure."

"Preacher?" Phantom asked with obvious awe in his voice. "Your guy is Preacher, the conspiracy theorist? I heard he died."

"He probably started that rumor," Hook chuckled. "He does shit like that just to see how long it takes for word to get around."

"What was your take on the men today?" I asked Sin once the other men were quiet. Sin pulled a list out of his pocket and unfolded it before he slid it across the table to me.

"There were 116 men total from both groups and then the women in the office. You didn't include any cleaning staff or other office employees in the meeting, so I didn't get a bead on them. However, there are 14 officers, including one captain, three sergeants, and three detectives, who were exhibiting behaviors that make me think they're a little off-color if not completely shady as fuck. If you've got some of the higher-ups involved in bad shit, I guarantee there are more than 14 of the officers involved too. It's the law of averages, and the bigger fish need minions to do their dirty work."

"There's a lot of shit going on in this town, and you don't hear much about arrests. I've started to wonder if some of them might just be lazy, or if they're on the take. Same thing with the detectives. We've got a dozen of them, and they can't figure out an armed robbery even after they were given tapes of the suspect *and* the license number."

"Shit. I didn't know all that."

"There was a report on my desk this morning about open cases, the information they've got, and what's been done up to this point. It's updated for me before I come in every day."

"That's handy," Hook said with a laugh. "Crime statistics with your morning cup of coffee. Start the day out with some depressing bullshit."

"And it's based on what they turn in, so half of it very well could be bullshit, especially since they aren't showing many arrests or closed cases." I took a sip of my beer and blew out a long breath. This was turning into much more of a clusterfuck than I imagined I'd run into during my first day on the job. "I guess they're inept and crooked more than they're just lazy.

"That's not good. They could be fucking off all day at home and just blowing smoke on that report so that it looks like they've done something. Or they could be out starting fires and doing illegal shit on the clock."

"Shit, Hook. You're just a fountain of rainbows and positivity, aren't you?" Sin asked my brother before he tilted his beer up for a sip. "I agree, though. They're probably not lazy as much as they're crooked. You've got your work cut out for you, Boss. That's for damn sure."

"Considering all of the red tape I had to go through, none of my brothers from the club can get inside the department to serve as my backup. However, out of all your law-abiding, military-experienced, honorable men, you wouldn't happen to have a guy who's always dreamed of being the deputy chief of the Tenillo Police Department, do you?"

Sin turned his head and looked at one of his club brothers sitting at the end of the table. The man, Wrecker, put his hands up like Sin was pointing a gun at him. Sin smiled, and Wrecker shook his head back and forth as he shot both of us a glare. When Sin's smile got wider, Wrecker finally sighed and said, "Both of you are fucking crazy. I'm retired, remember?"

JENNIFER

"Ms. McCool?" The young man in charge of the construction crew called out to me through the screen door on the back porch.

"Come in!" I yelled from the living room as I frantically searched for the remote. Again.

"If you don't mind, I'd rather not."

"Well, shit," I whispered while I used the arm of the couch to brace myself as I stood from my knees. I yelled loud enough for the kid to hear me, "I'll be right there!"

I rushed through the living room to the back porch and opened the screen door for the young man before I said, "I'm so sorry. I forgot your name again!"

"It's Tyler, ma'am. I'm sorry to bother you, but can you come get that rooster again? I'm not sure how he escaped, but he has two of my men up on top of the platform we're building, and he won't let them down."

"None of you guys have ever dealt with a rooster before?" I asked Tyler as I walked past him out the door. I could see the two employees he was talking about, and he hadn't been exaggerating. Ed Earl had them pinned on top of the platform they'd been working on.

"I'm from the panhandle, and I was raised on a farm, ma'am, but I've never seen anything like that. It's just not natural."

"He's just a cranky little rooster."

"Cranky?"

"Well, look at how he's behaving!" I pointed at the rooster who had the men pinned. "That's what you meant when you said it's not natural, wasn't it?"

"No, I meant I've never seen a rooster that size before."

"He's a Brahma rooster. I've got the vet coming to check him out again because he's just getting meaner. He's nice to me, but I'm the only one."

"Have you had him long?"

"I just bought this place six months ago. Ed Earl came with the house as did the chickens."

"Did the people before you leave because of him?" Tyler asked with a straight face.

"I didn't think to ask, but you might be onto something there. He attacked one of the other men from your company when they worked on the house. The poor guy never came back."

"I remember that."

We were finally close enough to the pen for me to get involved. The second he heard my voice, Ed Earl turned toward me and hurried my direction. Tyler veered away so that he was out of his line of sight, and the men who'd been stranded jumped down with relief.

I opened the gate and let Ed Earl out so he could hang with me on the porch for a while, and as he passed me, he nuzzled his head against my thigh and made a noise deep in his chest. I didn't know much about roosters, but I thought this behavior might be considered abnormal somehow.

I'd researched and figured out that my guy was a Blue Partridge Brahma rooster and that he was probably 12 pounds or so. Because of his breed, he had feathers all the way down his legs and over his feet, and that made him look like he was standing on some huge paws, rather than the regular skinny chicken legs and claws.

All in all, this guy looked like he'd been introduced to gamma rays as a chick and had then turned into a beautifully feathered version of the Incredible Hulk. His hens were all different shades, but also relatively large. My other rooster and a few of the hens were normal-sized and looked like the chickens you saw on television, which made this guy and his harem seem even bigger.

"Cool Cat!" I heard a man's voice, and I looked toward the walkway that wound around my house. I smiled when I realized that it was the veterinarian whose property bordered mine. It was always nice to visit with him, and it didn't hurt that he looked so damn good too. "Sorry I'm late. I was having coffee with a friend, and time got away from me."

"You're not late. It's still morning. I was just about to take the big guy inside and have another cup of coffee. He's being a menace today and won't let the guys finish up."

"Is that Tyler?" Doc York asked as he tilted his head to peer around me at the crew in the yard.

"You know Tyler? He's such a nice guy, and he's so polite. I've told him more than once that he can just walk into the house if he's looking for me, but he never does it. He stands right there on the porch and calls for me to come to the door. He probably thinks I'm some crazy person, so he's afraid to go inside."

"I'm sure he's got his reasons for staying on the porch and thinking you're crazy isn't one of them," Doc York said in an odd tone. "Good to know he's following the rules, though."

I ignored my first instinct to ask him what he meant by that rules comment and instead asked, "Will you come in for a cup of coffee?"

"I'd be honored. So, Ed Earl is feeling feisty today?" Doc York was asking about the rooster and unconsciously rubbing his hand where he'd been bitten last time he came to visit.

Even as docile as Ed Earl seemed right now, if Doc York got too close to me, he'd attack. For some reason, the rooster had fallen head over heels for me and liked to be right by my side all the time. Luckily, my dog, the animal that was supposed to be my constant companion, didn't give a shit that he'd been replaced. If anything, he enjoyed the time off. Although, if I started taking Ed Earl out in the truck instead of Moe, there might be a problem.

Considering that the rooster was bigger than my beagle, I wasn't positive who would come out the winner of that fight.

"He is as ornery as ever. I'm wondering if it has something to do with the food he's been on since your last visit."

We'd just stepped onto the patio, and Dr. York held the door open for me to go inside first. I glanced back and saw that Ed Earl was right behind me and thanked God once again that my entire first floor was all tile and hardwood.

"I think he's just attached to you, and he's having an identity crisis."

"A crisis?"

"He thinks he's your pet, and you're his human."

"Well, he is. I am. We are. I mean . . . I don't know what I mean. Can a person have a pet rooster, Doctor York?"

"We've known each other long enough that you should just call me Hook, darlin', and you can have any kind of pet you want. One of my brothers from the club has a pet skunk."

"Eww."

"She's completely domesticated and doesn't have her scent glands anymore. She thinks she's a cat."

"You're kidding me."

"Nope. Her name is Elvira, and she hangs out with the three cats he found just a month or so after he found her."

"That's sweet."

"I'll tell him you think so. Now about that coffee."

I walked over to the pot and poured us both a cup of the fresh brew, and since he'd been at my house more than once, I knew exactly how he took his coffee. I'd always resisted calling him by his nickname, even though he'd given me one of my own. Doc York was more than handsome. He was charming, funny, and intelligent. Still, for some reason, I didn't want to give him any ideas that this was anything but a professional relationship and maybe a friendship.

I decided to just put that right out there, so I said, "I'll call you Hook since you call me Cool Cat, although I'm not sure how in the world that moniker came about.."

"Your last name is McCool, darlin'. I'm not sure how no one's called you that before."

"Well, you're the first," I told him as I slid his mug in front of him. "And just so you know, I'm glad we're friends."

"Have I given you any indication that we might not be?"

"No, I just wanted to . . ."

"You wound me, Cool Cat. Shooting me down before I ever even thought of taking a shot."

"Well, I just wanted to make sure we're on the same page."

"Same book, same chapter, same page, darlin'," Hook assured me as he lifted his mug up and held it halfway across the table in a toast.

I tapped my mug against his and said, "Good."

"And, as friends, I came over here to not only see about your guard bird but to give you some good news and ask a favor in the process."

"Do tell."

"I know you said you'd always wanted a llama, but I was wondering what you know about alpacas."

"I know they're a smaller version of llamas. Right?"

"You could say that. Alpacas are smaller and more domesticated. Some people even keep them as house pets."

"You're kidding."

"Nope," Hook said as he pulled his phone out of his pocket. "Here, look at this picture. This is a llama." Hook turned his phone so I could see the picture of the llama, then he scrolled through his photos for a second and said, "This is an alpaca."

"Those are even more adorable than the llama!"

"I'd have to agree. They're very clean animals too. They find one spot, and that's sort of their latrine. You don't have to worry about wading through their shit all over the yard because it's always in the same area."

"They sound amazing, but you know me, I love anything cute and cuddly. That's how I ended up with your herd of pygmy goats, isn't it?"

"I believe that's how I hooked you, as a matter of fact."

"I'm a sucker. I'll be the first to admit it."

"I'd prefer the term 'big-hearted' if I were you."

"What are you circling around, Dr. Yo . . . Hook?"

"A farmer came to me yesterday and said that his alpaca died, and he didn't have any use for her crias."

"Crias?"

"A baby llama or alpaca is a cria."

"Oh. Good to know."

"Yeah, he's got a set of small twins. Too small. They need to be bottle-fed every four hours for the next few weeks, kind of like having a newborn baby."

I felt myself perk up at the thought of having a baby that needed me, even if it was a furry one. Or two.

"He doesn't want them?"

"They're not made to have twins. That's what killed the mother."

"Oh, that's so sad," I whispered.

"Sadder than that, he said if I didn't take 'em, he'd put them both down."

"He didn't!"

"He did. So I've got a set of three-day old alpaca brothers who need some tender loving care."

"Aww."

"I thought you might be interested in meeting them."

I thought about my schedule for the next few weeks and calculated what it would take to feed and care for babies every four hours. I wouldn't get much sleep, and I still had things I wanted to do around the property, but I did have help scheduled for those tasks, so I wasn't strictly tied down to work on them.

As if Hook knew he almost had me, he finished with, "I brought them with me. They're out in a kennel in my truck."

"Really?" I squealed before I could stop myself. Hook's laughter boomed as he nodded his head. "Let's go see them!"

I jumped up from the table and rushed toward the back door, waking Ed Earl from his nap on the kitchen rug. I heard Hook walking behind me and the click of Ed Earl's nails on the hardwood before I opened the screen door and rushed onto the covered porch. I hurried around the house to Hook's big diesel and ran around to the bed. Hook pulled the tailgate down, and I got a look at the precious cargo he was hauling.

In the big black wire kennel were two of the cutest little animals I'd ever laid eyes on. Hook opened the crate door, and both animals stood up and sniffed his hand when he held it out to them. The dark one was a fluffy chocolate brown, and the lighter one was almost blonde.

"It's about feeding time. Want to help me out?"

"Oh my God. Are you freaking kidding me?"

Hook just laughed again and pulled the darker baby out of the crate and handed him over. "They're smaller than

43

they should be, and my guess is that they'll always be that way. Right now, they're each around 10 pounds when they should be closer to 20."

"Oh, sweetheart," I murmured as the little guy rubbed his nose against the side of my neck. "Sweet baby."

"I know it's a lot of work to take care of them, but I'll get staff over here anytime you need help. If you want to take them in, that is."

"You knew the second you saw them that they were going to come live with me, didn't you?"

"I wouldn't want to impose."

"Bullshit," I teased him. "Is that box there full of their stuff?"

"Maybe."

"Give me that baby, and carry all their shit into my house. I need to find a spot to put their kennel that's not right under a vent." I was really just talking to myself at this point. Hook had already handed me the other baby and picked up the box of supplies and tucked it under one arm while he hefted the crate out of the pickup with the other. I was halfway to the house with Ed Earl dogging my footsteps, curious about the animals I had in my arms. I turned around and saw that Hook was still back at the truck, getting something else out of the backseat. "He knew just what he was doing when he brought you here, didn't he?"

"I didn't plan this!" I heard Hook yell from the end of the walkway.

"My ass, he didn't plan this," I told my new babies. "Let's get you two in the house so Mama can take care of you."

"Do you have any idea how long it might take? I've got to pull my trailer next Friday so I can set up at the winter festival."

"Hmm," Saint, the big man who Hook had referred me to at a place called Infidel's Custom Motors, ran his hand over his goatee a few times as he stared thoughtfully at the back wall of the cab of my truck. "And you're saying you want a simple doggy door you can open and shut with a flap that hangs down over the hole."

"That's it. Just simple and to the point. No frills, really."

"And this is for a dog."

"And two small alpacas."

Saint blinked a few times slowly and then turned his head to stare at me. "Alpacas?"

"Yes. They're like a small llama."

"I know what they are," the big man said before he smiled at me like I was crazy. Not funny crazy, more like a danger to myself and others crazy. "You're going to have a dog and two alpacas riding in the bed of your truck, and you want to give them easy access to the cab?"

"Exactly. Well, sort of. I'm not comfortable with them riding back there while I'm driving, but while I'm parked with the trailer, I'd like for them to have the freedom to come outside for some air or to go potty in their tray if they need to."

"You want to install a doggy door, so they can come out and potty while you're working."

"Yes."

"Won't they get hot in the cab? Shouldn't they be . . ."

"Oh, I'll leave the truck on so they have air conditioning inside."

"Of course you will." The big man blinked his bright blue eyes at me a few times and then tilted his head. "Did Boomer talk you into this?"

"Boomer?"

"Yeah."

"Who's Boomer?"

"Who was it?"

"Who referred me to you?"

"It was Boomer. It had to be."

"No. Doc York, the vet? He's the one that told me I could trust your company. He said you'd do right and not cheat me, that your club was friendly with his club."

"Doc York? You mean Hook?"

"Yes. Hook. He's letting me foster the alpacas, and he knows they have to be fed every four hours just like human babies. When I called him yesterday and asked him if this idea was even possible, he said anyone could do it. Well, he said that your company could specifically. Was he wrong?"

"You really want a pet door for a dog and two alpacas so they can escape the nice air-conditioned cab of the truck for fresh air and a potty break?"

"I know it sounds stupid, but if you knew anyone who's really attached to their pets, then you'd understand where I'm coming from. If I need to go . . ."

"My brother Sin loves his boy Zeus this way. I understand."

"Your name is Saint, and your brother is Sin?"

"The man that sent you to us is called Hook."

"True."

Saint let out a snort and shook his head. "I can get this done. Probably this weekend. It's going to take some fabrication, but the supplies should be easy to find."

"That would be great!"

"Leave the truck with me, and I'll call you on Monday with a progress report."

"Okay," I told him as I handed him the key fob to my truck.

He looked past me into the parking lot and then back at my face. "How are you getting home, sweetheart?"

"I'll call a cab."

"Me or one of my guys will drive you in the shop truck. A lady doesn't need to take a cab alone."

"I've been in plenty . . ."

"I'll get you home," Saint said as he turned around and started walking back into the garage.

The man was sex on two legs. He had the dreamiest blue eyes and the face of a movie star, but he was much too alpha male for me. He must be a solid 10 years younger than me. Bossy man, I thought to myself as I reluctantly followed him back into the office. I'd had enough overbearing men in my life. Hell, Ethan was enough to turn me off of men forever. If I ever *did* find another man to spend time with, he'd be nothing like the man I was following.

I'd find one who was friendly and agreeable, calm, studious, and attractive. I didn't need some hot shit alpha male trying to tell me what to do in the bedroom or outside of it.

As hot as it seemed, I'd never let that happen.

BOSS

"Come on in. I've got bottled beer and canned sodas in the cooler out back. I'll meet you out there in just a minute; let me get the steaks," I told my visitors as I held the door open for them. I motioned toward the patio door on the other side of the dining area and said, "Patio is out that way."

"Thanks, man," Sin, the president of the Ares Infidels MC and Harvey Korbyn's nephew, said as he led his men through my house.

I followed them through the living room but turned right into the kitchen so I could grab the tray of steaks I'd had marinating. I walked out onto the large patio and saw that Sin and his men had made themselves comfortable, and each of them had a drink in hand.

"Everyone okay with medium-rare?" I asked the group. I heard yesses all around and turned to the grill and started putting the steaks down one by one. When I was finished, I walked over to the cooler, grabbed myself a beer, and tossed the top into the bucket I had for my collection. "My guys are on their way. One of them got held up with work shit, and the other one is just always late. He doesn't even bother with excuses anymore."

As I walked back over to the grill, Smoke, one of my cats, and Elvira, my pet skunk, sauntered up onto the patio. Sin and his men jumped up and hurried away from Elvira. I was impressed at how quickly such big men could move.

"She's a pet, don't worry. She can't spray, but she'll claw the shit out of you if you ignore her." I reached down and scooped Elvira up into my arms and held her against my chest as she snuggled against my neck. "I've had her since she was just a few days old."

"Shit! That scared me. I *do not* want to go home smelling like a skunk," one of the men said with a laugh as he watched the animal in my arms.

"Fuck. That is so freaky." Sin chuckled as he watched me pet Elvira. He walked closer and said, "I'm going to regret this when Zeus gets a whiff of me and stays pissed off for hours, but can I hold her? I've never held a skunk before."

"Sure. She'll go right to anyone," I told Sin as he took Elvira out of my arms. "I'm going to wash up and then come back and turn the steaks over."

Sin walked back over to the chair he'd been sitting in before their scare and sat down with Elvira in his arms. I hurried inside and washed my hands. As I was drying them on the towel, my front door opened, and Hook and Captain walked inside.

"Sorry I'm late. I was at the neighbor's checking on the alpacas I took to her place last week."

"I'm just fucking late," Captain admitted. "Only 10 minutes, though, so there's that."

"Are you late to court?" I asked him.

"Oh, hell no. I get fined for that shit."

"Next time you're late, you can pay me $50," Hook told him. "That shit pisses me off."

"Company's already here. Elvira scared the shit out of the commandos." I smiled when Hook glanced out the patio door and laughed. "Steaks are on. We'll make introductions and eat while we talk."

"Sounds good," Captain agreed as he slid the patio door open. I walked through it with Hook behind me, and I heard Captain slide the door closed again.

"Gentlemen, I'm sure I've met all of you at one point or another, but I'm Boss, this is my VP, Hook, and our secretary, Captain," I told the group as I walked toward the grill. I flipped the steaks as the AIMC men introduced themselves to my brothers and shook hands. I listened to the men make small talk as they sat around the long table I'd set up. After a few more minutes, I put the steaks on a clean platter and carried them over to the table. "I think I've got everything we need out here. If not, my kitchen's right through that door, and you can serve yourself. Martha Stewart, I am not."

A few of the men chuckled as they started to pass around the grilled corn and baked potatoes I'd prepared earlier. Once everyone had food in front of them, I looked over to Sin, and he nodded at me.

"Sin and I heard some disturbing news while we we're having coffee with the geezers yesterday morning. We thought we should get some boots on the ground and started kicking around to get some answers," I told the men as I topped my baked potato with sour cream and butter. "You all know Harvey, I'm sure, and our mentor is Pop, who I'm also sure you've seen around. This morning, word around the table was that some small business owners around town have some little punk ass in a fucking suit shaking them down. He says they need to pony up protection money or something might just happen to them, their business, or their family."

"Protection? From what? The rednecks who get drunk over at Lucky's?" Pitbull, one of Sin's men, asked.

"Lucky was the one who told Pop and Uncle Harvey about it," Sin told the table. "Said $500 was due on the first of every month, or they'd put him out of business."

"What the hell?" Hook asked.

I sighed loudly and told the men, "Pop asked Mary at Frontera if anyone had approached her, and she looked around the room like someone was watching her. She shook her head no, but her eyes said yes. I figure I'll go in for lunch sometime this week and feel her and her daughters out. Maybe get one of them to talk to me."

"You think she'll talk to a cop, or would she talk to one of us? I know Mary's daughter. Maybe I can get her to spill," Phantom said as he glanced from Sin to me and then back at Sin. "I eat there at least once a week, and I've done tattoos for both of Mary's daughters and a granddaughter that works there."

"That's probably a good idea. I know Mary, and if she wouldn't talk to Pop, she damn sure won't talk to me." I nodded at Phantom and saw that Sin did the same thing.

"If they've gotten to Mary, and they're working on Lucky, it only makes sense that Uncle Harvey will have a target on his back soon," Sin told his guys.

"Oh, hell no." Executioner, the SAA of the AIMC, growled. "They can leave Harvey the fuck alone."

"We can't match your manpower with just the three of us in town, but we'll do what we can to help," I assured Sin and his men.

"There are only three of you in your club?" Saint, the AIMC VP, asked.

"We've got over 50, but we're the only three here. The rest are all over the place. Hell, there's a brother living as far away as Australia now."

"How does that work?" Saint asked.

"We're not a club like yours that sticks together and lives close to one another. Pop started our club years ago so men like us - convicts, felons, ex-cons, and all-around fuck ups - would have a group we could depend on and find some common ground. When some men get out of the pen, they don't have a reason to keep themselves on the straight and narrow. Pop brings the ones he can into the fold, gives them a home, a job, and a purpose. If they want into the club, they prospect while they're adjusting to the outside world. One of the things that Pop does for every man who comes to the compound is to find them a bike frame and help them build their own ride. Nothing fancy, but something that gives them the freedom to come and go."

"That's smooth," Saint said before he shoved a bite of potato into his mouth.

"Do the men who live here and get to know Pop have a higher success rate than other men who are released back out into the world?" Talon, the treasurer of their group, asked.

"It worked for the three of us and the rest of our brothers," Captain told him.

"You're all ex-cons?" Talon asked as he looked from me to Hook and then Captain.

Captain nodded, and Talon looked shocked.

"I'm a veterinarian, Captain's a lawyer, and you all know Boss is the new police chief," Hook told the men, holding back his laughter at my title.

"Just petty stuff, right? You guys didn't kill someone or some shit, did you?" Talon asked, and I could hear the disbelief in his voice.

"When you were in the military, did you kill anyone?" I asked in a calm, low voice. "If you did, do you like it when people talk about it at the dinner table?"

"Talon," Sin said softly as he glanced from his man to me and then back.

"My bad, Boss. I apologize. My curiosity got the best of me, and I let my mouth run away."

I nodded at him, and all was forgiven. I felt the tension in the air start to fade a bit.

"Rest assured that the crimes we committed weren't the kind that can't be forgiven. But not a single one of us was ever accused of hurting women or children. Pop doesn't allow anyone that has done something like that around the compound or any of his businesses." Captain assured the men around the table who were just getting to know us. "Everyone here at this table has committed some kind of crime, whether it was in the eyes of the law, the eyes of God, or just the eyes of their mama. We served our time, got on with our lives, and want to make the town we live in safer than it was when we got here."

"Amen. We served our time, too, just in a different institution," Sin said as he lifted his beer toward the middle of the table. The rest of the men, including me, raised our beers and toasted to Captain's decree and Sin's final words on the subject, "To Time Served and the Ares Infidels, making the world safer one day at a time."

The phone on the nightstand rang, and I didn't even open my eyes as I hit the button to answer.

"Hello?"

"Chief, we've got another missing girl," Lorene, one of the lead dispatchers, calmly said over the phone and woke me up instantly.

"Shit. Another one? There's more than one missing tonight?"

"No, this is the same scenario of those other three girls that went missing six months ago. Her car is outside her apartment with her purse, keys and cell phone inside it. She's not anywhere to be found."

I'd already jumped out of bed and had my pants and boots on when I asked, "Fuck. Where?"

"She lives in the dorms at the college. Campus police called us three minutes ago."

"Who's the investigator tonight?" I hit the speaker button on my phone and tossed it onto the bed while I pulled on a long sleeved t-shirt and my uniform button-up.

"Marshall's on call, but Detective Clinton worked the other cases, so I called him instead," Lorene informed me.

"Why would you do that?"

"He yelled at me last time when he wasn't the first one notified and then he tried to have me written up," Lorene's voice was barely above a whisper, and I understood that she was talking to me in confidence.

"Nobody's gonna fucking write you up if you call the man who's on the roster. I'll make sure of it. It's not your place to babysit these fuckers, Lorene. That's my job."

"Yes, Chief." Lorene sounded relieved, and I promised myself I'd explore that issue when I was more awake

"I'm on my way to the scene. I'll be on my motorcycle since my car's getting a paint job."

"I'll radio the deputy chief."

"Do that. And Lorene?"

"Yes, Chief?"

"Anybody fucking raises their voice to you again, you tell me. If you can't get me the minute it happens, you do it as soon as you can, or you call the deputy chief. I won't have that shit on my watch, and neither will he. You get me?"

"I get you, Chief. It's cold outside. You should wear a scarf if you're riding your motorcycle."

"I'll see if I can find one," I lied with a smile on my face.

I grabbed my keys and wallet off the dresser and checked the weather on my phone as I hurried down the hall to the garage. It was in the 50s outside and that could get nippy at 70 miles an hour, but I sure as fuck wasn't wearing a goddamn scarf.

It wasn't far to the college from my place out on Pop's property. When I pulled up into the parking lot of the dorms, it was easy to find the girl's car. Two patrol cars, one unmarked detective car, and two motorcycles were already at the scene. Once my bike was parked, I made my way over to a huddle of men who were watching the crime scene technician process the vehicle. When I stepped up between Wrecker, my new deputy chief, and Detective Marshall, one of the prospects for his club, the air in that group was tense.

"What's the situation?" I asked the men in general.

The first one to answer was the investigator Lorene had mentioned, Detective Clinton. He glared at Wrecker and Marshal for a split second before he turned his gaze to me and complained, "These assholes are fucking up my crime scene."

"Are you on call tonight?"

"I took the last three calls for the missing girls, so dispatch sent me out."

"Have you found those girls yet?"

"All our leads have dried up and . . ."

"Then maybe we need fresh eyes and a crime scene tech before this one's leads dry up. You run on home, Clinton, and you can brief us about the others first thing in the morning."

"This is my case!"

"Pretty sure he told you to get, man," Wrecked said in a deadly calm voice. "We'll talk about this in the morning."

Wrecker and I both stared silently at the detective until he turned around and walked to his unmarked car. He sped out of the parking lot, and I noticed from the light inside his vehicle that he had his phone up to his ear before he even turned out onto the street.

"Now who in the world would he be calling at this hour?" Wrecker mused out loud.

I pulled my phone out of my pocket and dialed the non-emergency number to get Lorene. When she answered, I identified myself and asked, "Clinton call you a second ago?"

"No, Chief."

"Thanks, Lorene. Let me know if you hear from him. On the down low."

"Yessir."

"Well," I told the two men standing on either side of me. "He wasn't calling dispatch to check out, and from what

I remember, he's not married, so he wasn't calling his wife at home."

"He was fired up when he found me here," Wrecker told me. "He got real pale when the techies got here too. Is he on that list Sin made for you?"

"Right at the fucking top. What do we know about the girl?"

"She's 5'1", blonde hair, blue eyes. Just a little slip of a thing," Detective Marshall drawled.

"Shit. Did you get a list from campus security to start making calls?"

"I did, but I'm curious why whoever took her wanted us to think she disappeared out of this parking lot."

"Why do you say that?" Wrecker asked Marshall.

"Driver's seat is pushed all the way back, as is the backrest. Little 5' nothing girl's gonna be right up on that steering wheel just to reach the pedals, and she wouldn't even be able to see out of the window with her seat back like that. They planted this car here."

"Look at the big brain on the prospect," Wrecker whispered.

"I'm going to have a chat with the techs and get in their business. I don't want one of them *accidentally* fucking up evidence."

Wrecker and I watched the detective walk over to the car and say something to the technician. We were quiet for a minute and then I turned my head and looked at him before

I asked, "Have you heard anything on the news in the last few months about these girls disappearing?"

"Nope."

"And did anyone think to brief you on that shit since you started?"

"Nope."

"Me neither. You might want to ask Sin if he's got any more decent cops in his arsenal because you and me are about to fucking start cleaning house."

JENNIFER

"No! I can talk," I wheezed into the phone as I tried to catch my breath. I walked out of my home gym and down the short hall to the kitchen table so I could sit down. "I was working out and lost track of time. If anything, I'm glad you called! My arms are noodles, and I can't have that today. I've got too much to do."

"How are your babies doing?"

"Did you see the pictures I sent you this morning? If they get any fucking cuter, someone from Hollywood is going to take them away from me and put them in the movies."

"That's the truth. If they move them to Hollywood, you'll be closer to Seattle! You can come take your spot at the company back."

"I'll sell that bitch first, Connie. I am not coming back for anything but a quick visit to piss off Ethan's friends on the board."

"He's been all over the place looking for you, Jennifer. I don't know what he wants or why he wants you, but he's got something up his sleeve."

"He doesn't know we talk."

"Well, no. And I'm not telling him either. That phone I gave you is under my grandson's name and part of my son's phone bill. He won't find you through me. Why are you hiding from him again?"

"Because, honest to God, if I see that son of a bitch I'm going to beat him until my arms fall off."

"I would watch a video of that on repeat, just so you know."

"We could send *that* to Hollywood and make a mint. I'd even get dressed up to thank the academy for my award. Hold on, I'm putting you on speaker," I told Connie as I pushed a button and then set the phone on the kitchen table in front of my chair. I started to unwrap my hands as I continued, "Business is going well, I assume?"

"Seriously flowing. I made some changes in a few of the departments and within three days, I got so many ideas sent that I had to hire a third assistant."

"Good. You're so much better at that job than me and Ethan ever were. Of course, your heart's in it unlike mine. You know I"d been checked out for years. Ethan didn't have a heart, he just wanted it for the money. Without him sucking the company dry, you're going to be rolling in it."

"I'm working on it. How's the coffee truck going?"

"There's a winter festival that starts tonight. I've got my last pan of monkey bread in the oven right now."

"Oh, I miss your monkey bread." Connie sighed wistfully. "I bought a lemon bar at the cafe down the street yesterday, and it sucked so bad that I almost cried."

Since my hands were unwrapped, I picked up my

phone and scrolled through the apps until I found my calendar and set a reminder for myself. I would send Connie two dozen lemon bars to freeze and keep on hand for dessert emergencies.

"I don't know what the hell Ethan is thinking, trying to find me, but keep your ears open, and let me know if you find out."

"I'll do that. I just wanted to call and check in. I've got a meeting in ten, so I've got to let you go."

"Talk to you soon, babe."

After we hung up, I tossed my phone back onto the table. I stood up and walked across the wide expanse of the living room to the stairs that led to my bedroom. I held onto the rail since my legs were wobbly from my workout. I heard a noise behind me, and I turned to see Sammy and David were both following close behind me, their nails making a tapping sound on each step.

"You boys finished your nap?" I asked as the three of us walked up the stairs. Of course they didn't answer me, but they both hurried past me toward my bedroom. We walked past Moe who was sleeping in his favorite bed next to the fireplace. I led David and Sammy over to their new beds and ordered them to lay down. We'd been working on commands since the day they had arrived, and I was happy to see that they were both learning quickly. Once they laid down and settled in, I walked toward my bedroom door. Rather than shut the door, I pulled the accordion gate across it and latched it on the door frame.

I'd had two baby alpacas join me in the shower

yesterday, and that was not an adventure I wanted to repeat anytime soon.

Once I'd finished my shower and dressed for the day in a long-sleeved, cherry red henley, a pair of faded jeans, and my favorite sneakers, I opened the accordion gate and went over to my vanity to put on my makeup and do something with my hair.

I went into each day thinking I'd try a new hairstyle and maybe even one of the new makeup trends I'd seen online, but I almost always ended up with my hair in a ponytail and just a smudge of eyeliner, and a coat of mascara.

I didn't expect miracles - I *was* 44 after all, but I'd like to think a little makeup could spruce me up, and a new hairstyle might do the same.

Of course, three minutes in, I was done with the whole routine. I just couldn't sit there for a fucking hour and put on layers of shit when I was just going to sweat it off or get it covered in flour. I had on eyeliner, mascara, some brow powder to give me some definition, and tinted lip balm.

I did, however, put my hair back in a loose twist and clip it up rather than my going with my usual ponytail.

As a concession to how I knew the day would go, I slipped a few bands over my wrist for later when I'd need to really pull my hair up because I knew that this cutesy clip wouldn't make it to the finish line.

"This is as good as it gets," I told my reflection. I leaned forward to inspect my laugh lines. I squinted a few times and then smiled widely to see what sort of progress Father Time was making on my face.

Before our divorce, Ethan had been trying to convince me to try some cosmetic procedures. I hadn't realized it at the time, but, in essence, he wanted me to replicate Homewrecker Barbie. I'd resisted the fake boobs and the liposuction, but almost fell for the botox and fillers. Almost.

And now, glancing at my reflection and liking what I saw, I was glad I'd resisted. Ethan could eat a dick and enjoy paying for his own botox.

Finished with my daily routine and still buzzing from my workout, I went downstairs and double checked my supplies in the trailer before I pulled the last batch of goodies out of the ovens and put them in warmers that would hold them while I traveled.

All set for the evening, I gave Moe, David, and Sammy each a good rubdown and said my goodbyes before I took off. One of Hook's employees would be here for feedings in two hours and then again in four if I wasn't home yet. I'd already had my truck outfitted for my pets, but since the alpacas were still so small, I'd decided to leave them at home for the evening. They could come with me once they'd gained some weight.

With the truck loaded and trailer hitched up, I pulled off of my property onto the long road that would take me into Tenillo and the park hosting the festival. Once I arrived, I found my assigned spot and pulled in, ready to work for the evening.

I'd enjoyed my job in Seattle to a point. I worked with people that I'd become friends with through the years, but it was a boring office job that stifled me over time. I'd always enjoyed the food trucks around the city and almost every time

I found a new one, I had thought about how I'd love to just buy one of my own and leave everything behind.

So I did.

I'd purchased the trailer and had it customized by a company out of Longview, Texas. While they were working on it, I'd applied for my tax license, food license, and all the other things necessary to run a food business.

I'd hired a construction crew to build a commercial kitchen in my house and then had it inspected by the powers that be so I could become a legitimate business owner in my new town.

After only a few months, I had a great following online - customers sought me out wherever I parked. Word of mouth had gotten me maybe even more business than social media. One of the best parts of my job was meeting new people, catching up with those I'd started to consider my regulars, and watching kids light up when I handed them their free cookie.

In my coffee truck, S'more of That, I created specialty coffee drinks with recipes I'd found online and tweaked to my own tastes. I kept a slow cooker full of spiced Mexican hot chocolate, another of regular hot chocolate, and a third full of cinnamon apple cider. I made desserts, too, but there was no set menu.

The best part of being the owner and operator of my own small business was I worked when I wanted and served what I wanted.

I kept my drink choices the same and created new recipes on the fly, but my baked goods varied according to what I felt like making for the day. Today I was serving monkey bread, mini Key lime pies, red velvet cupcakes, pecan pie bars, and assorted cookies along with my usual drinks.

I always made the kids' cookies slightly smaller than the ones I sold and did something special with them that the kids would like. This evening's cookies were soft sugar cookies with the Captain America shield stamped into the middle of each one and topped with red and blue sprinkles .

Once I had the generator on, everything ready inside the truck, my apron tied on, and a smile ready for my customers, I slid the metal gate up to a line that was already 20 people deep.

"Hi, guys!" I greeted my first two customers, some bikers who I'd seen more than once around town. "What can I get you gentlemen this evening?"

BOSS

"Just wait until you see this little girl, Boss. She's got the body of a goddess, the smile of a movie star, a personality that gets a man's motor running, and she can bake things that make you want to slap your mama."

"Pop, what would Ms. Maddie say if she caught you crushing on another woman, especially one that bakes?" I asked my friend and mentor as I glanced around at the crowd and then behind us at the people lining up at Pop's favorite food truck.

"Maddie and I have an unspoken agreement, son. She's the only woman who feeds me regularly, and I'm the only man who makes her breathless behind closed doors," Pop boasted, and it was all I could do not to shudder at the picture he was painting. Ms. Maddie was 70 if she was a day, and as much as I liked the woman, I wasn't keen on imagining her doing anything that might make her breathless behind closed doors. "Besides, she's got you young'uns to fawn over whenever you go to her diner. I have on good authority that Captain really trips her trigger when he smiles sweet at her."

I glanced at Hook, who was standing just a few feet away in line with us. I watched him pull his lips in and look at the ground so he didn't laugh out loud.

"She's sweet on Captain, huh?"

"She's sweet on me, boy. She likes to look at Cap."

I heard a metal gate roll up and a woman's sultry voice cheerfully greeted the first customers in line: Torpedo and Boomer, two of the men from the AIMC I'd met through Sin. I tilted my head to get a look at the woman Pop had been raving about just in time to see her turn away from the counter and give me her back.

And what a fantastic backside it was too. She was tall, and the ass on her was enough to make my cock instantly wake up and say hello. I couldn't wait to get a look at the woman's front, but I had to admit, if it was anywhere as fucking hot as her backside, I might just embarrass myself.

I heard Hook chuckle and looked over at my friend. He was staring at me with a big smile on his face, and when I glanced at Pop, I saw that he was doing the same thing.

"What?"

"Did you just growl?" Pop asked me before he started laughing at me.

"I did not growl. You're hearing shit, old man."

"Oh, you sure the fuck did," Hook argued once he could control his laughter. "We both heard it. You going to rip your shirt off and start beating your chest now? One look at Cool Cat, and you've turned into a fucking caveman."

"Cool Cat?"

"She's my neighbor. Her name's Jennifer McCool."

Shit. Even her name was hot.

Pop finally stopped laughing and asked, "She's a shiny one, isn't she?"

"Fuck both of y'all," I snarled at my friends with a glare. I looked back at the window and saw that the woman inside the trailer had turned back around, and I could see her face. "Well, fuck me."

I didn't even realize I'd said anything out loud until Pop and Hook started laughing again. I didn't give a shit. The only way the woman inside that trailer could look any better was if she were naked and tied to my headboard. With that thought, my cock decided to really join the conversation, and I thanked God I was wearing a long hoodie over my uniform shirt.

Jesus Christ. One look at the woman, and I was a 12-year-old who couldn't control his hard-on. It didn't get any better as I watched her interact with the people in front of us.

One man was holding a toddler, and I watched the woman lean out of the window and hand the little boy a cookie with a smile that could light up the town.

It damn sure lit up every nerve ending in my body.

It was finally our turn at the window. I swallowed and tried to figure out how I was going to speak coherently if she turned that smile toward me.

"Look at the handsome devil at my window," the woman said as she smiled at Pop. "Are you feeling adventurous, or do you want plain coffee?"

"Give me an adventure, sweetheart," Pop schmoozed. "These here are my boys, Hook and Boss. Boys, meet your future mama."

"I told you last time that I'm not the marrying type. We can live in sin or go our separate ways." Oh, I'd like to sin with her, but she hadn't even glanced in my direction yet. She looked at me before addressing Hook. "Hi there, Hook. I didn't realize you knew Pop. What can I get you? Adventure or plain old coffee?"

"Hit me with something good, Cool Cat. No coconut, though. That's not my thing."

"And you, sir?"

"It's Boss," I told her as I stuck my hand out to shake hers. She glanced at my hand and then put hers in mine for a split second. I was surprised at her grip but hated when she took her hand away so quickly. She looked up at me with eyes so green, they were almost yellow. When she smiled, they crinkled at the corners like they were used to that position, her smiling. "I'd like for you to take me on an adventure."

"Oh, you would?" Ms. McCool asked saucily. She looked back at Pop and winked before she turned around and started making our drinks. I didn't even care who saw me do it, I studied her back and profile while she worked. She was efficient and wasted no movement, pumping syrup and other ingredients into our cups while the espresso machine did its thing. While she poured milk into our cups and stirred the concoction, she called out over her shoulder, "Do you want something sweet this evening, Pop? What about your boys?"

"We'll take whatever compliments your creation, honey," Pop answered.

I watched Ms. McCool use tongs to fill three cups with some sort of sticky goodness before she set all six of the cups on the rail in front of her and tallied up our total. Once she announced it, I was quick to hand her my card to pay for the drinks. While she took care of that, I slid Hook his coffee and snack, and Pop took his off the rail and sniffed at the lid.

"Smells delicious. And what's this in the cup?" Pop asked.

"It's monkey bread. Oh, hold on!" Jennifer told him before she spun around and picked up two of the sugar cookies I'd seen her give to the children in line before us. "Since these are your boys, I need to give them each a treat. I do it for all the customers' kids, you know." Ms. McCool reached out and stuck a sugar cookie in my dessert cup and then another in Hook's. "There you go. A snack for Pop's good boys."

Hook snorted before he said, "You shouldn't have wasted those cookies on us, Cool Cat. We quit being good boys long ago."

"If you never aspire to greatness, you'll never reach it," she told him before she winked at me. "You guys have a good night. Hook, I'll talk to you tomorrow."

"Yes, ma'am."

Pop, Hook, and I walked away from the trailer, and I listened as her voice followed us when she greeted the next customers.

"Are you already in there?" I asked Hook directly. I needed to know if he had his eye on her, or even more than that before I let my thoughts roam in the direction they were going. I watched his face as I took a sip of my hot coffee.

"Nah, I've already seen the size of her cock, and I don't think I could deal with that on a daily basis." Pop and I both choked on the coffee we'd just drawn into our mouths, and I realized that Hook was laughing at us as we tried to clear our throats and start breathing right again. "Fuck, I've been waiting to say that since we stepped into line. It worked out even better than I thought."

JENNIFER

Once the latest rush of customers was served, I took a shot at a quick break and made myself a coffee. The band playing in the gazebo had just started, and in a few minutes, the comedian who was scheduled to perform would get up on stage. The local talent was booked until midnight tonight, meaning I had another three hours here in my trailer unless I sold out.

At the rate things were going, that might just happen. The monkey bread was a hit, and I made a mental note to add it to my box of successful recipes to use on occasion. Honestly, there hadn't been many items I'd sold that weren't successful. Like today's monkey bread, some were such instant hits that I worried I wouldn't have enough to last even half of my scheduled time at the event.

As I sipped my coffee, I leaned onto the counter in front of my large open window and looked around the park at the other trucks serving customers. I had quite the competition for a town this size, but none of them served my specialty coffees or such a diverse array of baked goods.

I'd never been able to settle on a regular menu. What I had going on now kept me on my toes as far as quality and creativity went, and it kept my customers coming back just to see what I'd have.

One of the other trucks served coffee, but it was drip.

They had an ice bucket full of creamers they bought at the grocery store - no comparison to my liquid goodness.

Another vendor served sweets and desserts, but they stuck to cookies, brownies, and caramel apples. I'd snuck away from my truck and bought samples of their food only to realize that the owner's mom has a bakery in town, and they were selling her day-old fare.

Amateurs.

Not a single one of these people would survive a weekend in the Seattle market. As unique as my truck seemed, I might not survive long there myself. But this was Tenillo, Texas. The town had one mall, three Walmarts, and a rivalry between the two high schools that had a level of drama worthy of a made-for-tv movie. Football season had kept me busy with all the events they had scheduled, and I'd learned that these people took their high school football *very* seriously. I'd witnessed my first Christmas in Tenillo recently, and it was a mixture of a Hallmark movie and Christmas Vacation. Lucky for me, I liked both of those things.

My first round of holidays alone had been hard. I'd been so down that I'd eaten my frozen turkey dinner in the barn while my herd of pygmy goats napped around me.

Sitting there in the cold barn surrounded by sweet animals, I'd decided that was the last time I was going to wallow. I was on a mission to make friends here, and I'd gotten off to a good start in the new year, as far as I could tell. I considered Hook to be a solid friend besides being my neighbor. It didn't hurt that the man fed my addiction to fluffy animals that needed me just as much as I needed them.

I'd also met a woman at the nail salon, and we'd exchanged numbers and had lunch together twice. Her name was Paula, and she was divorced from a douchebag that sounded a lot like my ex. She'd been here a few years, and like me, she was concentrating on building her business from the ground up. The fact that she was absolutely hilarious was the icing on the cake.

I saw Pop, Hook, and the other man walking across the grass in my direction. Since they were far enough away that they couldn't see my eyes, I studied the third man.

I knew that Hook was Dr. York's nickname, and Pop had called this guy Boss, so I assumed that was what he went by. That nickname combined with the fact that he was tall and had such a commanding presence, along with a deep, sexy voice, let me know he was one of those alpha-male types and I was *not* interested.

Okay, I was *very* interested. I couldn't lie to myself. I'd made that promise to my reflection in the mirror 10 minutes after Homewrecker Barbie left my office that day. I wouldn't put my head in the sand again, and I sure as hell wouldn't put up with some bossy man who thought he could run me over.

But Jesus, take the wheel. That man was something to look at. He was at least 6'4" with legs like tree trunks and muscular arms that stretched the sleeves of his hoodie. His face was enough to make all my soft spots melt and yearn for what I was sure he would be willing to give if I only asked.

If the man came back to my truck, and I saw that his hands were big, strong, and calloused, I'd probably forget everything I'd promised myself and proposition him for a one-night stand that lasts at least six hours. I'd even figure out how to supply a little blue pill if needed.

Six hours might not be enough. It had been over a year since I'd had sex, and that last time was with Ethan, so I didn't even have an orgasm. I rarely ever did after we got married, and both of us got busy building our company. His mind was always on business, and he was just as selfish in the bedroom as he was outside it.

I'd need 10 hours, maybe 12. Fuck it. I needed a weekend that would leave me walking funny for a week.

I'd been lost in my own naughty thoughts for so long that when I came back to myself, the three men were in front of my window again. Hook was smiling wickedly, and he was the first one to say anything.

"I told them about your big cock, and they were so shocked they both damn near choked to death."

"It wasn't shock, honey; it was jealousy. I'd put money on the fact that mine is way bigger than either of theirs."

Pop started cackling and shook his head. "A dirty mind and a body like that to boot . . . when are we going to run away together?"

"I don't like to run, but you can take my hand and lead me wherever you want to go, Pop," I teased. "Do you want another coffee or some of that spicy hot chocolate you like?"

"Spicy hot chocolate?" Boss asked as he tilted his head and leaned forward to look past me into the trailer. "I'd like to try that. What else do you have in there that's delicious? Other than yourself, I'm sure."

"Oh, the big man flirts," I mumbled as I stared into his blue eyes. I pulled my thoughts together and said, "I've got a few things up my sleeve. Do you like pie?"

Boss chuckled, and when I glanced at Hook, I saw that he was fighting a smile.

"Oh, I like pie. I could eat it for *days*. What are you offering tonight?" Boss asked me with a grin.

"Tonight, I have pecan pie bars to go along with your spicy hot chocolate, or I have cinnamon apple cider, if you'd prefer."

Boss held my eyes and kept grinning but didn't give me his order.

Pop jumped in with, "I'll take that spicy hot chocolate and some more of that monkey bread, sweetheart. You've got a way with sweets that's going to make my doctor cuss at me."

I tore my gaze away from Boss and looked at Pop and Hook before I asked, "What about you, Hook? What can I get you?"

"I'll take cider and a few cookies. Whatever you've got, even if it's just more Captain America. Those were good but barely more than a mouthful."

"I make them for the kids. I'll get you a couple that are grown-up size. You have a problem with raisins?"

"Nope. Hit me with whatever you've got back there."

"And Boss, what can I get you?"

"I'll take your number and some of that pie. Oh, and let me try the spicy hot chocolate."

"Hmm, I can manage all of those things." I reached over to the side and pulled one of my business cards out of the holder. I slid it across the countertop and tapped it twice before I turned around to fill the men's orders. I listened to them talk and then their voices were replaced with the sound of police radio chatter that made my blood run cold. When I turned around, Boss was holding it in his hand as he listened to dispatch give details and assign a car to the call. I turned back around and filled the cups out of the different pots, grabbed the cookies, pecan pie bar, and monkey bread, then turned back to give the men their drinks and sweets. As I pulled my hand back across the counter, I brought my card with it and let it fall to the floor before ringing up Hook and Pop's purchases. I told them the amount, and when Pop argued that it couldn't be enough, I smiled tightly and said, "I don't charge police officers. I didn't realize earlier, or I would have given Boss his first order free too."

"You can't give me all this goodness for free, sweetheart," Boss argued. "I'll pay like the rest."

"Oh, no," I told him before I took a deep breath and smiled at Hook when he handed me cash. As I made the change and handed it out the window, I said, "I'll take care of it. It's the least I can do for one of the boys in blue."

"He's not just one of the boys," Pop boasted, "he's the new police chief."

"Well, isn't that something. Congratulations on your new position, Boss."

"Thanks," Boss said in a softer voice as he stared at me again, trying to catch my eye. I guessed he could feel the chill in the air now, but there wasn't much I could do about that. All thoughts of that wild weekend in bed with the man were dashed. I couldn't get involved with a cop no matter how good looking he might be. Boss looked at the counter where the card had been and then down at the ground to see where it had fallen. Just then, another customer walked up, and Pop and Hook moved to the side. With another glance at me, Boss did the same, but I could tell that he was curious about the sudden change. I'd probably have to talk to him directly to make him understand.

I decided to put a pin in that for now, and I greeted my next customers as the three men walked away.

After another hour of steady customers, I finally got a break, and I decided it was time for a snack. I'd already sampled the wares I was serving, so I reached under the counter and pulled an orange out of my purse. While I was peeling it, a man I'd noticed standing near another truck walked up and glanced at my menu and then inside my trailer.

"Can I help you?" I asked him as I put my orange to the side and pulled on a pair of disposable gloves.

"You're new in town, aren't you, honey?"

"Not that new," I answered tightly. Something about the man rubbed me wrong, and I didn't like the way he was studying me, the cash register, and the other things on the counter behind me. "What can I get for you?"

"It came to my attention that you get quite a few

customers here." The man wasn't dressed like most of the others here at the festival. He had on a wool jacket that I could tell cost a pretty penny, his hair was slicked back, and he had a thick gold chain around his neck that dipped down into the chest hair exposed from his unbuttoned shirt. As he reached up and rested his hand on the counter, I glanced down among the scarred knuckles and saw one of those gold nugget pinky rings that had been popular in the '70s and '80s. He reminded me of Joe Pesci's character in Casino for some reason. When I looked up at his eyes, I realized they were just as crazy as Pesci's, and he'd seen me assessing him.

After I'd held his gaze for a second, I answered, "Baked goods and coffee are always popular."

"That's good. There's a fee for working at these gatherings, you know. I realize you haven't paid yet, but I'd like to strike a deal with you instead."

"There wasn't a fee when I signed up, and I have my license in order with the health department. Do you want something to drink, or are you one of the organizers?"

"Yeah, an organizer. I like that. Are you the owner of the business, or is there someone else?"

"I'm the owner."

"No husband hiding in there to help you?"

"What exactly can I do for you?"

"I have a business proposition for you, but I'd like to talk to you about it tomorrow. Do you have a number where I can reach you?"

"I'm not interested in a business proposition, sir. I like things just the way they are."

"Sometimes we don't have a choice about changes that come along."

"I always have a choice. I've got customers walking up, so I'll have to ask you to move along unless you're ordering."

"I'll see you in the next few days," the man said as he studied my face. "I'll make sure it's a reasonable offer, and I'm sure we can work something out. Until then, be safe, sweetheart."

The man walked away, and I let the breath out I'd been holding in a long whoosh as I watched him go. That was the strangest conversation I'd ever had with a customer at one of these events. Actually, he hadn't even bought anything, so the man wasn't even a customer. I had no idea what he was exactly, but I knew I didn't want to deal with him again. That was for damn sure.

Luckily, he didn't have my business card. There wasn't anything on the outside of the truck other than my phone number. I helped the next customer, and after a few minutes of constant movement, I let the tension the man had caused flow away.

I was probably making too much of it anyway. He was likely just some creepy guy trying to hit on me.

BOSS

"Did you see what she did with that business card after she realized you were a cop?" Hook asked me after Pop walked away to greet some acquaintances.

"She slid it off the back of the counter, didn't she?"

"She did. If I hadn't been looking at her hands, I'd have never seen it."

"I wonder what the fuck that was about."

"She gave you your coffee for free, so she doesn't *hate* cops; she just doesn't want to go out on a date with one. I wonder why."

"I've a good mind to just ask directly. Until I pulled out my radio, she was into me. I could tell."

"Well, times have changed, I guess. Used to be with some girls you could pull your *radio* out when you first met, and they'd be happy to see it."

"You're such a fucking pervert," I told Hook as I let my head hang down. Finally, I couldn't hold it in anymore and let my laughter out.

"I like the woman, Boss. I've talked to her more than a handful of times, and she's got her shit together. I don't know her story, but I know she's been single since she came to town. She's not hurting for money, I can tell you that. She's turned that old farmhouse into a magazine spread, and her barn is state of the art. Those animals of hers are living the good life. Fuck, they eat better than I did while I was in prison. They eat better than I do now!"

"You think she was married to a cop?"

"You're gonna have to ask her, man. I couldn't tell you. She's all alone over there right now. Why don't you go back and talk to her? I'll keep Pop at bay. You're flirting with his new favorite gal, so he's gonna cockblock you at every turn."

"He can try," I growled as I turned around and headed toward the S'more's truck and Jennifer.

As I walked across the grass, weaving around people seated in folding chairs or laid out on blankets, my radio squawked again. I pulled it off my belt to listen and shook my head with a sigh. This was the third call this week about someone breaking into a car and just tearing the shit out of it. There weren't any items missing, but the interior was fucked. We'd thought it was a prank the first time, or that maybe the owner of the car had an enemy. The second had us confused, and now with a third, I had no fucking idea what to think.

I made a mental note to call my newest detective, Sin's guy, Marshall, tomorrow morning and hear his thoughts on the issue. All three had to be connected. Maybe just some stupid kids fucking shit up on a whim. There was no telling at this point.

I got close enough to see Jennifer's face, and I didn't like the expression on it when she noticed me. She squared her shoulders, and her face went blank. I could see the wall going up in front of her.

I was curious now, and when that happened, I couldn't be deterred until I'd found an answer. As if I wasn't already interested in the woman for that hot fucking body, her divine skills in the kitchen, and that sassy personality, now I had a mystery to solve.

The woman wasn't going to know what hit her. I could be charming when I wanted to be, and for a woman like that, I wanted. I wanted a lot.

"Are you hungry or thirsty? Or both?" Jennifer asked when I got closer to her trailer. She was smiling, but it didn't quite reach her eyes.

"Curious."

"About?"

"If you'd met me before I put on this badge, say, maybe six months ago, would you have let me get that card, or would you have still palmed it when you thought I wasn't looking?"

I saw her eyes flare when she realized she'd been busted, but her recovery was quick. "A girl can change her mind."

"She certainly can. I'm just curious about why she would."

"I have to think about something." Jennifer leaned down and rested her arms on the counter. "Is this where I blow smoke up your ass and play to your ego, or is this where I give it to you straight and hope we can remain friends?"

"I am one to enjoy a good cigar on occasion, but that's about all the smoke I can tolerate. I think my ego can take what you dish out. Besides, if you give it to me straight, maybe I can find an argument or two that might bring you back over to this side of friendly."

"I'm not some meek and mild nitwit who's gonna put up with an alpha personality who thinks he can run me over. I also have a healthy respect for police officers. Being the daughter of one, I know how it feels to be the person who opens the door to find the captain there to tell you that your boy in blue is no more because some scumbag got a lucky shot. I don't do alpha, and I don't do cops. That's two strikes on your first at-bat, Boss man, and things aren't looking very good for that last pitch. I took the card back in the hopes that you'd get the hint that I'm not interested and back the fuck off."

"Now I've got some thinking to do."

"Nothing to think about. It's always good to have a wide circle of friends. You and your officers are welcome to come and get snacks and drinks from me free of charge any time. Game over."

"I enjoy baseball just as much as the next guy, but I'm not about playing games, sweetheart. I'm going to put it to you bluntly. Let me know when you're ready."

Two couples walked up, and I stepped aside so Jennifer could get their orders together. Once they'd paid and walked off, I stepped back in front of the window, and Jennifer leaned back down to finish our chat.

I didn't say anything, waiting for her to make the next move and let me know that she was ready for my rebuttal. I was prepared to be straight with her, and I didn't know if she'd shoot me down or drag me through the window and have her way with me on the floor when I was done.

"I'm braced and ready, Boss. Go for it."

"I'm not sure about the alpha personality bullshit, but I'll admit I'm a strong-minded man. That being said, I like to spend time with a strong-minded woman and not some nitwit who's going to go right along with whatever I say. How fucking boring would that be in the bedroom or out of it? And I'm sorry for your loss as far as your daddy. That's gotta fuck with a child to have that happen. However, if you think it through, that daddy of yours was a strong and opinionated man who did his best every day to make sure you were happy and supply you with what you needed to grow physically and thrive mentally. I'd bet my last dollar he started you on this path to being a strong, independent woman. Why the fuck wouldn't you want a man around who could nurture that part of you that you lost when he died?"

I could tell that Jennifer was stunned at my argument, but I wasn't finished by a long shot.

"I'm not asking for your hand in marriage. I've been there and done that, and I'm not quite sure I'm willing to do it again. I am asking you to let me get cleaned up, put on some decent clothes, pick you up on my motorcycle, and take you out for dinner at Daltons where you can enjoy a glass of wine with our meal. When we're finished eating our dinner, we can critique the dessert they offer because we both know you could make one a thousand times better. When we're finished at the restaurant, I take you back home and do one of three things."

"Uh-huh," Jennifer whispered as she leaned forward, waiting on me to tell her where that idea was leading.

"Would you like to know about those three things?" I

asked in a low voice as I leaned against the counter, putting my face just an inch or two away from hers as I stared into her eyes.

"I suppose I would." She let out a sigh.

"The first scenario is we had a great dinner, sit on your porch for a cup of coffee, and realize maybe we *can* just be friends. The second scenario is I kiss you at the front door until you're breathless and wanting me. When you pull away, I realize you're not ready, so I get on my bike and go home to await the next time I can take you out, get to know you some more, and try that kiss again."

"Interesting."

I waited a few beats, knowing she was curious about the last option. I could see it on her face. Her eyes were glazed, her lips were parted, and I could feel her panting against my face. She fucking smelled like oranges, and I wanted to devour her lips with mine right about now. I could control myself but just barely.

She finally whispered, "What's number three?"

"The third scenario is that we have a great meal, skip the dessert because we know it won't measure up, ride my bike back to your place, and kiss on the porch. But the kiss will be so fucking hot that we have to take it inside. We'll end up naked in the hallway with my mouth on your pussy, your hands in my hair, and you screaming my name when you come. Then, being the alpha that I am, I'll take you into the bedroom, lay you out on the bed, and feast on every inch of you. I'll worship those thighs, that ass, and those hips with my tongue and lips until you're writhing and begging for my cock. And when you're so fucking hot, and I'm ready to explode, I'll put those legs over my shoulders and fuck you so hard that neither of us will be able to walk right for the next three days."

Jennifer's breathing was fast now. She let out a soft moan as her eyes closed for a second and a shiver shook her entire body. Her hands were clenched as she tried to catch her breath and collect herself. "Holy fuck."

"Now, are you gonna give me that card so we can let this shit play out?"

Jennifer's face, just inches from mine, never moved. Her arm went to the side, and she slid a business card across the counter to me. I reached up and took the card and slipped it into my back pocket without losing eye contact for a second.

"I want number three so bad, I can fucking taste it. Since we haven't had that date yet, I'll have to go home and take care of business on my own. You gonna do that, too, Jenn?"

"I am."

"Maybe after we get to know each other, you can call me while you do that, and I'll do the same while I listen to that sexy voice of yours. Or maybe, just maybe, I'll drive to your house while I'm listening to you touch yourself, and then I'll take care of you as soon as I get there. Let's make that the fourth scenario. What do you think?"

"When?"

"I'll pick you up at seven o'clock tomorrow evening. Wear something you can ride in - plan on boots and a coat, for sure. It's cold as fuck after dark. I'll get you a nice dinner and some wine and then we'll pick a number."

I leaned in just a few more inches and touched my lips to hers. It was a soft kiss, nothing like what I'd described, but it did the trick. When I leaned back, her eyes were still closed, and her face was flushed.

"Tomorrow. Seven o'clock." I reminded her as customers walked up. "Be ready, sweetheart, because I'm shooting for number three."

BOSS

"Talk to me, Preacher man. What sort of goodies did you unearth snooping through the internet?"

Preacher, one of my brothers in the club who was also our information and technology expert, laughed on the other end of the phone. Of course, like the rest of the men in my MC, he was an ex-con who'd turned his life around with Pop's help.

And turn it around, he did. He has an almost cult-like following because of his podcast and videos talking about conspiracy theories on everything from coffee pods to what the colors of the president's ties meant regarding world affairs.

I listened to him out of sheer loyalty at first. I thought most of his shit was crazy as hell. Some of it actually made logical sense, though - the guy was not lacking smarts. He researched every single thing and had contacts worldwide, so it made sense that we came to him for help vetting both employees Pop hired from outside and some of the customers who ordered custom parts or wanted multi-million dollar construction work. Preacher always got us any scoop there was to be found. It was rare that he came up against a brick wall that he couldn't bust through. That's why his answer shocked me.

"I'm still running through a few leads and waiting on

some information, but those men you had me look into are some serious shit. Most of their stuff is completely black, and what I could find is totally badass. That Sin fellow has a reputation among the men he served with that says he could lead a team of men straight into hell, and they'd pack a bag with an extra water and follow him right down. He earns that much respect. I can't find anything that's a bright red flag. However, some of the stuff I unearthed lets me know that these guys either all need a fucking shrink, or they have some issues that only violence and some wild sex can work out."

"That bad, huh?"

"Uh, yeah," Preacher said with a snort. "They've been through some hairy shit, all of them, and they came out on the other side and got medals for it."

"Trustworthy?"

"These are some fucking boy scouts with a tendency toward violence, so, yeah, I'd consider them excellent allies. They'd damn sure make terrifying enemies."

"What about the rest? Start with the chief that just retired. What did you find out about him?"

"His wife got sick. There was a shit ton of debt that their insurance didn't cover. He took out two additional mortgages on his land and his house to keep them afloat. His credit was in the shitter. He was making every penny of every paycheck scream, he was living so tight. Then, all of a sudden, the medical bills are caught up, and his wife starts seeing a specialist in Houston, flying down there for treatment like she owns stock in the airline, mortgages were paid off, and trust funds were started for each of his children and grandchildren. He's got a considerable amount of money stashed in a money market account that's gonna see he and his wife living the high life whether they are in the cabin he bought in the mountains, the house on the beach in Galveston, or the bungalow they bought in California to be near the grandkids on holidays."

"That's serious money. Fuck. The big guns. I thought maybe a bill under the table here and there, but that's not what this sounds like at all."

"It's definitely not just money under the table, man. They gave him the entire fucking table and the chairs to match. Can't trace it, though. I'm coming up on wall after wall. The last one I hit was somewhere in the Cayman Islands. They keep their banking shit tight."

"Talk to me about one of the investigators. I sent you a list of names."

"Two of them are bad. One of those is worse."

"Clinton?"

"And he's psychic all of a sudden!"

"I knew there was something off about him. We went on a call the other night, and he was freaked that I didn't let him run it. Middle of the night, and he had the phone to his ear before he was out of the parking lot. He was whining to someone."

"He's got some debt. I'd be surprised if his Vegas bookies don't send him Christmas cards and take him to Outback for his birthday every year."

"Shit."

"The wife left him five years ago, and he pays her a chunk in monthly child support. I can't find any record of him seeing his kids since she's been gone. She's up in Pennsylvania with family and doing fine. Remarried and had another kid since she left, living the good life as Sally Soccer Mom with some business executive. They own three horses, and I must say they are some beautiful beasts. I'll send you a picture of the white one. Fucking magical."

"I'm good. How about the other one?"

"He's saving up for a rainy day. Although I did find out that his mother was attacked in her home about a year ago. She got the shit beat out of her, and they killed her fucking dog, man. No one has ever been arrested. You know cops would have been all over that shit. She spent a few weeks in the hospital, and while she was there, he hired movers to pack her house up and put most of her things in storage. She left the hospital and took off to Montana to live near her sister, or at least that's the story he told people."

"That was a lie?"

"Mom was an only child, and I can't find her in Montana."

"He's still getting money?"

"Yep, and he's socking it all away. Got an account in Cayman like the other guy, and his family is slowly disappearing off the grid. He's got two younger sisters and a younger brother and some nieces and nephews. The kids were yanked out of school the day after his mom's attack and disappeared along with the man's siblings, never to be heard from again. My theory is that the bad guy has them, and that's why your investigator is cooperating."

"Or he's cooperating to keep the heat away from his family until he can get out too."

"Or there's that."

"Office staff?"

"Almost all of them married with the tendencies of the Golden Girls. One plays bingo and is a church lady. Another one volunteers at the cancer center where her sister was treated before she died. One of them crochets afghans and makes money selling them in online auctions so she can support the local veterans club. All good as far as I can see. I need to go more in-depth with my research on the office manager. There's something about her that doesn't fit. She's taken great pains to stay off the radar, and that's not a good sign."

"Fuck."

"That would also explain why she went into your office and dusted the furniture herself, all the while trying to inconspicuously get a look at the cameras you guys fucked up. She didn't touch them, she was just feeling them out. From the minute she walked in to 'clean' your office, she was on the phone. And when I say clean, I mean she used the dust rag on three shelves and the corner of your desk while she listened to whoever was on the other end and nodded her head."

"Leaving it unlocked the other day while I went to lunch worked as planned then."

"Yeah. The day before that, there's video of her turning the knob and walking right into the locked door that was always open before. Bloodied her nose. It was fucking hilarious."

"So she was suspicious as fuck, but we don't have anything damning on her from her time in there."

"Nothing at all. She made it look like she was just sucking up to the boss with a can of Pledge."

"Okay. Keep working on the others and get back to me. I've got to go."

"How's Pop? I haven't talked to him since last week when I had to walk him through working that new television Cap got him. That was some funny shit."

"He's good, but he wants to go back to his old console TV with the foil on the rabbit ears. Says he doesn't need to see the veins on the newscaster's nose, but he's got a great view of the weather lady's panty line during the evening news now. He misses Dan Rather and Walter Cronkite."

"I'll give him a call tomorrow before his Sunday nap. In the meantime, I'll keep digging for dirt on the rest of your staff."

"Thanks, Preach. Good to know who I need to pay closer attention to for now, at least."

"There's more to come, I'm sure. Do you want me to run the coffee lady for you before your date tonight?"

"Talked to Hook before you talked to me, I guess?"

"Maybe. Or maybe I'm following your movements

with a satellite and know everything you do and say, down to and including that singing shit you do alone in the shower."

"Leave her alone. I'd like to explore her all on my own. As far as the singing shit, you knew about that because you fucking lived next door to me for a year."

"I did. If you want to get the good stuff from the pretty coffee lady, don't serenade her. Ever. She'll either take an ice pick to her ears or to you. Or both."

"Fuck off. I'm out. Talk to you soon."

"Adios," Preacher chirped before the call disconnected. I laid my phone on the armrest and let everything he told me resonate for a few minutes while I stared at the ceiling.

"My singing isn't that bad, is it, Elvira?" I asked my pet, staring at me from her spot on my chest as we relaxed in the recliner. She blinked a few times and then looked away. Merlin, one of my cats who was laying on the couch a few feet away, let out a howl of disagreement. I glared at him for a few seconds while he stared into my eyes. Finally, I broke the silence and told him, "Shouldn't you be out hunting mice or something?"

As usual, the look on his face and his apparent disdain for me as a pet owner showed me just what he thought about my opinion. He blinked once and then laid his big head down on the couch before he closed his eyes for a nap.

I had a lot of information to mull over, and I knew it was just the tip of the iceberg. I'd have to tiptoe around Julia in the office and see if I could get one or two of the women to spy for me on the down low. Lorene was a likely candidate.

Clinton had gone into the office the day after she'd dispatched me for that missing person call and chewed her ass out. I'd shut his shit down and sent the little fucker home for the day before I walked Lorene over to Jitters and bought her a hot tea to help calm her nerves.

I'd speak to Lorene and see if all was good among the office staff. If Julia was hiding something, she probably had a loyal accomplice. If two of them were tight and excluded the others, there would be some hurt feelings, and that could help bring the other women over to my side of the fence.

As I stood up, I mentally kicked myself yet again for going along with the batshit crazy idea to put me in as chief. I did not handle politics well and couldn't fucking keep my mouth shut around backstabbers and the cloud of bullshit that always accompanied them.

Being right in the middle of a shitstorm and surrounded by people I didn't know or trust was not my idea of a goddamn good time.

I'd put it all out of my head, shower, and get ready for my date with the beautiful lady. I had plans for her that included lots of naked time, lots of good screaming, and a nap between each round. But first, I'd need to take care of business in the shower while I thought about her. It might take the edge of this hard-on I'd been sporting since our talk last night.

I wanted to make a good impression so I could see where this might lead us. If I went in like a three-pump chump, I'd most likely hit a dead end. I couldn't have that.

Ms. McCool had so much more to offer than just her body, and I wanted to explore those avenues too.

But since she'd set her mind against me, I'd have to blur her decision with orgasms. Considering how sexy the woman was, I didn't see that as a chore.

JENNIFER

"You're fucking with me." Paula, my new friend here in Tenillo, had frozen with her coffee mug halfway to her lips and sat there as she stared at me in shock. "Shit like that doesn't happen."

"I'm not fucking with you. I had an orgasm, and *he never even touched me.*"

Paula set her mug on the table with a thump and tilted her head as her eyes blinked rapidly and her eyebrows rose up toward her hairline. She suddenly narrowed her eyes and recounted what I'd told her. "Standing right there in your coffee trailer on the edge of a park full of people, and he got you so hot you spontaneously combusted and had an orgasm on the spot."

"Yes. And *then* he kissed me."

"Holy shit. He's got sex voodoo."

"I don't care if he's got an inch-long penis and doesn't know what the hell to do with it. If he can kiss like that, talk like that, and make me forget where I am, I obviously don't need penetration for him to get me off."

"But what if the rest of the package is as good as that imagination of his?" Paula whispered as she leaned forward.

I shivered at the thought and took a deep breath. I didn't know if I could handle the man at full throttle packing a dick worthy of that dirty mind.

I didn't know if I could handle it, but I'd die trying.

"Has anyone ever died from having too many orgasms? If he's got the whole enchilada, I might."

"Honestly, he could be all talk and no action if the talk's that hot, right?"

"I've been telling myself since my divorce that I need a man who's not gonna try and boss me around or give me any shit when I do what I want to do. This guy is the opposite of what I want."

"What you *think* you want."

"No. What I know I want. I want a man I can get along with, talk to, enjoy spending time with and basically be friends with for the long term."

"You just described a gay best friend."

"I really didn't. If I'm ever in a relationship again, he needs to be easygoing and let me have my way. I argued enough for a lifetime with Ethan. Every single fucking thing was a discussion and then he'd bulldoze right over me while he made me feel like shit about myself. I'm not that woman anymore. It's not going to happen."

"I never met your ex, thank God, but he sounds like a small-minded bully with a pinch of chauvinism and a dash of asshole thrown in for good measure. Now, as far as the easygoing man? You'd be disgusted at him being a pushover in life besides just with you. You'd be done in a month. A man that keeps you on your toes, knows how to compromise, and can put you where he wants you in the bedroom while he gives you multiple orgasms is what you need. I think the pussy whisperer police chief is that man."

"One date, a wild night of sex, and I'm out. Anything further than that is unacceptable."

"But what about the phone conversations that end with him driving to your house? If you just have a one and done, you won't get that, and those sound really nice," Paula said wistfully.

"That sounds better than nice, Paula. Too nice."

"Whatever, woman. We're going to get manicures and pedicures, then you're going to go home and make sure that what hair you've got on your body is flawless and inviting. Then you're going to put on your face, leave your hair down and sexy, get dressed for a motorcycle ride, and let him wine and dine you. After all that foreplay, you'll let Mr. Chief of Police take you for a different kind of ride where you'll be making noises louder than the siren on his patrol car while he fucks you into a sex coma. When you wake up tomorrow, you'll call and give me details, and we'll reassess your decision to make this a one-night stand."

"If he's as good as he thinks he is, I might not have the energy to pick up my phone."

"For your sake, I'm hoping that's the case."

JENNIFER

"You know I wouldn't generally leave you out here, but I'm going to have company this evening, and I don't want to scar you for life," I whispered as I leaned down and hugged Sammy, the blonde alpaca. "I've got someone coming to feed you in three hours, and I've got my alarm set for four hours after that. By then, he'll be gone, and I'll come down here to the barn and get you two and Moe so I can take you back to the house, okay?"

Neither one of them seemed to have a strong opinion about my abandonment. David was in the stall rolling around on his back in the fresh hay I'd put down a few hours ago. As soon as I let Sammy go, he joined him. Moe lifted his head and gave me a bored look, but he seemed content to lay on the dog bed I'd brought out into the barn for him weeks ago.

"Ed Earl, you're gonna have to stay in the barn too. Go on in with your ladies and get settled for the night I'll come out to visit you in the morning." I reached down and touched the rooster on the head as he leaned against my thigh. After some coaxing and a shove or two, I got him through the door that led to his section of the chicken coop.

All of my chores were finished now. I was dressed appropriately for a motorcycle ride. My hair was covered in a bandana that I could take off when we got to the restaurant and I was wearing a thick sweater with a henley underneath, faded jeans, and the boots on my feet were classic Doc Martens that looked kickass as I walked down the main aisle of the barn.

I was ready to go. If he didn't get here in the next minute and a half, I'd lose my nerve. I was that freaked out. As I turned and shut the barn door behind me, I heard a motorcycle driving up the road. As I walked toward the house, I watched it slow and turn down my long driveway.

His motorcycle seemed larger than most I'd seen, but considering the size of the man himself, it made sense. The bike was matte black with barely any chrome, and its loud growl made my insides quiver almost as much as looking at the man driving it.

I wasn't sure how tall Boss was since I'd been standing inside the food truck, and he was outside on the ground. He had to be huge, considering he was a little taller than Hook, who was much taller than me. I'd seen him walking toward the food truck, and I'd watched him walk away. Both views were enough to make me drool.

I hurried through the house to the front door. By the time I got there, I couldn't hear the motorcycle anymore, but I did hear heavy footsteps on the porch right before I pulled the door open. When I looked up into his rugged face, I found out just how tall he was.

Damn, the man was handsome. His hair was mostly silver. Not gray at all. And sexy as hell. There were still areas of it that were dark, almost black, but the longer hair on top was all silver and windblown from his ride.

As if my staring made him self-conscious, he ran his big hand over his head to take care of the hair that was out of place. How in the hell could he make just that so fucking sexy?

"Are you ready, sweetheart?" he asked in that gravelly voice, and I had to stop myself from shivering.

I really needed to get my shit together, or I would be a puddle of drool on the floor of the restaurant by the time dinner was served. When I was able to form a coherent sentence, I answered, "Yeah, I'm ready."

"You sure?" Boss chuckled and reached out to hold the screen door open. "You look fantastic, babe. You need to grab a jacket, you think?"

"I've got a thermal on under the sweater. Will that be okay?"

"It should."

I glanced at the leather vest he was wearing and back up into his eyes before I joked, "I don't have a fancy leather vest to wear, so I'll have to make do."

"Let's see how shit plays out and then maybe we'll get you one. Take your time gathering your things. I've got a table held for us, but we don't have to be there at a specific time."

"They're holding a table for you? Shit, where are my manners? Come in for a second while I lock up." I stepped back and let Boss into my house. Once he was through the door, I thought to myself that I should get moving, but my legs just wouldn't work. I couldn't take my eyes off the man.

He was staring down into my face with a half-smile, and then I heard his low chuckle. "Sorry. It's been a long time since I went on a date. I got ready too early and had time on my hands, so I took the animals out to the barn. Hook's got a guy coming over to feed them in a few hours just in case I'm not home, but I've got to set my alarm so I can remember to feed them four hours after he does. I hate making you wait on me, so I'll . . ."

"Relax, Jenn. I've got nothing but time." Boss's voice was soft and rough at the same time. It was sexy as hell. He moved closer to me and got into my space, but I couldn't step back because the door was behind me. "I think I can help. Do you want me to?"

"Help what? Help me relax?"

"Yeah," Boss whispered, even closer now. My head was tilted back so I could hold his stare. My chest was touching his, and that made me forget to breathe. His face moved down to mine ever so slowly. He reached up, put his hand on my jaw, and held my chin in his hand. He tilted my head just a bit and then touched his lips to mine.

It was a soft kiss, but just like the other night, it was explosive. Every nerve ending in my body burst into flame at the simple touch of his lips on mine the other night, but now, his rough hand was touching my face, and I really was ready to combust.

Before he pulled back, he kissed me a few more times, just simple nibbling kisses on my lips, before his hand moved toward my ear and down to the back of my neck as he stared into my eyes.

"Now that we've gotten our first real kiss out of the way, there's no sense in being nervous. It's like tasting the wine before you pour a glass. Just a sip to get a feel for what to expect."

"Oh."

"You smell good, baby, and you taste like oranges. I love oranges, and for years, I couldn't have them. When I kiss you, it's like tasting them for the first time all over again." Boss leaned forward and kissed me one more time, this one with a little more tongue. Not too much, not too heavy - just a taste. Like I was a fine wine. When he pulled back, he let his hand drop before he grinned and said, "Go do your thing, sweetheart. I want to get you on my bike so you'll put your arms around me. Then I want to get to know you over dinner so that when I bring you back here, we can do that again. For hours, maybe days."

"Fuck a duck. You really need to come with a warning label," I muttered as I took a deep breath and shook my head. "I just can't with you."

"Can't what?"

"Can't breathe, can't speak in coherent sentences, can't remember what the fuck I'm supposed to be doing right now. I just can't. I'm like the shy freshman girl when the senior football captain says good morning in the hall. I turn into a puddle of hormonal goo and forget how to function."

Boss's laughter boomed and echoed through my house. I looked up at him with a smile before I shook my head again and walked toward the back door. I heard Boss's heavy boots following me across the hardwood, but they stopped somewhere behind me as I walked out onto the back patio to make sure the outer door was locked. When I turned around, he was standing at the bar looking at a contraption I was working on for Sammy and David.

"What's this?"

"I saw a video on YouTube where they were bottle feeding a herd of baby goats using this cool stand, and I was trying to make one. I guess the saying you can fix anything with duck tape doesn't really hold true in this case."

"You'll have to show me the video over dinner, and let me see if I can help."

"Okay," I agreed as I locked the back door. I walked over to the bar and dug my wallet out of my purse. I found my ID and debit card and slipped them into my back pocket before I dropped my wallet back into my purse. I turned to Boss and said, "I'm ready."

He looked out of the back windows and then turned and looked out of the front windows before he looked down at my purse.

"That's an engraved invitation, sweetheart."

"What?"

"You can see right through this place, and a dirtbag would absolutely see a leather purse sitting right in the middle out in the open. A leather purse that probably costs a mint *and* is likely full of goodies. An asshole wouldn't think twice about busting out a window to get to that. Drop it back behind the counter?"

"Oh. I get what you're saying, but there's a treatment on the windows so no one can see inside." I picked my purse up and set it on the counter behind the bar and then smiled up at him. "Now I'm ready."

"Keys?"

"Well, shit!" I hurried around the bar, rifled through my purse, and then rushed around the bar to go out to the garage. I found them in the cupholder of my truck and came back into the house. "Found 'em!"

Boss was staring at me like he was trying desperately to keep a straight face, and he held his hand out to me as he walked across the room. When he got to me, he took the keys and reached around to rest his hand at the small of my back before he nudged me toward the front door. Once I was outside, he pulled the door shut and locked the deadbolt before he looked down at my jeans and then at the jumble of keys on my keyring. "Just a sec, sweetheart."

He turned around and unlocked my door and then walked toward the bar while he fiddled with my keyring. I heard him drop my keys into my purse before he walked back out. Once the door was shut and locked again, he handed me my house key with a smile.

"Those jeans fit like a work of art. It'd be a sin to ruin that masterpiece."

He put his hand on the small of my back again and walked me toward his motorcycle while I processed that compliment.

'Oh, shit, that man is trouble!' a little voice in my head was screaming at me. It was probably the part of my brain that had decided to stay away from alpha males who were large and in charge. I let the sex-crazed puddle of goo part of my brain slowly suffocate the little voice until it was gone before I climbed up on the bike behind Boss. I listened to his instructions about where to put my feet and how to hold on, and then I was settled.

Once that nagging voice was silent, I let myself wrap my arms around Boss's solid body and held on as he roared down my driveway. With the wind in my hair, the motorcycle rumbling between my legs, and the hot as hell man against my chest, I let my head fall back and stared at the sky.

I was going to ride this adventure out and look back on it fondly for years to come.

BOSS

"You're the president *and* the chief of police?" Jennifer teased before she took a second sip of her wine. "Tell me how you got elected."

"I'm the president of my MC, and my brothers elected me when the former president took off for that perfect fishing hole in the sky."

"Oh no. He died? I'm sorry!"

"It's alright, babe. He had a heart attack and died while fishing, which was probably his second choice of how he wanted to go out. Maybe his third."

"What would his first two choices have been?"

"I don't know his choices exactly, but my number one would be in the arms of a beautiful woman with her legs wrapped tightly around me while she screamed my name as she clutched me while I came inside her." I watched Jenn's breath hitch and resisted a smile. She really liked dirty talk for such a put-together woman, and I did not mind giving it to her. "The second choice would be on the bike doing 80 on the highway with the sun on my face and the wind whipping by. I guess third would be on my porch with a beer in hand while I watched the sun set."

"I like your first one, but from the other side of that scenario. My second would be sipping coffee as I watch the sunrise. I guess I don't have a third."

"Didn't like riding the bike?"

"Oh no! I loved it, but if I fell off, how would you know?"

"I was aware of every single second that your arms were around me, Jenn. I'd know."

"Your club is called Time Served. Why?"

I stared at her for a minute and then took a deep breath. It was going to come out sooner or later. I guessed that my answer and her feelings about it would decide how the rest of our evening went. I looked her in the eye and said, "Every member of our MC has spent a significant amount of time in prison."

"And since you're the police officer, you're the one in charge? I bet they're not happy about that." Jenn laughed, and

I knew she didn't get what I was saying, so I repeated it.

"*Every* member of our club has spent a significant amount of time in prison, darlin'. Every member."

"You too?" Jenn asked, shocked. I nodded slowly and took a sip of my beer, letting my eyes scan the restaurant as Jenn decided to either cut this evening short or give me a chance to explain and maybe salvage what we had going here. She leaned forward and whispered, "I don't think I've ever met an ex-con before. If I did, I didn't realize it at the time. Is it rude to ask what you did to get there? I mean, even if it is, I really want to know. I would hope that it wasn't something horrible, but what do I know? I mean, your version of horrible and my version of horrible could be two totally different things. To me, cheating on taxes isn't horrible, but to some people, especially the IRS, it is. But then again . . ."

"Jenn. Shh." I whispered as I reached out and touched her hand. I'd noticed that she rambled when she was nervous, and I hated that I'd made her feel that way again, this time without the dirty talk and the kissing. "I can tell you what I was convicted of flat out, or I can tell you what led me being charged with that crime. Which version would you like? Simple or longer?"

"Longer."

"I was married. Happily married. We were high school sweethearts. It was just like in the movies: I was the football captain, and she was the cheerleader. We got married fresh out of high school and had our daughter not long after that. Seven months after that, actually." Jenn started to say something, but I squeezed her hand just a bit, and she stopped so I could finish. "I was a cop and had been for 10 years. I was moving up in the ranks even though I wasn't quite as easy to get along with as some of the men in my department. By easy to get along with, I mean I didn't turn a blind eye when I saw something wrong going on. I was approached by another officer who offered me money to forget some details on a report I was writing. When I refused, he told me that if I knew what was good for me, I'd never testify in court. I told him to fuck off. A month later, I was scheduled to testify against the man. While I was at work, three men broke into my house. They took my 16-year-old daughter and my wife hostage. From what I found out later, the men were ordered to take them away and keep them safe until after the trial. Without my testimony, the man would walk, and by taking my family, he knew I'd cooperate."

"Oh no," Jenn whispered before she bit her lip and shook her head.

"They didn't keep them safe. They didn't even take them out of our house. When I got off shift, I went home and found my wife and my daughter dead. They'd both been violated by more than one man and then beaten before they were shot. I laid my wife and my baby girl to rest side by side in the plots my wife and I had bought for ourselves. After that, I went to the officer who'd tried to stop me from testifying, and I beat him until he told me who was behind what happened to my family. A few days after that, I was arrested for putting the cop in the hospital. Before I could even hire a lawyer, they charged me with the murder of a man who had previous convictions of burglary and rape. He was one of the men that broke into my house. I pleaded no contest for a lesser sentence and was convicted and spent 10 years in prison. I got out five years ago and moved to Tenillo where Pop helped me adjust to life out in the world. He gave me a job, a home, and the will to keep going, just like he's done for all the other men in my club."

"Oh my God, Boss."

"This is where you've got to make a choice, Jenn. And it's your choice. I won't judge you for it. You can ask me to get up and leave you here to wait for a ride home, you can let me drive you home and leave you there alone, or we can finish our dinner, bitch about the quality of the dessert choices, and proceed from there. It's all you, babe."

"What happened to the other men? You said there was more than one man. Did they go to prison?"

"No."

"Did you kill them too?"

"I was prosecuted for one murder."

Jenn sat there quietly, and when I started to pull my hand away, she turned hers over and held on, twining her fingers with mine. She stared into my eyes for a few seconds and said, "Give me a minute to process, okay?"

I nodded and watched her face as she gazed sightlessly around the dining room. Finally, she turned back to me and smiled.

"I think we should just skip the dessert altogether like we talked about last night. I tried out a new recipe today, and it's at home in the fridge if you wouldn't mind trying it and giving me your opinion. I resisted a taste test, hoping you'd help me out."

I felt the vice that had been tightening around my

chest loosen in small increments until I could finally take a deep breath.

"It would be an honor if you let me be your taste tester, babe. We barely know each other, but I've got a feeling there's nothing you could do, say, or create that's going to disappoint me."

Jenn smiled at me, and her light green eyes glowed in the dim lighting of the restaurant. I'd made it through some shit times, been broken down so severely that I didn't want to live. I'd lost 10 years of my life for doing something I didn't have a single ounce of remorse for, but with that smile, I saw something I'd never dreamed I'd get.

That smile and the woman giving it to me was going to be my reward for coming out the other side without losing everything good inside me.

JENNIFER

After two glasses of wine and a motorcycle ride under the stars, I found myself walking hand in hand with Boss up my porch steps. This was the scenario he'd described just last night when he'd convinced me to go out with him.

We'd talked about his history, and he shared even more details after that, including the fact that his real name was almost as sexy as his nickname or road name, as he called it. We'd talked about my ex-husband and how he treated me, and he'd laughed at my description of Homewrecker Barbie. He'd told me about his daughter, and I could see the pain and the pride in his eyes as he talked. He'd made sure to let me know that he'd come to terms with the loss of his wife after all these years and knew she'd want him to move on.

He'd told me about his pet skunk, and I'd told him about my dream of owning a yard full of animals. He'd asked me about children, and I'd held back my tears when I explained that a baby of my own wasn't in the cards for me. He admitted that he didn't understand how I felt, but he sympathized. He understood why I wanted all my fur babies.

We'd laughed over dinner when he told me some of the things he'd seen in his short time as police chief and a few stories he remembered from his time as a cop before he went to prison. I'd shown him the app I'd created while I waited on my divorce, and he'd laughed as he played it for a few minutes and marveled at how smart I must be to create such a thing.

He'd told me how hard he'd worked to take care of his wife and daughter while he got his associate's degree. I told him about my double major in computer science and business and how I'd gone back and gotten a degree in business law because I didn't trust the lawyer my husband had chosen for our company. He'd laughingly told me that now he knew his place in our hierarchy. I was the brains, and he was the brawn.

And through all that, I'd realized that option number three was exactly what I wanted. I also wanted to add breakfast to tomorrow's agenda as well as relaxing beside him on the porch with a motorcycle ride thrown in somewhere between more time naked in bed and a nap or two.

As we reached the top step, he held his hand out for my house key so he could open the door for me.

"I've made a decision about those options you gave me last night, but I'd like to add something." He didn't say a word, just unlocked the door and pushed it open before he turned to look me in the eye. "I want option three, but I want it to flow over into tomorrow morning where I make you breakfast and watch you eat it in my kitchen without a shirt. Then I'll leave the dishes in the sink and let you thank me for cooking. When you're finished showing me your appreciation, we can shower together and then sit on the porch and enjoy the sunshine for a while before I cook you lunch, and you thank me again. We'll nap, maybe take a ride for a while and then come back so I can cook you dinner, and you can thank me for that meal too. Does that work for you?"

He didn't say a word, but his hand shot out and

wrapped around the back of my neck so he could pull me close to his body. Our mouths met, and it was a scorching hot kiss. Not at all like the soft ones we'd shared before. No, this one set my body on fire. When his hand fisted in the hair at the back of my head, and he turned my body with his hand on my hip, I went willingly, walking backwards into my house. I heard the door slam and knew he'd kicked it closed since both of his hands were still on me.

Finally, he pulled away just far enough to growl, "Still want the hall floor or want to start this in bed, babe?"

"Bed. Start to finish. This time."

"Fuck yeah. This time." Boss's slow smile lit me up inside, and he kissed me again before he let my hair go and pushed my hip to spin me around in front of him. I heard the deadbolt engage behind me as I walked toward the stairs. Boss was right behind me, and I realized he appreciated the view when his hands came up and cupped my ass as I climbed the stairs in front of him. I heard him growl, but I wasn't sure if he was talking to himself or telling me, "I can't wait to get that ass naked in front of me."

Either way, I was all about giving him what he wanted in exchange for getting a whole lot of what I wanted, namely being worshipped like a goddess and figuring out if multiple orgasms were really a thing. I guessed that at my age, I'd have experienced it by now if there really was such a thing. But considering I'd slept with only one man in my entire life, and he was a selfish bastard, I didn't think I had much to measure other lovers by.

We'd see.

We got to the top of the stairs and turned left through the sitting area on our way to the bedroom when I heard Boss's footsteps stop. I turned around and saw that he was staring down at the living area from the railing that surrounded my upper level sanctuary.

"Your house is fucking great, baby," Boss told me as he looked around. "All sorts of things that make it yours, and all sorts of places I'd like to make ours." He pointed downstairs at the baby grand I had in the corner and then at the bar, the kitchen table, the couch, the back door, and porch. "There are all sorts of flat surfaces I'm looking at here, and although they look like a picture out of a magazine, there's one thing that can make them better."

"What's that?"

"You. Naked. Spread out on top of 'em with me between your legs."

I had another one of those whole body shivers and heard Boss laugh when I grabbed his hand and yanked him behind me as I said, "Bedroom's this way, big talker."

I'd barely made it through the bedroom door when one of Boss's arms went around my waist. He stopped me from walking closer to the bed and fit his large body behind mine. I felt one finger move my hair across my back and over my shoulder a second before his lips were there, trailing soft kisses from my hairline to the edge of my sweater. Before I realized he'd let me go, his hands were at my waist, and my sweater and shirt were bunched in his hands as he ordered, "Arms up."

Once the sweater was off my body, I saw it tossed over

to the side. It landed on the floor, and I didn't care. Boss had swept my hair back over my shoulder and was trailing kisses down my spine. I felt him unhook my bra and then his hands pushed the straps down my arms and I let it fall to the floor.

"It's like opening a present on Christmas morning," Boss whispered as he put his hands on my shoulders and slowly turned me around to face him. "Oh, fuck yeah, and what a present those are."

His hands came up and cupped my heavy breasts before he bent forward and licked first one nipple and then the other. I was staring at his face when he looked up at me as he pulled one nipple into his mouth and sucked hard while his other hand tugged at my other nipple, gently at first and then with a little more force.

Boss stood up and kissed me as he unbuttoned my pants. My hands went to the button of his pants. He moved his hips out of reach before he took his mouth off mine and said, "You first, babe. If I'm naked, I'll be inside you. If I'm in clothes, I'll worship you with my mouth. I don't trust that I can control myself if I feel your skin on mine."

Panty-melting words if I'd ever heard them right there. I, Jennifer McCool, had the man so close to the edge that he didn't think he could control his own body. It was only fair because what he'd promised to do to me and what he was doing right now had me losing control of mine.

As we kissed and Boss worked my jeans and underwear down over my hips, he walked me backward to the edge of the bed. Once I was there, he knelt in front of me and pulled my clothes down with him before he reached up and pushed my body back so that I had no choice but to sit on the bed. He made quick work of my boots and socks and then I was naked with him kneeling between my legs. He looked up at me as he ran his hands from my ankles to my knees and up my thighs toward my sex.

"Days, sweetheart. I could eat pie for days."

"Fuck a duck," I moaned as I flopped back on the bed. I heard his soft laughter and lifted my head to watch him. His hands were moving slowly up and down my inner thighs, pushing my legs wider with each pass as he studied me intently.

"I do believe that's the prettiest pussy I've ever seen in my life, sweetheart," Boss said as he kissed the inside of my knee. "I'm going to worship it," he whispered as he kissed a little higher up. "I'm going to taste it." Another kiss even higher up on my thigh. "I'm going to nibble on it." Another kiss just an inch away from my sex, so close I could feel his breath on my clit. "And I'm going to lick it until you scream my name and pull my hair. You want that, Jenn?"

"I want that."

"No going back once I'm in there, and I don't just mean in your pussy, sweetheart. I'm in there, there's no going back."

"No going back."

"I've got condoms in my wallet. Two of 'em. We need 'em?"

"I can't get pregnant. No eggs."

"You told me that. That's not what I'm asking. Do you

trust me?"

"Oddly enough, I do," I whispered as I took a deep breath, waiting on him to speak again so I could feel his hot breath on my clit one more time. "You trust me?"

"Fuck yeah, and I don't have a goddamn clue why," Boss admitted before he put his mouth right at my center and sucked my clit between his lips. I let my head fall back with a moan at the pressure, the *perfect amount of pressure*, as his tongue swiped back and forth across my clit while his hands pushed my thighs up and apart. I felt his thumbs part my sex and move upwards toward his mouth, opening me up before he let go of my clit and swiped his tongue upwards until he was back at my clit, breathing on it, licking it, nibbling it. Finally, he flattened his tongue and pressed in just as he pushed two fingers inside me, and I was gone. I clutched at air, the comforter at my sides, my legs, and finally found purchase in his hair as I came so hard that it took my breath away.

He didn't let up until I was finished and then he tugged his hair out of my hands as he kissed his way down my thigh to my knee and worked his way back up again slowly. I was boneless now, my legs splayed out to the side as my feet rested on his shoulders. I felt him close to my sex again, then he kissed his way up one side of my pussy until his tongue touched my clit again and flicked back and forth slowly. He kissed down the other side and then down my thigh to my knee before he moved back up and did the same thing, only this time he used his fingers again along with his tongue. I was a writhing mess in front of him, calling his name, begging for more, and pleading for him to fuck me. Once that orgasm waned, he pulled back. I heard his pants hit the floor and movement as he got out of his boots and clothes. I lifted my head to watch him and saw that his eyes were roving over my body until they finally looked up at my face.

He smiled as he ran his hands over his mouth and short beard. He was cocky about it, and he should be. He'd done just what he said he'd do and had me screaming his name before I'd even seen him naked. I decided to fix that issue, and I let my gaze wander down his body. His muscled chest had a sprinkling of silver hair that tapered down over his firm stomach, no rippling abs, just a firm and thick body that screamed *power*. My gaze went lower, and I saw his belly button and, less than an inch below that, the head of his cock.

I'd wondered last night when I saw how big his arms, thighs, and hands were if the rest of his body matched, and now I had my answer. As I stared at him, one of those big hands I'd admired wrapped around his dick and started moving up and down, his thumb passing over the top of the head with each stroke. I was mesmerized until I heard his gravelly voice order, "Move up the bed, Jenn. I'm gonna fuck you hard, and you're gonna need to brace."

'Oh, hell yeah!' my wicked inner voice screamed as I scrambled up the bed. He put one knee on the bed and let his cock go as he moved up between my legs. When his mouth was even with my pussy he gave me one last swipe with his tongue and then kissed his way up my belly between my breasts before putting his mouth on mine for a long, deep kiss.

I felt his cock at my entrance and moved my hips to guide him to me, and I heard him laugh deep in his chest as he kissed me.

"Hungry for it?"

"I'm fucking starving."

"What did I tell you would happen?"

"What?" I whispered as I tried to shimmy lower to get him inside me.

"I told you you'd beg me to fuck you. You gonna beg?"

"Fuck no."

"Good girl," Boss growled as he pushed inside me. He moved steadily, slowly, until I was stretched around him, my body full of his until I wasn't sure I could take any more. Then he pushed in even farther, and I realized I could, and I wanted to. "Can't beg for what's already yours, sweetheart."

And with those words, he fucked me just as senseless as he'd promised and proved that when a man wasn't a selfish lover, his woman could come over and over again.

BOSS

"What the fuck is that noise?" I grumbled when a nuclear reactor alarm started warning of impending doom. "Jesus."

"Gotta get up, honey," Jenn whispered before she kissed me on the tip of my nose and wiggled out of my arms. "Go back to sleep. I'll be back in a bit."

"What the fuck? Where are you going?"

"Gotta feed the babies and bring them inside for bed. Go back to sleep."

"You're walking outside alone in the fucking middle of the night, and you want me to lay here like that's okay?"

"It's not like I'm in the middle of the city, and there are criminals around every corner, Boss. I'll be okay. Sleep."

"Fuck that," I grumbled as I sat up in bed and twisted to put my feet on the floor. I stood up and grabbed my pants from where I'd dropped them and pulled them on with nothing underneath. "You got socks I can wear?"

"Socks?"

"Just white socks. Can't put on dirty socks, babe."

"Gotcha. Here you go." Jenn tossed a pair of white athletic socks my way, and I sat down on the edge of the bed to put them on my feet. I pulled my boots on and didn't bother adjusting my pants over them. I planned on being dressed for as little time as possible. I pulled my shirt on as I followed Jenn out. She was dressed in a pair of sweatpants, a sweatshirt, and a pair of flip flops. Miraculously, my dick got hard again, watching her ass move around in those loose pants with every step she took.

Once we were at the bottom of the steps, Jenn reached up and pulled her hair back. She used her teeth to get an elastic band off her wrist and used it to put her hair in a ponytail. While we walked across the yard, she made quick work of braiding her long tresses and pulled another elastic off her wrist to tie off the end.

"These are those babies Hook brought you?"

"Yes. David and Sammy. We'll bring in my dog Moe while we're out here."

I watched as Jenn punched in a code and then I heard a lock tumble before she slid the door to the side. All was quiet in the barn, and as we walked down the broad aisle in the middle, I looked through the iron gates of each stall. I found two sleeping pigs, little things, not much bigger than a dog. In the next pen, I saw a donkey that was so small, I was sure it had to be a baby, so I asked her, "You gotta feed that baby donkey too?"

"Oh, he's fully grown. Hook brought him to me just yesterday. Some asshole bought him as a pet for his daughter when she was small. Now that she's too big to ride on him, they didn't want him anymore. They dropped him off at Hook's place."

"People are dicks."

"That they are. The man who had David and Sammy was going to put them down rather than take care of them. Fucking lazy asshole."

"Tell me how you really feel, babe."

I heard a rooster start to crow, but Jenn cut him off in a harsh voice, "Dammit, Ed Earl! Don't you start your shit with me!"

"Ed Earl? Really?"

"The Chicken Ranch. What can I say? I had a thing for Burt Reynolds when I was young."

I couldn't stop my laughter, but I did try and keep it

down in consideration of the sleeping animals around me. Jenn stopped at the end of the corridor and pointed her finger at the biggest fucking rooster I'd ever seen.

"What in the fuck is *that*?"

"Hook told you my cock was bigger than yours, but there's no need to be jealous, Boss. I like yours, too, just in a different way." Jenn opened a door in the fenced area at the back of the barn, and the rooster strutted out and rubbed himself up against Jenn's leg. "He thinks he's a cat, or I'm his woman. Something. Hook's never seen anything like it. Ed Earl, if I let you in the house, you're staying on the porch, buddy."

"You let him come in the house?"

"Well, yeah."

"And the baby alpacas?"

"Their beds are upstairs, over against the wall by the couch."

"I just thought you had three dogs or something."

"Nope. David and Sammy are house trained, and they sleep inside, which is good because I still have to feed them every four hours."

"You are fucking kidding me." Jenn looked at me with one eyebrow raised, and I laughed at her trying to be a badass. "I've got a pet skunk that lives in my house, honey. I'm not throwing shade; I was just shocked by it all."

"I've never heard of anyone owning a pet skunk."

"Says the woman who lets a rooster that's bigger than most dogs live in her house."

"On the patio. Ed Earl can only roam the house when I'm with him. He's not house trained yet, and I like to make sure and get the mess when it happens."

"Jesus."

I followed Jenn back down the aisle, and she opened a gate on the right. A beagle who was a bit overweight and looked irritated that his sleep was disturbed walked out, followed by two of the cutest fucking animals I'd ever seen in my life. They strutted out and rubbed against Jenn's legs as she petted their heads. "Sammy Hagar's the blonde, and David Lee Roth is the brown one."

I laughed again and asked, "What's the donkey's name? Eddie or Anthony?"

"Lee Majors."

I laughed even harder as I followed Jenn, the giant rooster, the pissed off dog, and two crying baby alpacas out of the barn. Once we were inside, the dog nudged Jenn's leg until she squatted down and kissed him on the head while she rubbed his neck. When she stood up, he walked to the stairs and went up, presumably to his bed by the fireplace I'd seen earlier. Jenn pulled two large bottles out of the mini fridge under the counter and held them in front of her.

David and Sammy went apeshit and sucked the milk down in minutes, making grunting noises as they gorged themselves. When they were finished, Jenn rinsed the bottles out, left them in the sink, and then washed her hands. After she dried them on a hand towel, she opened the refrigerator, pulled out a Tupperware container before she went to a drawer and got two spoons.

"I'm hungry again, and I blame you, so you have to share this with me in bed."

"By all means," I agreed as she walked toward the stairs carrying the food, the little animals following in her wake. Once we were upstairs, they moved right over to their beds and laid down while I latched a gate across the top of the steps at Jenn's instruction. I followed Jen into her bedroom and shut another gate, penning the animals upstairs but out of the bedroom. "Love your house, babe, but I have a question. If you can see down into the kitchen from your bedroom, they can see you. Also, when it's dark, you can't see anything in the yard, but anyone on the road can see us moving around in here."

"There's a film on the glass up here too. As far as seeing into the kitchen, there are shutters in the ceiling that come down if I hit that switch, cutting me off from the rest of the house if I have company."

"Good call."

"I drew the plans myself, and Pop's company made it happen."

"Also a good call. We've got some great guys working for us."

"They're part of your club?"

"Some of them."

"Is Tyler?"

"Yep. He's a prospect and a really good kid who's turning his life around."

"He's very polite but stubborn. I kept telling him to just come in the house if he needed me, but he'd stand at the back door and call for me instead."

"Ex-cons who want to stay out of trouble keep themselves out of positions where they can be in trouble or even assumed to be looking for trouble."

"What does that mean?"

"If Tyler never walked into your house, then his fingerprints won't be inside if something comes up missing. He's protecting himself, and I get that."

"Oh. Now I know. Hook said he was following the rules, and I didn't . . . holy shit! Hook's in your club!"

"He's my VP, babe."

"That means he's been in prison?" I smiled at her but didn't answer. That was Hook's business and story to tell if he wanted her to know. "Well, fuck a duck. I had no idea."

"Babe. Love talking to you, but it's two in the fucking morning. Feed me, fuck me again, and let's take a nap."

"I like how you think, Boss. I like it a lot."

BOSS

"How long has he been in there?" I heard Soda ask Hook from a few feet away. Hook answered, but I blocked out his voice. Pop had been in surgery for too long. I wasn't a fucking doctor, but I knew there were problems.

The man was almost 80 and, even though he was as healthy as a man his age could be, he was still too old to come back from a gunshot to the chest on top of the heart attack and CPR that happened in the ambulance three hours ago.

I'd been at Jenn's all day, and we'd gone to bed hours ago. I planned on going home to shower and put on my uniform when I woke up in the morning, but when I glanced at my phone, I saw that it was just past 4 a.m. now, and Pop was having a goddamn fit.

"Hold on just a minute, Pop! Someone cut the fence? Did you see who did it?" I asked as I sat up in bed and put my feet on the floor.

"Fuckers cut the chain on the fence out front and drove right through the goddamn yard to the back. I got in my cart and followed them, but they'd cut through the fence already and were gone. I told that son of a bitch when he came sniffing around yesterday that I'm not gonna have any part of him cutting through my property, but he didn't listen to me. I'm gonna find them and fuck them up, son. Beat their ass enough to make it worth the money it's gonna take to

fix all that shit."

"Don't you follow them, old man. I'm on my way now, and I'll wake up some of the guys. We'll take care of it."

"Fuck that, sonsofbitches comin' on my property like they own it, driving through in the wee hours and tearing up my shit. I'm gonna find them. You get here when you can so you can help me bury them out in the field."

"Pop!" I tried to argue again, but I was talking to air. The old geezer had hung up on me. When I called back the phone went straight to voicemail. "Fuck!"

I scrolled through my contacts and called Soda, one of the prospects who was almost ready to patch into the club. He answered on the second ring, and I explained what was going on. He assured me he'd get the guys up and after Pop within the next five minutes before he hung up.

I was dressed now, and Jenn held my cut. I pulled it on before I leaned down and gave her a quick, hard kiss.

"Gotta go, babe. Call Hook for me and tell him what's up. He'll call Cap. Go back to sleep. I'll call you later."

I stepped over the gate at the bedroom door and then the one on the landing before I yelled, "Come lock the door."

I heard her yell, "On it!" from behind me as I mounted my motorcycle and turned the key. I'd taken the road home from Hook's place to Pop's a million times in the last year, and I knew at regular speed, I could get there in 15. Tonight, I needed to make it faster.

It took me seven minutes to get to my house, another

five to get in my truck and find the cut in the fence that was easily big enough for my vehicle to fit through. I could see taillights out in the field and hoped those belonged to Soda and the guys. I hauled ass over the hard ground to get to them, wondering the entire time why they were stopped out in the middle of the old base.

When I drove up, I saw why.

Pop was on the ground and bleeding from his chest. Soda was barking orders at the men around him while he held pressure on the old man's wound. I grabbed my radio and called for backup and an ambulance as I jumped out of my truck and rushed over to drop down beside Pop.

"Fuckers shot him and took off. I've got Sandy and Fish chasing after them, but they had a good lead on us."

"Oh shit," I whispered as I felt for a pulse. It was weak but there. I heard chatter on the radio and asked Lorene for the ambulance's ETA just as I heard sirens in the distance.

Another vehicle pulled up, and Hook dropped down beside me and reached for Pop's hand as he whispered something frantically. I realized he was chanting, "Don't die, old man. Don't die on us. Don't die, old man. Not today."

The next few minutes were a blur filled with sirens, lights, and a lot of frantic action. I got into the ambulance with Pop and heard Hook say he'd follow us while Soda assured me he'd take care of shit.

Right now, I didn't give a fuck about anything but the old man on the gurney in front of me. When the machines they'd hooked up to him started beeping, I leaned back to give the paramedic room as he started chest compressions.

The sound of Pop's old bones cracking under the pressure echoed in my ears as I chanted the same thing I'd heard Hook saying just minutes ago.

"Not today, old man. Don't you dare fucking die on me."

I stood at the window, looking down over the parking lot of the hospital, wondering what the hell I should do now. Do I take off and go hunting or leave it to the men who were still out there looking? If I left, would I miss the last chance to talk to the man who'd saved my life? So many questions, and I didn't have a single fucking answer to any of them.

What he'd said to me on the phone kept playing over and over in my head. Who in the fuck had done this to the old man? What had he meant when he said someone had been sniffing around asking to cut through the property?

"I think we should make some phone calls, Boss," Cap said when he walked up to stand beside me.

"I think so too. I'll do it. I'll call the guys. You put the word out to some of the others and have them call their men. Tell them to check-in by text with Hook since I'll be on the phone. I'll get Preacher on it once he figures out how to get here."

"Got it. You okay? Soda brought you some fresh clothes."

"I'm good."

"Go clean up, brother. You'll . . ."

132

"I said I'm fucking good, Cap."

I watched Cap's reflection in the glass and saw him nod before he walked away to talk to Hook and Soda. Just then, my phone buzzed, and I looked down and saw it was a text from Jenn.

Morning, handsome. Did you get Pop sorted out? I'm at your office with breakfast.

I stared at the text for a minute, wondering how to respond.

I'm at the hospital. Pop was shot and in surgery. Not looking good, babe.

I saw the three tiny dots blinking and knew Jenn was reading my message or responding to it. They disappeared after a few minutes, and I lifted my head to look out of the window again. I'd put it off long enough, maybe too long, and I needed to call my brothers. They needed to be here to say goodbye, if that was what it came to, and they needed to be here to help me find and kill whoever had done this. I knew that every one of them would be just as upset as me, Hook, and Cap were right now. I hated to be the one to deliver bad news, but it was my job.

Sometimes the weight of the world rested on the leader's shoulders, and I was feeling every bit of that load right now.

I turned around and found Harvey sitting beside Hook, his face haggard, knowing his best friend was fighting for his life. The door to the waiting room opened, and Jack came through it, followed closely by Maddie, Tom, and Hal. The geezers and their queen were here, and I knew that every one of them was praying to whatever God they worshiped, hoping Pop would pull through this.

"Hook, I'm going to find a quiet place to make some calls. I'll stay close. If he comes out, don't let the doctor leave without talking to me first, okay?"

Hook nodded before he looked down at his phone.

"Soda, any word?" Soda shook his head just as the door opened again. I looked up and saw Sin and Saint walking through, and both of them had murder in their eyes.

"A word?" Sin asked as he tilted his head toward the door.

I nodded, and Hook stood up beside me. The four of us went out into the hall.

"Any clue who this could be?"

"On the phone, he said someone came sniffing around, saying they wanted to cut through his property. He told them no, but early this morning, they cut the chain on the gate and drove through anyway. Cut the fence at the back, or already had it cut, I don't know. Either way, they went through the field to the old base. Pop chased them, and when Soda and the guys found him, the fuckers were hauling ass, and Pop was in the dirt bleeding from his chest."

"Fuck me," Saint whispered.

"He had a heart attack in the ambulance, and they did CPR. When we got to the hospital, they rushed him into surgery, and that was three hours ago. I've got men looking, but they don't know what the fuck they're doing. Every goddamn one is fresh out of prison within the last six months. I have to be here, but we're losing time . . ."

"Stay here. We'll cover you. Get me the phone numbers of the men you have out there. We'll meet up, get some information, and take over the hunt. We're not new at this, and we know what we're doing. We've got the manpower."

"I'm calling in my club, at least the core group. They'll have some input and expertise to lend. They'll want to lend that expertise just like I will when Pop comes out of this."

"Of course." Sin reached out to squeeze my shoulder. "Stay with the old man, gather your brothers; we'll take care of shit on the outside until you can join us."

I nodded because at that moment I didn't think I could speak past the lump in my throat and the pain in my chest.

"I'll talk to my uncle for a beat and then we're out of here. Hook, you got those numbers for me?"

"Let me introduce you to Soda. He may have seen something that can help but I don't know," Hook answered as the three men walked back through the door into the waiting room.

I leaned back against the wall. Still no text from Jenn, but I'd ponder that later. Right now, I had to get on the phone. I picked the first one on the list in alphabetical order.

The phone rang twice before Bug picked up. "Yo, Boss!'

"Bug," I said and realized my voice was so low he

might not be able to hear me. I cleared my throat and tried again. "Bug, Pop was shot last night and he's in surgery. Need you home, brother."

"Fuck!" I heard Bug hiss. "Who did it and are they dead?"

"No idea yet, and they will be."

"Save a piece for me, brother. I'm booking a flight now."

"Gotta make some more calls. Text me when you know your ETA."

"Just booked it. Flight lands at 5:14 this afternoon."

"I'll have someone there to get you."

"If you talk to him, tell him I'm coming, okay?" Bug said softly. "I'm coming."

"I'll tell him."

I hung the phone up and touched Chef's name next. He answered on the third ring. "Hello, Boss. What can I do for you this fine morning?"

I explained what was going on, and Chef did the same thing Bug had done while we talked. Within a minute, his flight was booked and would arrive by 5:30.

My next call was to Kitty, but before I touched his name on the screen, I saw movement out of the corner of my eye. When I turned my head, I realized that Jenn hadn't sent me a message because she was here to see me in person. She didn't say a word but held my eyes and didn't stop walking until she'd bumped into my chest and her arms were wrapped around my waist. I kissed her on the top of the head and pushed Kitty's name.

Kitty didn't say hello. The instant the call connected, he said, "I'm on the road from OKC now. I'll be there in less than three hours, probably closer to two."

"Bug and Chef are flying in, and they'll be here this afternoon. I'll go pick them up in Fort Worth."

I felt Jenn shaking her head, but I didn't want to keep Kitty on the phone any longer than I had to since he was driving, probably faster than was safe even without the distraction.

"Stamp got a flight too. He'll be in Fort Worth at 3:20."

I felt Jenn's arms drop and she turned so that she was still touching me from my chest to my knees but now with her back to my front. Her presence was comforting, an anchor holding me down. I wrapped my free arm around her waist and pulled her even closer to me, if that was possible. When I glanced down, I saw that she was texting furiously, her thumbs flying over the phone. The messages going out and coming in were scrolling quickly up the screen.

"I'll be there to get him. I'll send him a text to tell him to wait for me. We'll gather them all together at once and bring them home."

"I'll be there as soon as I can, Boss. Tell Pop I'm coming when you see him. Tell him . . ."

"You tell him when you get here, brother. I've got more calls to make. Drive safely."

Once I'd hung up the phone, Jenn pulled away and turned so she could look up into my face. She reached up and touched my cheek and then let her hand trail down so that it rested on my chest.

"I'm going to pick up your friends. I've made arrangements to borrow my friend Paula's Expedition. It holds six men with plenty of cargo room. If I need something bigger, I'll rent it, but you need to stay here so you're close to Pop when he wakes up."

"Jenn, baby," I started to argue, and she shook her head.

"No. Don't argue. No alpha badass right now, big guy. This is me doing what I can to take care of you and my flirty friend Pop. If that's driving my ass to DFW and sitting there until every single man you know flies into town, that's what I'll do."

"Thank you, Jenn."

"Now, call your people and make arrangements. I'll get their names and flight times from you, and I'll be on my way."

I leaned down and kissed my girl on the lips before she leaned closer and fit herself up against me again. Yes, after just one fucking date, I knew she was *my* girl.

My phone rang and I saw that it was Preacher. I answered, and he said, "Find someone to pick me up, or I'll rent a car. I'll be at DFW by 3:45 if there aren't any delays."

"Stamps coming in about that time too. My girl's coming for you guys."

"Your girl?"

"Hot as fuck - auburn hair and green eyes that glow even in the sunshine. She'll be at the coffee cart outside of the gift shop, but I'll send you her number and a picture so you can find her or get in touch."

"Gotcha. See you soon."

"Preacher's getting on a plane," I whispered, completely shocked.

"Is that weird?" Jenn asked as she tilted her head back to look at me.

"You'd just have to know him, babe. You'll see."

"How many more?"

"Just Santa. I talked to him yesterday, and he was in Amarillo, so he might drive. Not sure."

I dialed, and Santa picked up. He was out of breath and wheezed, "Just got off a flight in Denver, but I'm turning around. I caught a flight back, but they've got me on a layover in fucking Vegas of all places before I get to DFW. I'm on my way to that plane now."

"What time?"

"4:10."

"Okay. We'll get you home. My girl's picking y'all up. Text Stamp when you land, and he'll tell you where to meet them."

"Got it," Santa wheezed. Before he hung up the phone,

I heard a woman's voice telling him he'd barely made his flight.

"They'll start arriving at 3:00. Last one at 5:30 if there aren't any delays."

"Go ahead and send them my info. Between delays and a million gates at that place, they might need it." Jenn stepped back and let me take a picture and then waited while I sent that along with her number in a group text to all the guys who'd be arriving at the airport this afternoon. "I'm going to go check my animals and pick up Paula's Expedition. By the time I'm done, I'll need to be on the road just in case there's an early arrival."

"You've known me less than 24 hours, and this is what you do."

Jenn shrugged off my comment and tipped her head up for a kiss. I gave her a few before I hugged her tight and let her go. I had to be missing something because there was no fucking way a man like me could be lucky enough to have a woman like her.

JENNIFER

"Connie, calm down," I told my friend over the Bluetooth speaker in my *other* friend's Expedition. "I don't have a picture of him, but I'll send it over when I get one."

"I'll print it out, frame it, and put offerings of rare gems, a bottle of lube, and some Viagra to take him through those rough days. I'll set them on a gilded plate below his picture and chant to him every day if he's really as awesome as you say. Okay, he deserves those things anyway. How many orgasms again? Hold on, I'm checking Amazon for rare gems."

"You're such a fucking dork."

"I'm a dork that hears the smile in your voice, and just for that, I'll find the gems and have them shipped to the man. Are you in the car?"

"Yeah, I'm on the highway," I admitted. "You're on Bluetooth, though."

"Where are you headed?"

"To pick up five of Boss's friends from the airport an hour away. They're, well, Pop's not their family, but close enough. Mentor might be a better word to describe it. He was shot early this morning after someone came onto his property and he gave chase. I left Boss at the hospital waiting for him to get out of surgery, and I'm headed to DFW to pick up his brothers. I guess they're not really his brothers. They're in a motorcycle club together."

"Like Sons of Anarchy?" Connie whispered in awe.

I laughed for a second and then answered, "Something like that."

"How does he run guns and kill people if he's a cop?"

"He doesn't sell guns, Connie. Jeez."

"Does he kill people?"

"I sincerely doubt it. He is the chief of police, after all." I thought about what Boss had told me in confidence last night. He hadn't admitted that he'd killed the man, only that he'd been convicted. I had a feeling he'd killed that one and the other three. Fuck the feeling part. I *knew* deep in my bones that he'd killed them, and I honestly didn't care.

They had done unspeakable things to his wife and daughter. If he'd killed all four of them, I didn't blame him. I even hoped he got to torture them for a while first.

What did that say about me?

"Are you sure?"

"That's television, Con. Seriously."

"You're right, but damn, those men are hot. Is he as hot as they are?"

"Hotter."

"What about his friends? Does he have a Chibbs? Or a Tig? Oh, please tell me he has a Tig. I want a Tig and a bottle of baby oil for Christmas. No, my birthday. It's closer. If he's got a Tig, I'm going to move to Texas, I swear to God."

"I've only met his friend Hook, and he's hot. Really hot. Of course, he's not as hot as Boss."

"I'm melting here. I really need a picture for my shrine."

"I'll get you one, and I'll be getting to know the rest of the core group while Pop recovers. If there's one that's a Tig equivalent, I'll give him your number, you freak."

"I've never pretended to be anything else! Shit. My meeting starts in five minutes, and I've got to pee. Call me later?"

"Yeah. Oh, any more from Ethan?"

"You know, I haven't heard anything from him in a few days. I'll put out some feelers."

"Talk to you later, dollface."

"Later."

I glanced at the stereo when Whitesnake started playing and then back at the traffic around me. I was close to DFW according to the GPS, and I could tell. Traffic was insane compared to the small town I'd gotten used to over the last six months.

Once I was parked in the short-term lot, I hoofed it into the building and made my way to the gift shop Boss had described. He'd sent the group text to the men with my picture and where I'd be along with my phone number, but they were all in the air somewhere, and none of them had answered.

I was so nervous that I couldn't sit still as I waited on some strange man to find me. Every horrible scenario I could think of was right there on the edge of my thoughts when I considered that I was meeting *five* strange men, all of whom had been in prison for various crimes. I was going to get in a vehicle and drive through the barren Texas countryside with them alone, all on the word of a man I'd met 24 hours ago.

What the hell was I thinking? One of them could be a serial rapist or . . . no! I shut that thought down. There was no way Boss, who had lived through his daughter and wife being raped and murdered, could consider a rapist his brother—no way in hell.

But he was a killer himself. I hadn't taken the time to analyze that or process it. My gut reaction screamed, 'Good for you! They deserved to die!'

And what did that say about me, that I was okay with that? Or that I was okay with spending the night with a man who hadn't denied hunting down and killing four other human beings? Was I so desperate for attention that I'd just let that go?

I'd forgotten every single rule I'd made for myself about avoiding the alpha male persona and finding a malleable man I could get along with and slept with the most alpha man I'd ever met 24 hours after I'd met him!

I needed a shrink. Or an exorcist. I was not behaving like Jennifer McCool, the 44-year-old Texas transplant divorcee with three college degrees, her own business, and enough animals to start a petting zoo. I was going with the flow and just letting my cooch make my decisions like I was a 19-year-old sorority girl trying to test out the efficacy of her new birth control implant.

I laughed at my own analogy and then looked around to make sure no one heard me when I saw a man leaning against the wall about 30 feet away. There was a duffle bag at his feet, and he had his phone in his hand.

The man was startlingly handsome in a dark and brooding way. He reminded me of the man who played Lucifer on that television show. I wondered if he might be a vampire or even Satan himself. I just got the vibe from his posture and his scowl that he was bad news. Sexy but evil in a bad boy way that was too much for me to even consider.

My phone rang, and I put it to my ear as I glanced at the man again.

"Hello?"

"Is this Boss's old lady?" I heard the voice on the phone ask at the same time the man I was studying spoke into his phone.

"What are you wearing?"

"Excuse me?" he asked, and I watched the man down the hall tense and stand up from his slouch.

"I think I see you. Look to your left."

The man slowly turned his head left, and his dark eyes caught mine. Oh, God. It *was* Lucifer, and I was his ride home. He bent down and picked up his bag as he shoved his phone into his back pocket. I stared at him in awe as he sauntered toward me. When he was about six feet away, his lips slowly curved into the sexiest smile I'd ever encountered. The man oozed sex appeal, but his eyes were still dark and dangerous.

Reminding myself that the man was the devil was hard to do when I caught sight of the dimples in his cheeks that wicked grin brought. He seemed familiar to me somehow, but I thought it might just be from paintings I'd seen in church as a child. He *was* the devil, after all.

"Jennifer? I'm Stamp." He stuck his hand out to shake mine. I put my hand in his and was happy that he shook it firmly and then let it go - none of that wimpy, limp shit some men tried on women. "It's nice to meet you."

"It's nice to meet you too. I know it's not the best of circumstances but . . ."

"Spending time alone with a beautiful woman, even in a busy airport, is a good thing regardless. Although the reason for my arrival is definitely heartbreaking. Any news on Pop?"

"I sent Boss a text letting him know I'd arrived safe, but he hasn't answered, so I don't have any current news."

"Who's set to arrive next? Do we have enough time to get some coffee and a snack? I haven't eaten since the hotel this morning and that was before dawn."

"Of course. Let's go into that bakery down the way. We've got 20 minutes until the next man lands."

"Who's next?"

"A man named Preacher. Is he your club's chaplain?"

I asked, unsure what the hierarchy was in the club other than what I'd already learned from Boss. He was the president, and Hook was his VP. I'd heard all the other names, but Preacher stood out as one that would probably be a man of God.

"Oh yeah. He's the chaplain. Keeps us all on the straight and narrow. Total man of the cloth." As we walked into the cafe, Stamp asked me, "Boss hasn't explained much about the club, has he? How long have you two been together?"

"Well, it's Monday now, and our first date was Friday evening, so we're approaching the three-day mark."

I was looking at Stamp when I answered, and the expression on his face didn't change at all. His only reaction was three blinks in rapid succession.

"You came to pick up a carload of men you don't know and drive us back to Tenillo. Alone."

"If I'm driving you back, obviously I'll have company."

"Do you know *anything* about us?"

"I do. Some."

"Give me a for instance."

"I know that the name of your club suits every man in it, but I don't know specifics, and I'm not going to ask. I'm going to trust that Boss wouldn't put me in any danger or surround himself with men he didn't trust implicitly."

"You're going to trust the opinion of a man you've

known for three days and put yourself in a vehicle full of killers, thieves, and arsonists?"

"It's a good thing I'm pretty because I'm obviously a few peas short of a casserole, huh?"

Stamp burst out laughing, and his entire face transformed from sexy and broody to the cheerful boy next door. It was amazing.

"I've never heard it put like that."

"I've got a million of 'em. A few years ago, I made a New Year's resolution to stop calling stupid people twatwaffles and dipshits - namely my ex-husband. Anyway, I branched out into more creative ways to say dumbass, and I reserve twatwaffle for the really bad cases."

"Like your ex-husband."

"Yep. Someday when he dies, I'm going to find his grave and replace his headstone with one that says 'Twatwaffle, may he rest in the same ignorance he wallowed in while he was living'."

Stamp laughed again and nudged me with his shoulder before he said, "I'm gonna like you, Jenn. I can already tell."

"Mr. Russo?" A woman who had stood up and walked toward us as we approached the counter called out. Stamp turned his head and smiled at her, She giggled like a school girl before she asked him if she could take a selfie and post it to her Instagram feed. He agreed and threw his arm over the woman's shoulder before he leaned down and smiled into her phone. Once they were finished, he signed a napkin for her with an ink pen he borrowed from the cashier. The woman hurried back to her table, her fingers flying over the phone.

"What was that about?" I whispered, studying his face.

Stamp's voice changed, and he sounded like a game show announcer. "This week on Russo's Road Trip, we'll visit Tenillo, Texas - home of the three-pound burrito."

"Holy shit. You're Valentine Russo!"

"I am. Now, let me buy you a subpar brownie that was made six weeks ago and pumped full of chemicals and preservatives. Then we'll go find our man of God."

Once we had our drinks in hand, the large board in the hallway showed that Preacher's flight had arrived. We walked back out into the hall and sat down on a bench together as we sipped our coffee and nibbled on our snack. In just a few minutes, an incredibly gorgeous man with a very intense expression rounded the corner and walked straight toward us.

"Preacher man," Stamp greeted him as he stood up. The men did the handshake, half hug, back slap greeting that alpha men seemed to prefer, before Stamp turned and motioned toward me and said, "This is Boss's new girl, Jenn. She's here to drive us to Tenillo as soon as the other guys get here."

Preacher stared into my eyes for a long minute and then squinted just a bit as he tilted his head, never taking his gaze off me. Neither one of us spoke, and finally Stamp interrupted our staring competition and said, "Boss didn't tell her anything about us, but she realized from your name that you must be our chaplain."

Preacher's eyes darted to Stamp's for a second and then back to mine. I watched the edges of his eyes crinkle as he smiled. "You think I'm a preacher? Like a man of God, tell me all your sins, kind of preacher?"

"Aren't you? Your name is Preacher."

"Then why is his name Stamp? Do you think he used to be a mail carrier?"

"Well, maybe?" My voice rose with the question because I had no idea where they got these off the wall road names, as Boss called them. I turned and looked at Stamp when I asked, "But if you do a cooking show, shouldn't they call you Chef? I guess I don't get it. Boss never explained why he's called Boss either."

"He's called Boss because he's a pushy motherfucker who bulldozes anyone in his path until he gets his way," Preacher explained. "It's not rocket science, sweetheart."

I felt my eyes narrow as I processed Preacher's tone and words, and Stamp chuckled beside me because he knew I was irritated and about to say something shitty to his friend. Preacher seemed oblivious to how insulting he sounded. Still, I realized he knew exactly what he was doing when he smiled and said, "And it looks like he finally found one he can't boss around."

The three of us made small talk until we were joined by Santa, Bug, and the man who was actually called Chef over the next hour. Once we were in the truck, I got us on the highway, listened to the men catch up, and answered their questions when they quizzed me about Pop's phone call early this morning and what I'd gathered from Boss while I was at the hospital.

Once we were on the road, Stamp called Boss to let him know we were all together and on our way. Boss let him know that Pop was out of surgery but having complications, so they weren't allowed to see him yet. The doctor hadn't come out to brief Boss on Pop's condition, but the little information they'd squeezed from the nurses wasn't good.

I set the cruise control for 15 over the speed limit and hustled back to Tenillo so I could be with Boss in case he got bad news.

Considering I only knew Pop from the flirting he did when he came to my food truck, and I'd only known Boss for a few days, I wasn't sure what exactly I could do to help either man. I just knew that I needed to be there.

BOSS

I adjusted my arm over Jenn's shoulders again, pulling her a little closer to me. She mumbled something in her sleep and moved her head against my chest before she settled. She'd left the hospital earlier to go and check her animals and drop the guys off at the compound so they could change clothes, open their storage containers, and get their motorcycles ready to ride. I'd told Jenn to stay home, but instead, she'd brought bags full of baked goods and six large vacuum carafes of different coffee creations along with plates, cups, and napkins.

When she'd walked into the waiting room pushing a metal cart she'd borrowed from one of the hospital staff, I'd felt my heart stop for a second at the sight of her.

She'd showered and changed into more comfortable clothes, her hair was pulled away from her face and hanging down her back in big curls, she had on no makeup and a spot of flour on one cheek, and she was the sexiest woman I'd ever seen in my entire fucking life.

As friends of Pop, officers who worked for me, Sin's group of men from AIMC, and my own brothers trickled in over the next few hours, she fed them and gave them coffee, all the while reassuring me that everything was going to be okay.

Finally, I'd convinced her to sit down for a minute beside me. She was asleep in my arms seconds later. I was content to sit here holding her for the next few years or until she woke up on her own. Either way, I wasn't going to let her go.

In the wee hours of the morning, we'd finally gotten word that Pop was stable but sedated and on a ventilator. They needed him to be still because of his wounds from both the bullet and the heart surgery they'd performed. The man who'd seemed healthy as a horse had arteries full of coffee, donuts, bacon, and almost 80 years of hard living. They'd done a few bypasses and rooted around until they'd fixed him as well as they could. He'd need to recover from all that work along with the broken ribs and bullet wound he'd received *before* his heart attack.

I'd gone back to see him myself and stood silently by his bed for the allotted two minutes, plotting revenge as I studied his bruised and broken body. My brothers had taken their turns back there, also, and I was sure they'd done the same thing.

Sin, Saint, and a few of his men were here to talk to us about what they'd found out thus far and the plan going forward.

"I think all of you should stay a while if you can," I told my brothers, interrupting Preacher's discourse on how the government tracks our every move through our cell phone conversations and login information. "I want this handled swiftly, and me, Hook, and Cap can't do it alone."

"I don't have filming until the fall, and I can record my other stuff anywhere. I'll just rent a house with a decent looking kitchen and work to keep up with the advertisers so I still have steady income. My assistant is mobile, too, and he can pack our shit and be here by the end of the week. I'll need to find a place big enough for the boys to come to visit if they want, but other than that, I just need a big fucking kitchen."

"I plan to stay as long as I'm needed," Preacher informed us. "I've been living in the cabin and got everything buttoned up before I left. I packed up my audio and video equipment and dropped it off at a courier service. They'll have it here the day after tomorrow. I'll set up in my old house at the compound."

Chef nodded as he leaned back in the uncomfortable waiting room chair that was barely big enough for the man's thick frame. He sighed and said, "The lease was up on my apartment, so I was packed up to come home at the end of the month anyway. I'll stay at the compound for now until things blow over and then I'll find a spot in the country and settle in."

"We're all here to stay too. We've been talking it over in a group text all day," Kitty said as he leaned forward and rested his elbows on his thighs as he looked at the floor. "Our jobs are all about travel, so we just need office space here so we can go on with business as usual. We've got the condo, but it's just a place to sleep and hold our fucking clothes. This is home to us. All of us. Me, Bug, and Santa can set up in a snap. Our staff can pack our things for us. We'll just keep the condo for Vegas trips and a hiding spot, in case we need it."

"Same with my cabin," Preacher added.

"We can't even find your fucking cabin," Stamp argued. "How are we going to hide there if we don't know where it is, Preach?"

"If you don't know, and you're my brother, then that means nobody fucking knows, dumbass. That makes it a prime hiding spot, don't you think?"

"I know we just met and all, but I'd like to put in for some time at the Vegas condo and the cabin at some point when we get things around town settled," Sin quipped. "I promise I'm trustworthy. Scout's honor."

"From what I understand, you've already stood shoulder to shoulder with Boss and the guys, and you're putting your men and your club out there for more. You're welcome at our place in Vegas anytime you want it," Bug told Sin. "The key's available to any of your men."

"You want to hear about my cabin?" Preacher asked. "It's not really in the mountains. I say that as a diversion. My cabin is up on stilts right in the middle of a swamp that's filled with wildlife. Wildlife that eats whatever happens to be put in front of them, whether it's trying to crawl away, or it's been dead a week. I've got wild hogs, gators, and all sorts of critters that come in handy, especially since no one including Uncle Sam knows I own the place. I have all the swampland around me for 10 square miles. I'd like to toss the person who shot Pop out there, and I'd like for you guys to help me do it."

"Well, aren't you just a man of many secrets who's just chock full of alternative options?" Saint remarked as he smiled deviously at Preacher.

"You've got no idea, buddy. No fucking idea."

BOSS

"Two more women disappeared. Poof. Just gone. Same thing as that first one that made it look like she got lost walking from her vehicle into her own house." Wrecker and Marshall were sitting across from me at my desk filling me in on what had gone down during the four days I'd been at the hospital. "And we had another car vandalized - this one in a different neighborhood over by the mall. Same fucking thing as the others. Thousands of dollars in damage but not a single belonging missing."

"What is that shit? I don't get it," I admitted. "Who fucking does that? And why?"

"I'm working on a theory, but I'll need to access some older files, and I can't get logged into the computer," Detective Marshall explained. "For some reason, IT can't get my password to work. I've gone around and around with that bullshit. They've got my laptop ready. I just can't access any files other than mine."

"Who have you talked to about it?"

"The tech and his boss in IT. There's no further up the chain I can go other than you."

I stared at the man for a minute and then reached over and opened my laptop. I logged in, found the folder he'd need to access, and turned it around to face him. "Search for what you need. I'll get you a flash drive for now, and we'll go from there. What about your computer, Wrecker? All access?"

"I have no idea. I had the files I've been working with sent by crime scene techs."

"Check your computer and make sure you can get to everything. I'll put the fear of God into the fucking IT department and get his shit figured out. Until then, you have my laptop."

"Is that battery charged?" Wrecker asked abruptly. "And you've got access to the servers if you're connected to Wi-Fi?"

"Yeah."

"I think it's your turn to buy coffee."

I tilted my head and stared at him for a second before I stood up. "Then, by all means, let's get us a coffee. My girl's got her truck at the park for some craft festival going on this afternoon."

"I had her coffee at the hospital. It was like drinking a Reese's. I don't know how she got the flavor so exact - I feel like she's got some kind of voodoo shit going on.. It was not of this world. I'll take a gallon more of the stuff," Wrecker admitted.

"When I left this morning, she was pulling some sort of pecan caramel thing out of the oven. I'm gonna end up weighing 700 pounds just from the smells in her house. I'm constantly hungry."

The three of us walked out of my office, and when I turned to lock the door, Wrecker reached for my key. I looked at him curiously but handed it over and moved out of the way. He dropped the keyring on the floor and knelt down in front of the door to pick it up.

We got outside and down the steps with Marshall trailing behind us before I asked, "What was that with the key?"

"There's a figurine on the shelf behind your desk that I don't recognize from before. It's an eagle - did you put it there?"

"No. I didn't put it there. I've never even noticed it."

"There were scratches on the lock we installed, so it's been picked, and I'm guessing that bird records audio, at the very least. No telling what else is in there."

"Julia was in my office pretending to dust last week. She looked directly at the cameras but didn't touch them. You think they know we've found them?"

"We'll have to get back in and do another sweep. Is your guy with the camera feed set up to monitor remotely yet? The cameras we installed are motion-activated. There shouldn't have been any movement in your office while you were out if the door was locked."

"I'll text him, but he's on duty at the hospital with Pop, so he won't get to it until one of the prospects relieves him this afternoon."

"How is Pop, by the way?"

"Still not awake. They'll keep him under another week, sounds like, but they said he's healing and things look good so far."

The three of us got to the park and crossed it to find Jenn's trailer with a line at least 20 people deep. I noticed that Julia and a man who must be her husband were in line about halfway up. I kept my eye on the two of them while Wrecker and Marshall made small talk.

They seemed tense, barely saying a word to each other the entire time they stood there. Julia's whole demeanor changed once she was in front of Jenn's window. She lit up and talked animatedly while Jenn waited on her. I saw her take a business card when Jenn handed it through the window.

I glanced around and saw just five or six other trucks out today. At the festival where I met Jenn, there were at least 15 of them. Most of the trucks had a handful of customers in line, but one stood out. Rather than the soccer moms and people in business attire on their lunch break, this truck had a line of people that stuck out like a sore thumb. Three of the people in line looked like straight thugs. I could tell from where I was standing that a fourth one was coming down off something, probably meth if you took notice of his pallor and sunken cheeks.

What is that guy doing over there when he looks like he wants to be *anywhere* else?

I mentioned it to Wrecker, who seemed to have been tipped off by the same shit I had, but he voiced it out loud. We decided to casually head that direction once we had our coffee.

"Hello, handsome men," Jenn greeted us before she

leaned forward and let me give her a kiss. "You guys want anything special, or can I surprise you?"

"Surprise me with the coffee, but I want that pecan stuff you were taking out of the oven. Make it a triple. That shit smelled divine."

"I'll take the same. Even the triple order," Wrecker told her. "Boss said the smell made him gain 10 pounds. That's all the recommendation I need."

"Same for me, ma'am," Marshall told Jenn with a smile as he pulled out his wallet. Wrecker already has his wallet in his hand and was sifting through the bills inside.

"Oh, the three of you don't even try to pay me. I won't have it," Jenn warned before she turned around to make our drinks. I watched Wrecker pull a $50 out of his wallet and lean forward into the window so he could reach around under the counter. When his hand came back, it was empty, and he gave me a nod before he looked away. I smiled at him, knowing Jenn would be pissed if she figured out what he'd done. When she turned around, she had styrofoam containers and drinks ready to go. As she pushed them across the counter, she said, "Go sit on my tailgate while you eat. David, Sammy, and Moe are in the truck, and they'd probably like some petting."

"You're swamped. Need me to feed them?"

"Do you have time?" Jenn asked as she spun around inside the trailer. She put two baby bottles on the counter and then leaned out for another kiss. "Just leave the bottles in the truck, and I'll take care of them later. Will you come by when you get off work?"

"I'll be here, baby."

"Bye, guys." Jenn smiled at Wrecker and Marshall. As we walked away, I heard her greet the next customers in line.

"Sammy, David, and Moe?" Wrecker asked as we walked around the trailer to Jenn's truck that was parked behind it. "She's got kids in her truck?"

"Her kids, yeah," I answered as I dropped the tailgate and set my coffee and food over to the side where they wouldn't get knocked over. The doggy door opened, and Moe was the first one out, his tail wagging so fast that it was a blur as he rushed toward us. I was scratching his neck when I heard Wrecker mumble, "What the fuck?"

"Meet David and Sammy," I told him with a laugh.

"Are those llamas?" Marshall asked as he set his coffee and the laptop down.

"Alpacas."

"Well, holy shit," Wrecker mumbled as Sammy nudged his hand. "Give us those bottles."

I handed them each a bottle and then reached for my coffee as I watched the two grown men feed the animals, both of them enthralled with the cute little beasts. As usual, the formula was gone in just a few minutes and then both babies made their way back through the doggie door at the back of the cab to go lay down for their post-lunch nap. I sat down on the tailgate and waited for Wrecker to hop up before I put my coffee beside my hip. Marshall sat on the trailer's rail and sipped his coffee while Wrecker and I dug into our food.

"Have you said anything on the phone or had any visitors today that might be of interest if that eagle in your office is a listening device?" Wrecker asked me.

"You two were my first visitors. Before that, I checked my mail and dealt with paperwork that had piled up on my desk. The office manager was the only other one that came into my office."

"Is she the one your guy caught pretending to clean?"

"That's her."

"Odd that she pretended to dust your office and never walked into mine or anyone else's office with that rag. Did Preacher have any time to do a check on the office staff?"

"As far as I know, he hasn't made it that far yet. He was looking into the officers Sin pointed out and then working his way through the department roster from the top down."

"I'll set my guy on it. Two heads are better than one, after all."

"I'd appreciate that."

The three of us enjoyed our snacks and coffee in companionable silence for a few minutes. When we were finished, I gave Marshall my login and password information before he took my laptop home to use his own Wi-Fi and download files. While the laptop was with him, he would take it to their tech guy so he could search it for tracking programs. He'd also have an in through the department's firewall so he could nose around under IT's radar.

"When Pop and the geezers came up with the bright idea to get me elected as police chief, I had no idea I was walking into a shitstorm. I don't know who I can trust or who's standing behind me preparing to plunge a knife into my back."

"I wasn't too keen on coming out of retirement, but I'm enjoying the work, to be honest. As far as who's standing behind you, that would be me, and I'm pretty good in a knife fight, if I do say so myself," Wrecker assured me. "However, my guys have a few questions about some of your people."

"I'll tell you what I can."

"How did it work out that three of your men run a security company?"

"You're not gonna try and tell me that Sin didn't run checks on us, are you?"

"Oh, no. We know what all of you went down for; we're just curious about how an arsonist, a cat burglar, and a safecracker ended up with a security company."

"Bug was an arsonist for hire but made sure no one was ever injured while he worked. He went into a burning house to get a fucking dog, for God's sake. Kitty started out as a petty thief and began enjoying the high life, so he started breaking into nicer homes. He never found a security system he couldn't breach, and he always found a way in that left no evidence of how he got inside. Santa, well, he was a little more devious and played a part like he was going for an academy award."

"How's that? He cracked safes. How does one get in character for that?"

"He dressed as Santa during the holidays. He sat there

for eight hours a day talking to kids about their wishes and dreams. He fucked his way through the stores' upper management to get secrets and insights into the offices and security. When the season was over, he picked one business a month and wiped them out using the information he learned over Christmas. The next year he'd pick a different city and start over."

"And who better to teach you how to protect yourself from fire and burglary than an arsonist and two thieves? That's fucking brilliant."

"Honestly, that's their entire marketing strategy," I told him with a wry grin. "They make a mint off the fact that they're reformed criminals who are trying to give back to the society they wronged."

"And Chef?"

"He was a college football star that went pro for four years before a knee injury sidelined him. He'd always loved science and kids, so he used his degree to become a high school science teacher. His wife passed from cancer, and it was just he and his daughter. She rebelled and got in with a bad crowd, and he worked tirelessly to pull her out of it. There was this one guy, her pimp and dealer, and he had a death grip on her. One final time, she snuck out of Chef's house and went back to the asshole. He pimped her out and then she overdosed in the back room of his house. The coroner said she'd been dead three days by the time they called authorities. Chef was beside himself with grief. He'd lost his wife and then the only part of her he had left. He got obsessed and stalked the pimp, figured out when he was home, who was with him, all the details he could get. Then, one Saturday morning, he went to the high school and cooked up a deadly smoke bomb in his classroom. That night when the pimp's house was full of his cronies, Chef tossed it in through a broken window and then stood outside by his car and watched them all crawl out of the house for fresh air while they choked on their own blood."

"Fuck. But who could blame him, you know?"

"That's sort of what the jury thought. That's why Chef only served a few years. He was acquitted on the murder charges and served five years for misuse of state property because he made the bomb in a public school using their equipment and supplies."

"That's just bullshit."

"That he didn't go down for murder?"

"No, that they got him for five years. That prosecutor was just reaching for anything at all, wasn't he?"

"Fourteen men died that night or soon after from complications. The five years is nothing compared to death row."

"And Preacher?"

"He was railroaded into a short sentence by a crooked judge. The guy was pissed off that his baby girl was in love and going to give up her scholarship to get married to a guy who grew up in a trailer park and went to college on a scholarship for low-income students. While he was in prison, he was attacked and, in defending himself, killed two inmates and injured a crooked guard. If any man should believe the universe is out to get him, it's Preacher. He was born during an unlucky moon or some shit."

"And that makes up your MC."

"There are many more out there, but those are my core group. These men are more than just my club brothers. They're my family. They're the ones who think of Pop as their father like I do. Not just a father figure or a man they respect, he's the one that brought us back into this world and taught us how to thrive in it."

"I'm sorry he got hurt, man. I know it rips all of you up."

"I was terrified I was going to lose him, and I still am. But the more hours that pass, the more that fear is turning into rage. I want to find out who did it, who they work for, everyone they come into contact with, and I want to kill every fucking one of them slowly and painfully."

"That's the plan."

JENNIFER

"Hi!" A woman greeted me that I recognized from Boss's office and from seeing her in my line earlier today. Julie? Shit, I was horrible with names. "I'm Julia. I met you at the police department."

"Yes! Hi! What can I get you?"

"I'll take a s'more coffee. I just love *anything* with chocolate and marshmallows, so I'm excited to try it."

"Oh, me too!" I told her as I turned around and started her drink.

"Is that your dog in the truck? Oh, he's so cute!"

I glanced over my shoulder at the cheerful woman and smiled before I said, "That's Moe. If he's out, then Sammy and David will be coming out any second now."

When she gasped loudly, I knew she'd caught sight of Sammy and David. When I turned to hand her the cup of coffee, she was gone. I leaned forward out of the window and watched her cooing over the animals. The craft fair was coming to a close, and Julia had been my only customer in the last 20 minutes. I walked out the back door of the trailer and joined her at the tailgate.

"These are your pets?" Julia asked, in awe.

"They are. The dog is Moe, and the alpacas are Sammy and David."

"I'm in love! I've never thought of having one of these, but I've always wanted little goats. They're just so cute!"

"I have goats too. And a donkey."

"You're kidding me. What are they like? Are they friendly? Where do they sleep? Do they play in the yard, or do they need a pen? I have so many questions."

"In the barn, yes, yes, and I'll try and answer more you might have," I told her with a laugh.

"I know I just met you a few days ago, but can I come see your goats sometime? I'd like to watch them interact and see how you take care of them, so I know if it's something I can do at my place."

"Sure. You can come over some evening after you get

off work. I live out in the boonies, so it might be easier to follow Boss out from the police station."

"So he lives with you?" Julia asked as she turned her head to look at me. Her expression had changed as had the tone of her voice, and it unnerved me a bit. Then, as if she realized she'd tweaked my interest, she backtracked. It bothered me even more when she said, "It's just that living alone out in the country sounds scary."

"I'm rarely ever scared," I explained. I wondered if Julia got my double meaning and why I felt the need to warn her off.

"A woman alone, you know? You have a security system, I'm sure."

"Yep. I've got quite a few of them," I told her before I forced a laugh. There was something about how she studied me that I didn't like, and the look in her eyes wasn't friendly now. It was calculating.

"I'll get with Boss and figure out the best time to come out," Julia told me, but now I wasn't excited to make a new friend and show her the goats. I didn't want her at my house at all.

"Sounds good," I agreed, as I made a mental note to talk to Boss about his office manager and figure out why she'd set off my alarm bells. "I put your coffee on the counter when you're ready."

"Oh! Of course! I better get back to the office. It's almost time to lock up. You have a great day, and it was nice talking to you."

"You too." I watched Julia walk around to the front of the trailer before I gave Moe the order to get inside the truck. I walked around to the back of the trailer and opened the door.

I realized something was wrong the second I put my foot inside the tiny space. It didn't smell like coffee anymore, it smelled like cologne. My head snapped up, and I looked out the window. Out of the corner of my eye, I saw the man inside my trailer.

When I turned to go back out the door, I saw a man just outside of it - this one as creepy as the man inside, but he looked deadlier somehow. Maybe it was the face tattoo and the cold, blank eyes.

I looked back at the man who'd been lying in wait and stood there silently as I assessed the park outside the open window. There were very few trucks left and not many people milling around at this end of the park now.

"Coffee lady." The man from the other night, the one with the gold chains and the 80's jewelry, greeted me. "I'm happy to see you here today. I want to start that conversation we discussed the other night."

"Why are you *inside* my trailer, and why is *that man* stopping me from leaving?"

"Because I want to talk to you, and he's here to make sure we're not interrupted."

As I glanced around outside again, I saw three young men, probably college age, carrying boxes about 50 feet from the trailer. They were facing my direction, so I took a chance that they'd notice a disturbance and come to my aid.

Using every ounce of power in my sizable thighs, I bent my knees and launched myself headfirst out of the window.

I didn't even have to make myself scream bloody murder; that just happened naturally. I tucked myself as well as I could in the short distance to the grass outside and landed with a thump on my back.

My not so graceful landing knocked the wind out of me. While I tried to suck in air, I heard footsteps in the trailer just a few feet away before the door at the back slammed shut. The three guys I'd seen were at my side in just seconds, and I wheezed, "There was a man inside my trailer, and he wouldn't let me out."

Two of the young men disappeared while the third knelt over me and put his phone to his ear. I assumed he was calling 911, and I was okay with that since I wasn't quite sure I didn't need a full-body cast or at least a chiropractor.

I heard one of the guys yell followed by screeching tires on the other side of the trailer. The other two young men were soon back and nearly as short of breath as I was.

"Late model gold sedan, thug with bandana driving, no plate on the back," one of the guys said as he tried to catch his breath.

"There were two guys who jumped in. One was a gang banger type, and the other looked like he was from a cheesy porno," the second guy explained. "Which one was inside the trailer?"

"Cheesy porno guy," I told them as I rolled to the side to get my arm underneath my body so I could push up to a sitting position. My body didn't protest too much, considering I'd just tried to break it. Finally, I was sitting up on the grass with the three young men around me and a growing crowd of people who'd seen the commotion and wanted to get closer to it. I heard a friendly voice in the crowd and then my friend Paula was kneeling in front of me, her hand out to help me up.

"What the hell?" Paula asked. "Are you okay? I saw you fly out of the window and got over here as quick as I could."

"Can you grab my phone out of the trailer? Oh, but don't touch anything else. The cops might want to take fingerprints or something. I don't know."

"Sure, Jenn. I'll get it."

I bent forward to dust the grass off my legs as the people around me started to disperse. Before Paula was back with my phone, Boss was standing in front of me with his hands on my shoulders, his bright blue eyes drilling into mine. "What happened, sweetheart?"

I told him about the man who'd spoken to me before and then showed up *inside* my trailer today, but that was really all the information I had to give. He hadn't mentioned what he wanted to 'discuss' when he'd shown up previously, and I'd been so freaked out today that I hadn't given him a chance to get started before I found a way out.

"Did he ask for money or threaten you physically?" Boss asked, and I noticed that the officer standing next to him was taking notes.

"No. The other night, he said he wanted to talk to me

and asked for my card. I got a weird vibe and blew him off. Then today, I walked into the trailer and he was there. When I turned around to walk out, a scary-looking guy was blocking my way, so I jumped out the window."

"She fucking launched herself out the window," the young guy who'd knelt in the grass beside me and called 911 added. "Shot out of there headfirst and rolled like a gymnast."

"More like a cartoon character," I mumbled just loud enough for Boss and Paula to hear me. Paula smiled, but Boss did not. He was in cop mode now, and it was sexy as all hell.

"Let me get an ambulance here to check you out," Boss said as he pulled his radio off his hip.

"I don't need an ambulance," I told him as I rested my palm on his hard chest. "I'm probably going to need some Tylenol and a warm bath . . . maybe even a chiropractor, but I don't need an ambulance."

"I'll help her get everything put away so she can head home," Paula told Boss before she stuck her hand out to introduce herself. "I'm Paula Clewey, a friend of Jennifer's."

Boss shook her hand and gave her a firm nod as he told her, "I'm going to talk to the witnesses and some of the other vendors who are still here. Will you be okay sitting in the truck while I get someone over here for prints? I can get . . ."

"I'll be fine, Boss," I told him with a smile, happy to see that he was worried about me even if the situation was bizarre. At least I had that. "You do your cop thing. I'll wait in the truck until y'all are done and then lock up the trailer."

"Okay, sweetheart," Boss said as he searched my face and stared deep into my eyes.

"I'll wait with her," Paula assured him. "I'm already packed up. I was just walking over to say goodbye when I saw her fly out the window."

"Thanks, Paula," Boss told her before he looked back at me and said, "I'll get my bike and follow you home when you're ready. Don't you leave without me, you hear?"

"Yessir." I gave him a sassy little salute with two fingers, and one side of his lips tipped up with a half smile. He leaned down and gave me a quick kiss before he turned around and was all business again. I followed Paula to my truck and climbed up into the driver's seat as she got into the passenger seat. I took a deep breath and looked at my friend before I said, "Well, that was fucking terrifying."

"I bet. But from the looks of your hot cop, he's going to kiss all your bruises when you get home tonight."

I tilted my neck slowly from side to side and winced at how tight my muscles had already become. "That's probably going to take a whole lot of kisses."

BOSS

"How are you feeling today, babe?" I asked Jenn as I walked up behind her and wrapped my arms around her waist. She was wearing one of her many sexy aprons. The knot she'd pulled her hair up to on the top of her head was loose and hanging off to the side a bit, and she had a spot of flour on her nose. I knew that if she looked in the mirror she'd roll her eyes and try to 'fix' everything, but I thought she was hot as hell just the way she looked right this minute.

"The chiropractor did another magical snap, crackle, and pop on me and then I came home and worked out for an hour to keep myself loose. I think I'm back to fighting shape." While she talked, her hands never stopped kneading the dough in front of her. Jenn tilted her head to the side as if to invite my lips there for a kiss. I obliged and was happy when I felt her shiver and melt even farther into my body.

It had been almost two weeks since the incident at the park. That evening Jenn had been achy and taken a long hot bath before I tucked her into bed and went home. I called her the next morning, and she sounded tense. When I asked her how she felt, she'd told me she could barely move. The pain from her back and shoulders was excruciating.

I'd called my chiropractor, and since I was a repeat customer, he'd found a way to squeeze her in that morning. When I'd shown up to drive her, Jenn had been shocked that I was there to take care of her.

It made me want to find her ex-husband and punch him in the throat. Apparently, she'd never had a man try to help her when she was sick or hurt. It cut me deep to see how in awe and grateful she was that I'd taken the initiative and made her an appointment and then picked her up.

When I arrived at her house, I was glad that I'd come - she couldn't even lift her arms to wash her own hair or bend over and tie her own shoes. I'd helped her shower, then dressed her before I took her in for the appointment. That afternoon I'd filled the prescription for the muscle relaxers he'd prescribed and picked up takeout on my way back.

And again, when I'd shown up to take care of her, she'd been shocked.

That night, when I helped her lay face down on the bed and rubbed ointment all over her back while I gently massaged her sore muscles, she cried silent tears. At first I'd thought I was too rough and that I'd hurt her, but she explained that since her father died, she'd never had anyone take care of her like I'd done that day.

That tidbit made me want to punch her mom in the throat, and I wasn't the kind of man that had ever considered hitting a woman before.

"Back to fighting shape, but what about fucking shape?" I murmured close to her ear.

Jenn didn't answer me with anything other than another full-body shiver. I watched her drop the ball of dough into a large bowl and cover it with a dish towel before she turned in my arms.

"My dough needs to rest for about 20 minutes and

then I'll need to get back to it. I like it when we go slow and sweet, but I think I'll like it just as much when we go fast and hard," Jenn whispered as she wiped her hands on another towel she'd grabbed before she turned to me.

"Turn back around," I growled as I put my hands on her shoulders to help her spin. "Put your hands on the counter and brace, sweetheart."

"Oh, hell yeah," Jenn whispered as she did what I'd told her to do. I put my thumb into the waistband of the stretchy pants she had on and pushed them down her legs. Jenn stepped from one foot to the other as I pulled her pants off and tossed them to the side, leaving her naked from the waist down other than that sexy apron. "I need to get my apron off, Boss."

"Leave the apron," I told her as one hand slid up over the front of her shirt to cup her breast. My other hand slid over her hips and down between her legs. I nibbled her neck where it was exposed to me as I gently rubbed my hand over her sex. "You want me to fuck you right here in the kitchen?"

"Yeah," Jenn whispered.

"Next time you're standing here are you going to think about how I fucked you in the kitchen with your apron on?"

"I will."

"You wet for me, baby?" I asked her as I lightly rubbed my hand up and down over her sex. I pulled my hand away and started tapping at her pussy slowly, right over her clit, in rhythm with my thumb and finger squeezing her nipple. "You want me to use my fingers to feel how wet you are for me?"

"Do it," Jenn whispered. "Please. Yes."

I stopped the tapping and held my hand there, lightly covering her while I nibbled on her neck. It wasn't more than a few seconds before she bent her knees and spread her legs just a little bit more so she could rub against my hand. I smiled into her hair as she tried to find more traction so that I could reach her clit. Slowly, I bent my middle finger so that it curled up between her lips and entered her. Jen gasped, and I pulled my finger up a fraction so the wet tip of it could circle her clit a few times.

"You *are* wet for me," I whispered as I flicked my finger back and forth, making her gasp. I pulled my hand off her breast and opened the front of my pants. I pushed my boxers down under my balls and fisted my cock a few times before I rubbed it against her bare ass. "Is this what you want, my Jenn?"

"I want it," Jenn murmured as her head fell forward. She moaned and moved her hips in rhythm with my finger before she pushed back and nudged my cock with her ass.

"Where do you want it?"

"Inside me."

"But where inside? You want me to put it in your ass, Jenn? Have you ever done that, baby?"

"Never," Jenn whispered, but she didn't sound put off at the idea.

"You want to try that with me?"

"Yeah."

I moved my hand down and pushed two fingers inside her before I whispered, "I'll fuck your ass someday soon, sweetheart, but not today. Today you want fast and hard, and I'm going to give it to you. When I take your ass, it's going to be a slow burn that lights you on fire before I get in there and do it slow."

"Fuck," Jenn hissed as she rode my fingers. I could tell she was close, and I knew that she'd be screaming with her orgasm in just a few strokes. I wanted to be inside her when she did that, so I pulled my hand away and grabbed her hip to position her before I pushed up inside her from behind.

Rather than take it slow so she could adjust to me, I pushed in with one stroke. Jenn's head came up and fell back as she arched into me. I bent forward and reached around her again to stroke her clit as I started fucking her hard and fast, just like she'd asked for. The angle we were at felt different than anything we'd done before, and it was all I could do to keep moving without coming deep inside her. The sound of my hips slapping into her bare ass was loud in the room. The only thing louder were her moans and mine as we both sought our release. Finally, with a scream, Jenn came around me, clutching at my cock with her muscles as the orgasm took over. I pushed my cock deep inside and let go, collapsing against her back as her body milked every drop out of me.

We stood there connected until our breathing evened out, and I started to soften and slip out of her body.

"Give me that towel, sweetheart," I murmured before I gave her one more kiss on the neck. She grabbed it and put it down between her legs. As I pulled my cock out of her body, I held the towel there and cleaned her as well as I could with the damp towel. When I was finished, I balled it up and tossed it into the linen hamper I'd seen her throw dirty towels in before. "Turn around and kiss me."

Jenn slowly turned around and watched me pull my boxers over my soft cock and zip up my pants. I leaned down and kissed her softly before I pulled back and looked down into her bright green eyes.

"Your back okay?" I whispered as she stared up at me.

"My back's fine," Jenn whispered back. "That was the best thing that's ever happened in my kitchen."

"The best?"

"Absolutely the best."

"If that's the case, then the bar is pretty low, babe. I'll have to think of new and inventive ways to fuck you right here in this room so you have more of a scope."

"Do it," Jenn whispered before her laugh rang out. "I need to get cleaned up and put my clothes back on. Are you going to shower?"

"I am. Then I'm going to come downstairs and drink a beer while my girl gets dinner ready."

"What time will the guys be here?"

"In about an hour. Is that okay?"

"That's perfect."

"Have I told you today how happy you make me,

Jenn?"

"You told me this morning when you kissed me goodbye, then I thought about how happy you made *me* while I listened to your motorcycle fade off into the distance."

"Want me to stay again tonight?"

"Yeah," Jenn answered, but I saw something flash in her eyes.

"What's wrong?"

"Nothing," she answered immediately, too quickly.

"Talk to me, babe."

"Why am I not invited to your house?"

"Because I have a cat door that Moe and the boys can get out of but not a fenced-in yard."

"Oh." Jenn looked relieved, and I realized she thought I'd been hiding her away or something.

"Baby, you're welcome at my pad anytime, but let me tell you a little about it. It's a one bed, one bath house that's about the size of your living room. It wasn't built for comfort. It was built to let a man who'd been in a cell with no space of his own get adjusted to living in the outside world and have a place he could call home until he was ready to move on."

"Are you, um, going to move on? I mean, I was wondering if it would be soon, and if you do move on, will it be close by? I guess everyone has to, but you seem really adjusted to the outside world. I know you've been out for a few years now, and you just got elected, and that means four years, but . . ."

I'd noticed over the last month that Jenn rambled when she was nervous, and I even thought *that* was sexy.

"Jenn," I whispered before I leaned forward and gave her a soft kiss. "I'm not going anywhere. I've lived in that house for the last few years because it was close to my job and Pop. I've been saving up to buy a place out in the country. I always thought it would be somewhere I could be alone and watch the sun rise while I drank my coffee. Now I want it to be somewhere out in the country, so I can fuck my woman in the kitchen while she's half-naked wearing a sexy apron and not worry about the neighbors getting a peek."

"Can it be close to my house?"

"I'm a year or so away from having the money I'll need to afford the land and build a house, sweetheart."

"When you get closer to having the money to buy your own place, I mean, If I'm still around, and I'm the one you want to fuck in the kitchen, can we talk about where you're going to live? I mean, you could move close, but in a year we might want to see if you can move closer, and if I'm still around you might be staying here so often that it would make sense to . . . you've even got clothes here, and I made a spot in the garage for your bike so if you wanted to . . ."

"Jenn," I whispered, understanding where she was going with this but not sure I was ready for that quite yet. As I stared down into her bright green eyes, I realized I'd spent one night at my own house in the last month—one single night.

Every morning, I went home and spent time with my

animals while I got ready for work. Each afternoon, I came home and spent time with them while I took care of the mail and the bills before I made my way over to Jenn's house just as soon as Elvira and the cats got tired of looking at me. Sometimes, I encouraged Elvira to go her way a little earlier than she was ready because I was eager to get to Jenn.

I saw storm clouds gather in Jenn's eyes. She doubted herself and what she was feeling because I was just standing there staring at her in stunned silence. I wasn't surprised at the direction she was going, though - I was more shocked that I was ready to go there myself.

"You're really okay with me having a spot in your garage for my bike?"

"Well, yeah. I'm the one that made the space."

"You okay with me having space in your closet?"

"Of course. I made room for you there and in the dresser."

"You okay with me paying half your bills and bringing my animals over to join your menagerie?"

"I bought the house and the land outright, so I don't have a mortgage. Technically, the only bills I have are electricity and internet, but sure."

"You okay with me paying those two bills and kicking in for whatever else you need around here?"

Jenn stared into my eyes intently for a few seconds before she whispered, "Yeah. I am."

"You okay with my brothers coming and going at

wild hours when they need me?"

"I am."

"And my animals coming and going in your house?"

"Of course."

"I'll gather them up tomorrow afternoon and grab the rest of my clothes before dinner."

"Okay."

"Now, baby, your 20 minutes for the dough to rest was up a bit ago, and you're naked under that apron. My brothers will start trickling into the house any minute now, and I want to get a shower. Are we settled?"

"We are."

"If you change your mind after you think about it, we can . . ."

"I spent way too long with a man that never made a single effort to make sure I was happy or healthy to waste one single minute apart from a man who not only does all that but seems to enjoy it. I'm not going to change my mind considering I've been thinking about it since the day after I hurt my back."

"Okay."

"You're everything I never even thought about wishing for."

"Same, sweetheart. Same."

We were all sitting around the table in Jenn's dining room - well, hell, I guess it was ours now - with Stamp telling us about his visit with Pop earlier. "When I got to the hospital this morning, he had one of the nurses sitting on the edge of his bed., Her hand was in his, and he was telling her how a real man should treat a woman. I'd say he's getting better every day, but that would be a lie. He's milking this shit for all it's worth."

"What did they say about releasing him?" Preacher asked. "And when they do, who's going to move into his house and take care of him?"

"He's got to go to a rehab facility until he builds his strength back up," I told the guys. "I talked to his doctor this morning, and he doesn't want him without constant care for at least the next three months. He's weak but won't admit it. He gets tired and winded easily, and he's unsteady on his feet. At his age, he might not ever be steady again, and if he's out at the compound, he'll be all over the place in that fucking golf cart rather than taking it slow and taking care of himself."

"He's gonna hate it, but that makes sense, Boss," Hook agreed. "Soda has stepped up, and he's running shit the way it should be done. Sis is right there in the middle, helping him with everything. They go up to the hospital every afternoon and give Pop a play by play, ask for instruction and then go back to the shop and do shit the way they see fit. And, let me say, the way they see fit has brought some damn good changes."

"Like what?"

"Soda hired a cleaning service to come in twice a week and clean the bathrooms rather than letting the prospects muddle through and do a half-ass job. Sis got an artist to come out and paint the shop hours and info on the windows so he could take down all of the handwritten crap Pop had taped up over the years. Shit like that," Preacher told us. "I know Soda's got some time left as a prospect, but he's got a good head on his shoulders as far as the business is concerned."

"I agree," I told the men. "Over the last few months, I've noticed Soda was taking the day to day shit over gradually, and Pop was letting him. I say we let him keep moving forward, but we let him know we've not only got his back, but we've got our eyes on him at the same time."

Stamp nodded before he said, "He knows. I've sat and shot the shit with him over beers a few times, and he's arranged it so that Pop can step back in seamlessly. I think Soda would find it gratifying to continue on until that happens. We all know that it will probably never fully transition back to Pop. Pop needs to at least pretend he's his age and retire before he gets too old to enjoy it."

"I'll talk to Pop about it. Anything else?" I asked the men as I glanced over my shoulder and watched Jenn walk past the open area on the second floor, heading toward the stairs so she could come down.

"Is this our official meeting spot now?" Captain asked softly so Jenn wouldn't hear. He wasn't asking about the location of our meetings; he wanted to know whether or not they could trust Jenn with information that might not always be on the up and up. "Don't get me wrong, Boss, these digs are great, but there's a lot of open areas we can't see, and the acoustic in here lets sound travel."

"Let's call it our unofficial meeting spot since I'm moving in tomorrow after work."

Hook's eyes got wide, and Captain's mouth dropped open. The other guys hadn't been around before Pop's shooting, so they didn't know how long I'd been with Jenn - just that I was with her now.

"Need help getting moved?" Chef asked.

"I don't have a lot, but I could use a hand. I'm going to let Soda move into my place at the compound. It will give him a better house, and he'll have some distance from the other guys while being closer to the office and keeping an eye on the place."

Jenn walked behind my chair and trailed her hand along my shoulders as she went past us toward the kitchen. She checked what was in the oven before she glanced at the clock and walked out to the other kitchen without a word.

"What's out there?" Stamp asked.

"She's got a commercial kitchen that leads to the garage where the trailer's stored when she's not working. Makes it easy to load up when she's getting ready for a job."

"Sweet," Stamp said as he leaned back to try and see into the other kitchen. "I need to see if your girl will let me film here. I found a house, but I need to get a crew out there to remodel the kitchen and install new appliances before I can start production. Her kitchen is absolutely perfect."

"I'm done with new business if you want to go talk to

her. Sin and his men are working on some leads, but shit's buttoned up tight. They haven't found anything new. The only thing we've got is what I told you guys about the missing women. From what we can find in the records, there have been a total of 11 that have disappeared in the last year. Now, some of those are from the college and allegedly left word that they were running off. We're looking into that. Of those 11, seven are cases of women vanishing with their cars and shit being left out in the open."

"Trafficking," Preacher said in a low voice. "They're disappearing into thin air because they're being shipped off somewhere."

"That's what we think, but we've got not one fucking shred of evidence. The investigator that worked the original cases has covered his ass, but he did the bare minimum as far as leaving no stones unturned. We know he's crooked; we're just waiting on him to lead us to something we can use and hopefully hang himself."

"What's it like being surrounded by people you can't trust?" Chef asked.

"It's a lot like prison," I admitted. "The difference is that I can work with you guys and Sin's group to get to the bottom of this shit and take out the trash. And, of course, at the end of the day, I can come home to a smiling woman and forget my problems for a while."

13

JENNIFER

"They haven't gotten any further on identifying the man, as far as I know, but Boss is going to be with me while I'm out this evening. If he can't be there, one of his club brothers will be there to protect me," I assured Paula as I went through the list of ingredients I'd need for this batch of brownies. Once I had everything on the stainless steel counter in front of me, I started measuring ingredients into the large mixer.

Paula let me get all of that started before she spoke again. "I almost wish you had found out what that asshole wanted before you took a swan dive out the window."

"Honestly, I've thought the same thing. It's too late now, though. I'm going to meet with a police sketch artist in the morning. If they can find the guy, they'll at least get him for breaking into the trailer while I was talking to Julia. Boss talked to the prosecutor, and he said that he may be able to charge him for holding me against my will."

"That would be good. Can you have the artist draw a picture of the fucker that blocked the door too?"

"Definitely. He'll be pretty easy to spot with that face tattoo, I'd think. His eyes were just dead, Paula, but then again the skeezy guy's eyes were just as bad."

Paula sipped her coffee and thought about my description for a minute. "I think I might know who you're talking about. I've seen him but never spoken to him. He was standing at the end of the block when I walked out of the hardware store. I remember the man's eyes because he looked right at me."

"Did he say anything?" I asked as I cut out parchment paper to fit the pans.

"No. I just remember thinking the guy looked sleazy and then he stared at me, and his eyes were almost black. It was creepy. I got into the car as quickly as I could and drove off."

I heard the doorbell ring and glanced up at Paula in confusion.

"What? I didn't ring it." Paula laughed and then slid off her stool. "I'll get it for you. I take it from the look on your face that you're not expecting anyone."

"No, I'm not. I'm waiting on an Amazon delivery, of course, but they don't ever ring the bell. I'm lucky if the mailman even drives up to the house."

"Maybe it's a hot UPS guy. They've always got great legs."

"You need to get laid, sweetheart. You really need to get laid."

I could hear Paula laughing as she walked through the house and then I listened to her as she greeted the person at the door. I was fitting one of the papers into a pan when Paula appeared in the doorway and stopped, staring at me with her eyes wide.

"What? Were his legs that good?"

"There's a man at the door, and he says he's your husband."

"*What?*"

"That's what he said. Tall, slim, perfect hair, and shoes so shiny that he could probably see up a skirt in their reflection."

"Holy shit," I whispered. "That's Ethan."

"I left him on the porch, and he is *pissed!*"

"Shit. Did you lock the door?"

"Well, yeah."

"Check the back door and make sure it's locked. The patio door *and* the interior door."

"Is he dangerous?" Paula asked as she hurried out of the room.

"He's not dangerous, but I don't want his fucking stink in my house," I hissed as I wiped my hands on my apron and walked around the table toward the door. There were no memories of Ethan in my house, and I planned to keep it that way. The doorbell rang again . . . and then again. Ethan would stand out there holding the fucking button until I opened the door. Then he'd push his way past me and come into my fucking house before he stuck his nose in the air and insulted me, my friend, and everything about my new home.

"Doors are locked," Paula told me as she stepped up beside me. "How long is he going to stand there pressing the button?"

"Until he gets his way," I muttered. Moe was irritated at the sound echoing around the house, and he hurried down the stairs and started barking and howling at the front door. Sammy and David were right behind him. They'd spent so much time with Moe that they seemed to think they were dogs too. Any day now, I expected the little guys to start barking. "Fuck this. I'm calling Boss. I'm not dealing with Ethan on my own."

"Good for you. You've got a scary-looking hottie with muscles. Use him!"

I pulled my phone out of my apron pocket and hit the screen to dial Boss. He answered on the second ring but sounded distracted.

"Hey, babe."

"Are you in the office or out in town somewhere?"

"I'm walking into the courthouse for a meeting. What's that noise?"

"Can I use the group text from that day I did the airport run and see if one of the guys is close by? My ex-husband is standing on my porch, and I don't want to talk to him."

"Do what now?" Boss growled.

"I don't know how he found me, but he did. Ethan's here, and I want him gone. If I conk him over the head, can Paula and I bury him in the backyard and pretend you and I never had this conversation?"

"Fuck. I have to go to this meeting, babe. Send the text. Don't open the door. That motherfucker can stand on the porch until I get there, or he dies of fucking thirst. I don't want you to have to deal with him by yourself."

"I'm texting the guys. I bet Hook's the closest. He'll come over."

"I'll be there as quickly as I can."

I hung up and opened my texts, scrolling down until I found the group text. My fingers flew over the keyboard, explaining what was going on, what Boss had said, and asking if any of the men were nearby.

My phone started dinging with incoming messages almost instantly. Every single text said nearly the same thing. 'Do not open the door. I'm on my way.'

"Did you get in touch with somebody?"

"I sent a group text, and most of them answered that they're on their way."

"Oh, this is great!" Paula said as she bounced on the balls of her feet. "I get to meet all of them at once while they do that hot alpha thing and run your douchebag ex out of town."

"I doubt they'll . . . oh fuck, who am I kidding? They'll do that alpha thing, and they're all smoking hot, so you're probably going to need to buckle up. At the rate you're going, you might spontaneously combust."

"Is there such a thing as spontaneous orgasms?" Paula asked me with a grin. Then her face fell, and she was serious again before she said, "You're awfully calm considering who's standing at your front door."

"I've got the official papers that show I don't have to put up with that man's shit anymore. The divorce has been final for ages, and I can't even begin to imagine what the hell he thinks is important enough to chase me all the way to Texas."

Ethan stopped ringing the doorbell, and Moe instantly got quiet. I watched Ethan walk over and try to look through the windows, but I knew he couldn't see inside the house because of the privacy film I'd paid extra for. Right now, it was worth every single penny and then some.

"What are Boss's friends going to do when they get here?"

"I don't know. I didn't really think that through. I just want them for the intimidation factor, I guess."

"If you could choose, what would you *want* them to do with Ethan?"

"I want them to beat on him like a pinata until all his stuffing comes out, and he's small enough to fit in a shoebox I can bury in my backyard."

Paula burst out laughing, but I didn't. I really wanted them to beat the shit out of him. I wondered if I could get them to do it in the front yard and let me video it so I could watch it on repeat when I was feeling down.

That happened on days when the voice in my head wasn't my own, but Ethan's. After years of his voice telling me I wasn't quite good enough, smart enough, or pretty enough, it tended to echo through my mind when it got especially quiet.

The divorce papers were final, and Ethan was out of my life, but I wasn't sure he'd ever get out of my head.

"If they make yours a pinata, do you think I can hire them to do the same thing to mine?"

"You know, if we approach them with a sound business plan, I bet we could get them to sign up as ex-husband hunters. Maybe they'd hook us up with a BOGO."

"We could have a menu of sorts for women to choose from: intimidation, hurling insults, light stalking, waterboarding, whack-an-ex with a baseball bat, and even target practice with the weapon of their choosing. The most expensive and rewarding selection would be the Pinata Pound Down. We could even supply a decorative box for the remains that they can happily bury in their own backyard or exotic location of their choosing. We'll even include a video for them to watch whenever they need a quick pick-me-up."

"You're really an astute businesswoman, Paula, but with those bloodthirsty ideas, I think your talents might be wasted in Tenillo. You should apply for the mob."

Paula's laugh was odd, and I stared at her until she got herself together. She finally said, "I'll take that into consideration."

The doorbell started up again, and Paula and I both flinched when Moe started howling.

I got my wits about me and herded Sammy, David, and Moe up the stairs and gated them in so they couldn't run out the front door when the cavalry arrived. I'd done it just in time too. Over the sound of Moe howling at the top of the stairs and the doorbell's constant chime, we heard motorcycles. A *lot* of motorcycles.

Like little kids, Paula and I rushed to the windows at the front of the house and stood in awe as the bikes roared up my driveway. Ethan must have been in shock, too, because his finger *finally* came off the doorbell. I glanced at him on the porch and saw him edge closer to the front door as he watched the bikers come to a stop side by side just a few feet away from the bottom step.

I could only see his profile, but his pale skin and gaping mouth let me know he'd realized he was way the fuck out of his element and possibly about to become a human pinata.

I doubted it would happen, but a girl was never too old to dream.

Once the men had dismounted and were standing in a line in front of their motorcycles, I opened the door with Paula at my side.

Ethan spun around when I asked, "What do you want, dickbrain?"

"Jennifer!"

"Why are you here, fuckhead?" Paula asked him. I shot her a glance, and she whispered, "That's all I could think of in a hurry!"

"Let me in," Ethan hissed as he glanced over his shoulder at Boss's brothers.

"I think he's about to piddle himself," I told Paula gleefully as I watched Ethan's eyes go wide with obvious fear when he heard boots on the steps behind him. "Yep. He's gonna have an accident."

"What the fuck are you doing here, boy?" Chef's voice boomed out, and I swear, the power behind it made me sway. When Ethan turned around, he found himself nose to nipple with Chef. He tried to step back, but Chef grabbed him by the front of his shirt and picked him up off the ground until they were eye to eye. "I asked you a motherfucking question!"

"Who is *that*?" Paula whispered close to my ear.

"That's Chef. He used to be a high school science teacher," I whispered back.

I could see by Paula's face that she was going through the roster of every teacher she'd ever had and finding them sorely lacking in comparison to the man in front of her.

It sounded like Ethan was trying to talk, but it was hard to distinguish words from the garbled wheezes and squeaks coming out of his mouth.

"If you want him to answer, you have to give him at least one lung full of air first, brother," Kitty drawled as he slowly walked up the steps. "He's turning an alarming shade of purple. Jenn, honey, do you like purple?"

"I love purple. As of three seconds ago, it became my very favorite color."

"Don't let him breathe just yet, man. Jenn likes that color on him."

Chef didn't say a word, he just growled deep in his chest. As if to punctuate the sound, he shook Ethan twice. Ethan's feet were at least six inches off the ground, and his toes were pointed down as he moved his feet, trying to find purchase. His hands were up around Chef's wrist, and he was still making that garbled sound when Chef shook him again before he dropped him like a rock.

Ethan crumbled to the ground gasping for air as his hands came up around his neck. By now, Stamp and Preacher were on the porch, and the four men stood there looking down at Ethan as he tried to catch his breath.

"Why does his hair look like that? Is it plastic?" Stamp asked as he stuck one finger out and poked Ethan in the head. "It's crunchy." He poked him again so hard Ethan's head moved back a few inches. "What the fuck's wrong with your hair, man?"

"Did he shit himself?" Preacher asked the group. He reached out and poked Ethan in the head with one finger and asked, "Dude, did you shit yourself? You smell like sweaty nutsack and Old Spice."

I put my hands over my mouth to hold in the laughter, but Paula did nothing of the sort. Her laughter rang out across the porch, and Chef grinned at her. I saw a cruiser coming up the driveway and hoped it was Boss. When it got closer, I saw Wrecker, the deputy chief who Boss had hired to be his second in command.

The men around Ethan moved back as Wrecker walked up the stairs. When Ethan saw that it was a cop, he jumped up and started squawking, his words a jumble as he tried to tell Wrecker what had happened.

"Ma'am, is this man bothering you?"

"I'd like him removed from my property, officer. He has no business being here."

"I can do that," Wrecker told me with a slow smile. He looked back at Ethan, and his expression turned murderous. "Either explain yourself, or shut the fuck up, man. I'm fluent in a few languages, but pussy dipshit isn't one of them."

"That man assaulted me!"

"What man?" Wrecker asked as he looked at the four men around him. "I don't see anybody here but you and me. Did you bump your head when you tripped on the step, boy?"

"That man right there!" Ethan yelled as he pointed at Chef.

"Jenn, sweetheart, was there anyone else here before I arrived?"

"Nope. I haven't seen a soul," I lied as I smiled at the men on my porch. "I was standing inside praying that Ethan would choke on his own spit when all of a sudden, he tripped on the porch step and started wheezing. I thought maybe the time I had spent with the voodoo doll I made with a lock of his hair was finally working, and I'd get to watch him die right in front of me. He finally started breathing again and then when you drove up, he started in with that squeaky gibberish noise he's got going on now. It's annoying as all hell if you ask me. Grates on my damn nerves, you know?"

"I do. So, dumbass, what brings you to our fine town? You have 30 seconds to explain yourself before you mysteriously start choking again."

Chef put his hand out toward Ethan, and the man actually squealed as he jumped backward. It was one of the most gratifying things I'd ever seen.

The sound I made came deep from my belly, the kind of giggle that comes from the feeling of utter joy bubbling up straight from my soul.

When Ethan turned to look at me in shock, I did it again, but this time it was followed by loud guffaws as I bent forward and braced my hands on my knees and laughed harder than I had in *years*. Over my laughter, I heard Wrecker say, "You've got 20 seconds, dipshit."

"I'm h-here to t-t-talk to my wife," Ethan stammered. Those words stopped my laughter instantly.

"I am *not* your wife, you twatwaffle!" I exploded as I stood back up and pointed my finger at Ethan. "I'm your *ex*-wife. Our divorce was final months ago, and you moved in with Homewrecker Barbie to wait for your spawn to hatch."

"The baby's not mine," Ethan mumbled, and I felt my eyebrows shoot up to my hairline right before I giggled. Again. "She was sleeping with her ex-boyfriend on the side, and I didn't realize it. When the baby was born, it was a shock, to say the least."

"You knew the second the baby was born?" Preacher asked Ethan curiously. "You didn't take a paternity test? You just knew?"

Ethan glanced uncomfortably at Chef and then in a voice barely above a whisper, he said, "He doesn't favor either of us. The baby looks like his father."

"What's his father look like?" Chef growled.

"He looks like you, sir," Ethan said very respectfully before he swallowed loud enough for the people in the next county to hear it.

I reached out and braced my hand on the doorframe so I didn't fall over while I wheezed with laughter. Chef, realizing that Ethan meant the baby was black like him, threw his head back and roared with laughter.

"The cheater got cheated on?" Paula squealed. "Holy shit, that's perfect!"

When Wrecker was able to control his laughter, he asked Ethan, "What the fuck does that have to do with Jenn, and why the fuck are you standing on her porch with your finger glued to the goddamn doorbell?"

"I miss her. I realized that I'd acted rashly, and I'm here to convince her to give me another chance," Ethan admitted before he steeled his spine, mistakenly thinking that the men around him wouldn't do him any harm in the presence of a police officer. "I'm not going anywhere until she knows how serious I am about winning her back. If you're not willing to help me file a complaint against this man for assault, I'll go to your superior and have *you* brought up on charges."

"You're going to go to my superior officer? I'm the deputy chief, dumbass; there's only one man above me. He's not someone you want to fuck with on a good day, but especially not today when he's in a meeting he doesn't want to be at while he's wondering what in the fuck is happening on his own front porch."

"His own front porch?" Ethan asked with a quizzical expression as he glanced back and saw me smiling. "A man lives here with you? Already? That was quick, considering the way you look, Jennifer. I'd have thought it would . . ."

"What the fuck did you just say?" Wrecker asked Ethan. "Did you just insult her standing right here surrounded by invisible men who already want to stomp a mudhole in your ass and walk it dry? Really? You *are* a special kind of stupid. Asshole."

"I just mean that she's overweight and doesn't take care of herself. I didn't think it would be that easy for her to move on."

"I have never seen someone dig such a deep hole without using a shovel," Preacher said, stunned at Ethan's stupidity.

All laughter was gone now, and I asked Ethan, "How did you find me?"

"A woman called the tip line on your missing persons alert and told me you were in Tenillo, Texas."

"Missing person? You reported me missing?"

"Your mother did, and I encouraged it."

"Oh, fuck a duck," I grumbled. "Go the fuck away, Ethan, and don't ever come back."

"I want to talk to you, Jennifer. Your mother and I are worried about your safety. I must say, I'm worried about your mental health after you stood there and did nothing while this man assaulted me."

"No one assaulted you, Ethan! You tripped on the goddamn step and choked on your own spit! Jesus!" I stepped forward and pushed his chest so that he had no choice but to move closer to the porch steps. I shoved him again, and he reached up and grabbed my wrist. Without thinking, I turned my hand and grabbed his forearm while my right leg went out and swept his knees, knocking him backward. He fell down the steps, rolled once and landed in the grass. "Get off my fucking property, you asshole!"

Ethan scrambled to his feet, and I was off like a shot, my feet carrying me down the steps toward him as he started running toward his rental car. I'd never been a runner, and he'd been a track star in high school and college. He easily beat me to his car and had it quickly reversing before I even reached the spot where he'd been parked.

"We've got him," I heard Preacher yell right before all four motorcycles started up and roared off down my driveway, chasing Ethan's compact car.

I stood there panting from exertion and blinding anger for a minute before I felt a large hand touch my shoulder. I spun around and saw Wrecker standing close to me. The soft look on his face was almost enough to make me break into tears.

"From the look on his face, I'm going to guess you've never gone after him that way."

"Never once," I admitted. "I've never hit another person in anger before, but I guess there's a first time for everything."

"Did he always talk down to you like that?"

"It wasn't that obvious at first. There were subtle, occasional jabs about my weight or how I did my makeup. Through the years, it became normal. I didn't even think twice about believing what Ethan said."

"Why did you stay?"

"I wanted children, and he was my husband," I told Wrecker with a shrug. That one movement conveying that now even I didn't understand my logic. "After I found out I couldn't have kids, I didn't see any reason to rock the boat. We both worked all the time and didn't see each other very much. When I found out he'd been cheating on me, and his girlfriend was pregnant, I was more pissed that I'd been played than I was that my marriage was over."

"That makes sense, I guess."

"Thanks for coming out, Wrecker. If he comes back, I'll make it an official report and call 911."

"Do that, honey," Wrecker said with one more shoulder squeeze. "However, I have a feeling that your old man's club brothers are going to enjoy the new toy you got them until they either rip out the squeaky part, or he runs home with his tail between his legs."

"He doesn't have a home to go home to anymore. We had a prenup that his mother insisted on because she always thought that I would turn out to be a 'cheating whore' - those were her exact words. Since he was the one that got caught cheating, that backfired on both of them, and I got *everything* in the divorce. He had to move in with his girlfriend. I guess, considering that the baby came out looking like another man, that stream has dried up. He'll stay in town thinking I'll come crawling back."

"He's that stupid?"

"He's that stupid, but he's also broke as a joke and knows I've got all his money," I confirmed with a wry grin.

"If that's the case, I'm going to tell *my* brothers about him and let them play with the new squeaky toy too," Wrecker assured me before he started walking toward his patrol car. "You and your girl go back in the house and have a glass of wine. Boss will be here as soon as his meeting's over, I'm sure."

"Thanks again, Wrecker."

"Anytime, doll. Anytime."

I watched Wrecker's patrol car until he sped off down the road toward town.

"I don't believe that I've ever been in the presence of that much hotness or testosterone at one time," Paula admitted in a very soft voice. "I think my ovaries released at least three eggs, which is crazy considering I had a hysterectomy four years ago."

I burst out laughing and turned to look at my friend. She was staring down the road wistfully. She slowly turned her head and looked at me before she said, "I want one."

"Pick one out, and I'll see what I can do. There are more to choose from, just so you know. That was only four of Boss's club brothers; there are four more."

"I'd hate to choose and make one of them feel left out.

I'll just have one a day and two on Sundays. I'll be a legend because I'll be the first woman to die from an orgasm overdose, but what a way to fucking go."

JENNIFER

I laughed and then hooked my arm in Paula's and turned us back toward the house. "Let's go finish making the brownies, babe. I'll give you the beaters to lick so you can strengthen your tongue in preparation for the day you get all those muscled bodies in front of you. I'd hate for you to pull something."

"I can't believe your ex showed up out of the blue and expected you to welcome him into your house. Who does that?"

"Ethan. He does that. The world revolves around him. We're just the minions here to satisfy his every whim."

"Fuck that."

"Yep. Fuck that and fuck him. Oh, hold on, let me text Boss and let him know it's all clear, and he doesn't need to rush home."

"Home?"

"He's moving in tonight. We'll talk about that while you lick the beaters."

"Oh, goody. He's moving in, which means his friends will be in and out all the time. I'm going to start staying in your guest room."

"Whatever," I told her as my thumbs moved over the

keyboard. Boss responded almost instantly with a frown emoji. I didn't send him another text because I knew he was in an important meeting.

Paula and I chatted about Ethan, Boss, and his friends while I finished getting the brownies into the oven. As promised, I gave her the beaters. I hopped up on the counter and used a rubber spatula to clean the bowl I'd mixed the brownies in. We were surfing a sugar high when I heard a noise from somewhere inside the house.

"What the hell was that?" I murmured as I set my bowl aside and started to get down off the counter.

"I'll check. I need a glass of milk anyway," Paula told me as she slid off the stool and tossed the beaters into the sink. As she walked away, I hopped down off the counter. I moved over to the sink to start washing some dishes in preparation for the next batch of goodies I had planned.

I had just turned the water off when I heard footsteps behind me, so I asked Paula, "What was it? Did Moe escape?"

"If Moe knows what's good for him, he'll stay right where he is, Ms. McCool," I heard a man reply from close behind me. I had a wooden spatula in my hand and gripped it tighter as I came around, my arm moving in a powerful arc to surprise whoever was there. Just as the spatula hit him in the side of the head, I realized it was the sleazy guy from the park. He flinched and moved his head to the side from the smack, but it wasn't enough to disable him.

With one hand, he reached out and grabbed my shirt, yanking me closer to him so that I slammed into his chest.

"You little bitch!" he growled before he punched me

in the face. My head snapped back and I saw stars, but my body moved on instinct. I'd trained for years with a kickboxing instructor and former MMA fighter because that was the only exercise that didn't bore me to tears.

Today, all that training was about to come in handy.

I put one foot back to brace myself and used both hands to quickly jab Mr. Sleazy in the gut. My fists flew, and I hit him with all the power I'd practiced, happy to hear his breath whoosh out of him with every punch I landed. His head bent forward as he tried to move his body away, and I took that opportunity to slam my forehead into his nose.

He roared in pain as his nose flattened, but as he fell backward, he pulled me with him. I fell on top of him and made sure that my knee landed right on his groin with all my weight behind it. He howled like a wounded animal and finally let go of my shirt. I bounced up onto my feet, thanking God that I'd put on my favorite Docs this morning. My leg flew up with the strength of a horse to kick him squarely in the face. His head snapped back, and before he could recover, I kicked him three more times, letting the power in my thighs move him across the kitchen floor while I pretended his head was a soccer ball, and I was trying out for the Olympic team.

The sleazy guy didn't know whether to protect his balls or his face, but with another solid kick, his hands moved up to cover his head. I took that opportunity to go for his ribs, getting three good kicks in before he rolled away, giving me an open shot at his kidneys.

I kicked him in the back and kidneys until I was out of breath and seeing stars. By then, he was curled up in the fetal position halfway under the shelves on the other side of the room. Since he was moaning, I knew he was at least semi-conscious, so I grabbed one of the stainless steel saucepans on the shelf at my head and gripped the handle tight. I lifted the pan up over my head and swung with all the power left in my arms. The pan hit him in the back of the head with a loud thump.

The moaning stopped instantly, and I wondered if I had just killed him.

I realized that I didn't give a shit if he was dead. He had come to hurt me or worse, although I had no idea why I'd been chosen as his target.

"Paula!" I yelled as I watched the man on the ground for movement. I tried to catch my breath before I called for her again. "Paula! Are you okay?"

"Jennifer!" Paula's voice came through the doorway, but she sounded different, nasally, and out of breath.

"Are you okay? Are you alone?" I yelled as I propped the door to the walk-in refrigerator open with a huge bag of pecans I'd bought the day before.

"That man knocked me out," Paula said quietly from the doorway.

I looked over at my friend and saw her holding the side of her head. When she dropped her hand, I noticed that her eye was almost swollen shut.

"Fuck!" I roared as I pulled my leg back and kicked the asshole again.

"Holy shit!" Paula yelled when I turned back around

and stared at her. "You beat his ass!"

"I might have killed him," I admitted as she stopped by my side, and we stared down at the man on the floor. As if he knew we were talking about him, he moaned, and I saw his fingers twitch. "Shit! He's waking up."

"We need to tie him up with something."

I bit my lip and looked around the kitchen for something that might work. My gaze landed on the leashes and collars hanging beside the door that led to the garage.

I hurried across the room and got all three harnesses and leashes before I hustled back over to Sleazy.

"You get his feet, and I'll get his arms," I told Paula as I pushed him over onto his stomach and pulled his arms behind his back. "Just figure out a way to keep him still. We don't have to do much more than that because he's going to be hurting when he wakes up."

"Hurting or not, I don't want him to get up at all. Should we call the police?"

"I'll worry about that once we've got him secured," I told her, wishing with all my heart that I could just stick the man in the freezer and then bury him outside somewhere without Boss or Wrecker knowing what I'd done.

I'd never been that bloodthirsty before, but then again, I'd never been punched in the face by a man either. One glance at Paula, and I saw that she was probably thinking the same thing about him as she used her fingertips to gently explore the swelling around her eye.

I dropped down to my knees as Paula did the same, and we went to work making sure the guy couldn't get up and chase us or move his arms to hit us again.

I pulled his arms up at an unnatural angle and hooked one of the harnesses around them at the elbow. It was such a tight fit that I wasn't sure I'd be able to get it closed, but I managed, then did the same thing with another harness on his forearms. I heard a click and looked down at his feet where Paula had used the harness to pull his calves tightly together. If he was somehow able to get to his feet, he wouldn't be able to walk - he'd have to hop.

"Do you think they'll hold him?" Paula asked as she studied our handiwork.

"Do you think we can move him?"

Paula nudged him with her foot, and he groaned. She jumped back and nodded before she asked, "Where to?"

"We'll put him in the walk-in," I told her as I nodded at the big metal door I'd propped open. "There's a pin you can put in to secure the door. I've never understood why I'd need to do that, but now I'm grateful it's an option."

"After we get him in there are we going to call the cops?"

"Sure," I told her, again wishing that wasn't what we had to do. I'd never felt unsafe in my own home and knowing he was out there somewhere holding a grudge against me for the ass whooping I'd just dealt him made me afraid. I hesitated before I finally admitted, "I don't want to call the cops. If they arrest him, he'll just get bailed out. What would stop him from coming back?"

"Why did he come here in the first place?"

"I guess the cops can ask him."

"He looks like a career offender. I bet he won't tell them a thing."

"Maybe if we leave him in the walk-in for a while, *we* can ask him and *then* we can call the cops."

"That sounds like a good idea." Paula looked at me and nodded. "Let's put him in there and lock the door. We'll give it a bit, and after he's really cold, we'll ask him why he's so interested in you."

"Interested in me. Exactly."

"Let's move him," Paula said as she reached for his feet. She grabbed onto one foot and grunted as she tried to spin him around so that his feet were aiming for the refrigerator door. I grabbed his other foot and we got him settled in the right direction. We braced our feet and leaned back, pulling him along as we took baby steps toward the walk-in. Paula hissed her breath out as we took another step backward, moving him a few more inches. "I've never been so fucking glad I've got this ass and these thighs."

"Gives new meaning to that old song 'Put Your Back Into It', huh?" I asked her with a laugh. We had him halfway across the room now, and somehow the two of us were still managing to crack jokes.

"You can do it, put your back into it," Paula mimicked the female rapper from the song.

"You can do it, put your ass into it," I continued,

quoting Ice Cube.

"Put your back into it!"

"Put your ass into it!"

The two of us started laughing uncontrollably. I knew it was probably mild hysteria and shock setting in along with our funny misuse of an old Ice Cube song. We'd seemed to have found our rhythm, and we were already across the room and backing into the walk-in side by side as the big man slid across the cement floor, leaving a trail of blood in his wake.

"Oh, I've got one," I told Paula giddily. I burst into song. "She's got legs. She knows how to use them."

"Oh shit," Paula snorted before she laughed again. She started bouncing just a bit as she walked backward while she rapped Eminem's lyrics. "Come on, girl, shake that ass for me, shake that ass for me."

Finally, our backs hit the end of the walk-in, and we tugged the man in as far as we could. He'd moaned a few times while we dragged him, but he hadn't regained consciousness. Paula and I scurried around him to the door, and I kicked the bag of pecans to the side and slammed the door shut. It didn't latch - it just bounced back into my hand, almost knocking me over.

"What the fuck?" I asked out loud as I swung it shut again. I heard a distinct thump this time before the door bounced back again. I looked down at the floor just inside the walk-in and saw that the man's head was in the way. Paula saw it at the same time I did and giggled uncontrollably. I squatted down and pushed at the man's shoulders for a second and then shut the door again, this time successfully.

Once it was latched, I put the metal pin through the hole to hold the latch shut.

Paula was still giggling, and she sunk down onto the floor next to me. Our backs were propped against the metal door as we sat still and caught our breath.

"I think we just committed a huge health code violation," Paula said casually, as if we were discussing the weather. Paula and I were both staring at the trail of blood the man's nose had left as we drug him over the concrete. "He's bleeding, you know, and now that's going to be in your refrigerator. It might stain the concrete out here too."

"No, I had the concrete coated with sealer and epoxy for easy cleanup," I assured her. "There's a rubber mat on the floor inside the refrigerator. That will be easy to clean, too, I'm sure."

"Maybe you should replace it since there's going to be food in there."

"I'll use bleach on it. I'm sure it will be fine."

We sat there in silence for a few minutes until Paula whispered, "What the fuck did we just do, Jenn?"

"I think we just assaulted someone, and we're now holding them against their will. But we've both got temporary insanity on our side."

"And head injuries. If my face looks like yours, that will definitely fly in court."

"He was an intruder, right? We won't get charged with a crime."

"I sure wish you knew a cop who might be able to confirm or deny that," Paula hinted.

Just as Moe started howling, we heard the doorbell ring and the timer go off on the oven to let me know the brownies were done. Paula and I turned toward each other with wide eyes before we jumped up from the floor. I hit the timer and pulled the sheet pan out, then we both looked at the door, waiting for the doorbell to ring again.

"Do you think Ethan came back?" I asked her.

"Surely not."

"Whoever it is can't see in, so we should at least look."

"Okay," Paula whispered as if whoever was out there could hear us. We were almost through the door that led into my regular kitchen when Hook came in from the back porch. We stopped in our tracks and turned to look at him in shock. His expression was one of absolute disbelief and horror.

"What the fuck happened here?" Hook yelled as he rushed toward us.

"Nothing," we said in unison.

Hook skidded to a halt and studied us for a minute, confusion on his face.

"Hook, this is my friend Paula. Paula, this is Dr. York, but he likes to be called Hook. It's a motorcycle club thing, although I don't know how their names were decided."

"It's a pleasure to meet you, Hook," Paula interrupted my rambling and stuck her hand out to shake Hook's.

Hook looked down at her hand and then up at her face before he asked, "What the fuck happened to your face?" He glanced over at me and asked, "And yours? Did you two get into a fist fight? Who broke the window back there? What the fuck is going on?"

Paula spun around and pointed at her face before she asked me, "Does it really look that bad?"

"There's some blood." I pointed at my face and swirled my finger around my mouth and up my cheek. "It's kind of smeared a little bit, and your eye is swollen." I reached up and touched my nose and looked at my fingers before I asked, "Do I have blood too?"

"No, no blood," Paula assured me. "You need an ice pack, though. Your eye is swelling. I think mine is too. My whole face hurts now."

"So does mine."

"What. The. Fuck. Is. Going. On?" Hook's shock and curiosity were waning, and he was easing over to anger. "Did your ex get into the house? I thought the guys were coming over. I got here as soon as I could. Where the fuck is he?"

I bit my lip and wondered what I could say that might get him to leave so Paula and I could deal with the man in the refrigerator, but I was drawing a blank. I couldn't think of a single thing that might answer his questions while urging him to go home.

"The ex didn't get inside. Your friends came and scared the shit out of him before they chased him back to town. I was helping Jenn in the kitchen, and we, um, got dizzy from the, um, oven fumes, and we accidentally bumped heads."

"We're fine, though. It's okay. You can go home and take care of your animals. We'll put some ice on our faces and be fine. I'll have Boss call you when he gets here."

Hook was looking me in the eye when we heard the man in the refrigerator scream for help. Hook's eyes got wide, and I'm sure mine did, too, but both of us looked over at Paula when she said, "Man, my stomach makes some weird noises when I'm hungry. It was nice to meet you, Mr. Hook! I'm sure I'll see you again soon."

While she was talking, she put her hand on Hook's bicep and tried to turn him back toward the door. He was a huge man, at least twice her size, and he didn't budge no matter how hard she tried to push him.

Instead, he stared at me and then looked down at Paula with a glare. "Your hungry stomach sounds like a full-grown man screaming for help?"

"Did it sound like that to you?" Paula asked me with an exaggerated shrug. When the man screamed again, she closed her eyes and bit her lip before she blew out a long breath.

With a laugh that sounded more like hysteria than humor, I said, "There it was again."

Hook glanced down at his arm where Paula was still trying to move him and reached down with his other arm to pull his phone out of his pocket. With one thumb, ignoring the woman who was grunting with the effort, pissed off now that she couldn't even gain an inch, he pushed at the screen, and I heard Boss's voice come over the speaker.

"Did you make it?" Boss asked immediately.

"Yeah. I'm here. Are you close?"

"What's wrong?"

"There's a little, tiny woman here who's so hungry that her stomach is making weird noises. She and Cool Cat both seem to have lost their fucking minds. I don't know if they're drunk as fuck or high as kites, but I think I need backup. So, are you close?"

"I'm pulling into the driveway now."

"Come through the back door so you can get the same view I got when I came inside."

"What the fuck?"

"You're gonna say that more than once in the next few minutes, I'm sure."

The phone beeped when Boss hung up, and as Hook put it back into his pocket, I sighed dramatically. As if he was tired of her wasting her effort, Hook growled, "Stop it!" and put his free arm around Paula and pulled her tight to his chest. She made an 'oof' sound when she hit, but other than that, didn't argue about the contact. Instead, her hand came off his bicep and touched his abs before it drifted around his hip and settled on his back.

Just as Boss walked into the kitchen, the man in the walk-in screamed for help again. Boss's face went from shock at the state of my back room to anger when he saw the bruises on my face. Boss slowly turned his head toward the door leading out to the commercial kitchen when our captive screamed again.

"What. The. Fuck?" Boss whispered as he turned his head back to look at me.

"There's one." Hook mumbled as his other arm went around Paula.

"I have a question, and before we go any further with this whole screaming man thing, I need you to answer me."

"Okay," Boss drawled.

"Right now, are you here as the chief of police or as my boyfriend?"

Boss studied me for a second and asked, "Which one do you want here?"

"The boyfriend?"

"You sure?"

"In a perfect world, Hook wouldn't have shown up, and you'd still be in your meeting so Paula and I could take some time to figure out what we're fucking doing. Since it's not a perfect world, you're both here. Obviously, that sound is not coming from her hungry stomach. We'll have to explain what happened."

"Is whoever's making that sound why your face is fucking bruised and your eye is swollen?"

"Same with hers," Hook told Boss as he put his hands on Paula's shoulders and pushed her back far enough for Boss to see her face. Once Boss had a good look at her face, Hook pulled her back into his chest. Paula made another 'oof' sound when she made contact.

"That would be a yes."

"Is he dying?" Boss asked me.

"No. Maybe. I'm not sure. The guy's pretty fucked up and probably needs a doctor."

"Do you want him to get to a doctor, or do you want him to be dying?"

"I want him to not be able to break into my house and hurt me and my friend again. If him dying is the way to assure that, then no, I do not want him to get medical attention, and yes, I'd like for him to be dying."

"I vote for the dying thing, and I have a few ideas on how to do it if you need input," Paula said from her comfortable spot in Hook's arms. "I know we just met, but if the three of you knew anything at all about me, you'd understand that I'm really okay with this. I can even help."

"Want to get married?" Hook asked Paula as he patted her on the back.

"Sure. I'm free next Friday."

15

BOSS

"What the fuck are we doing, Boss?" Preacher asked as he glanced at the doorway of the room we were standing in.

"I don't know what *you're* doing, but I'm about to torture this fucker until he starts speaking in tongues. Then I'm going to give him a minute to gather his wits about him and ask him a few questions. Depending on how he answers, I'll either torture him some more and see if that loosens his lips, or I'll kill him."

"There are loose ends up there at the house, and you're trusting that they can keep their mouth shut," Preacher pointed out worriedly.

"I think I took care of that," Captain told Preacher as he held his hand up when he saw that I was about to argue. "First, they're the ones that incapacitated him. Second, it's Jenn's property we're on, and she's the one that pointed us to this location. Third, the two of them helped Boss and Hook get the fucker out here knowing good and well what was going to happen."

"What makes you think they know what's going to happen?"

"Jennifer was quick to point out the floor drain. She offered us a hose, bucket, and a bottle of bleach for easy cleanup. Paula stood there and gave me a goddamn anatomy lesson to make sure he didn't die too quickly," Hook explained. "I'm pretty sure they know what's about to happen. I'm a little pissed off that the woman knows anatomy better than I do, and I'm the one with a doctorate."

"And knowing all that, I explained to the women that if we go down for this shit, so do they. We've all come to a tentative agreement that we're in this together."

"Geez, Cap. I'm so glad it's a tentative agreement. Are you sure we shouldn't get something in fucking writing?" Preacher asked. His distrust of the human race was evident on a good day but more so right now.

"You wanna leave then fucking go!" Stamp barked at Preacher. "This motherfucker broke in and assaulted two women. If they hadn't stopped him, there's no fucking telling what he'd have done. I, for one, want to know why and will slit his throat myself once I find out."

"That's way too quick, man, and it leaves a helluva spray," Hook argued.

"Those hooks up there on the ceiling are for butchering animals, so you can hang them upside down and let all the blood drain out. We should utilize those," Chef said as he studied the ceiling. "I'm sure they'll hold him considering a good-sized buck is usually close to 300 pounds."

"Did you guys check out the room downstairs?" Kitty asked as he came up through the trapdoor a few feet from where I was sitting. Santa was close behind him and then Bug emerged. "Concrete walls and access to the outside through an insulated set of metal doors. I believe it's even soundproof."

"That's handy," Cap said from his chair on the other side of the bleeding man who was listening intently to our conversation. The guy whimpered around the dish towel Hook had stuffed in his mouth earlier. "And Boss is moving in this evening when we're done, so we'll have all access if we need it."

"And I thought my surgical room at the clinic would be our only location for shit like this," Hook said in awe. "Boss's new place comes with a soundproof room, so that's a step up."

"Guys," I shouted. "Focus. I have shit to do this evening, namely pack my belongings and move into my woman's house. Stamp, did you bring the tools I asked for?"

Stamp leaned down and grabbed the bag of things he'd purchased from the hardware store this afternoon and set it on the table with a thump. I gave the asshole a few seconds to look at the bag and wonder what tools I'd requested. I leaned forward and looked him in the eye while I said, "Now this is the part where you have to make a decision. If I take that towel out of your mouth, you can spill your guts and tell me what the fuck you were doing in my old lady's house. Then when I think you've told me everything I need to know, I'll hang you upside down from that hook and let my buddy slit your throat. If you don't immediately start talking, I'll put the rag back in your mouth and get to work. Make your choice now, bud."

I pulled the towel out of his mouth, and he worked his jaw for a second before he turned his head and tried to spit at me. His mouth was dry, so nothing came out, but the intent was there, and I understood it. I shoved the towel back in his mouth and pulled the bag my way.

"Get his arms, bring them to the front, and hold them out straight," I ordered Chef and Hook, the two largest and strongest men in the club. The man groaned and fought, but he was no match for my brothers. Within seconds, they had both of his hands held out in front of his body. I looked at him as I pulled everything out of the bags and said, "The way they're holding you right now, the more you fight, the more likely it is that you'll end up with your elbows touching and the bones sticking out of your upper arms."

The man stopped fighting, not quite understanding that what I was about to do to him would hurt just as bad, if not worse than that.

"Well, this is handy," I told Stamp with a smile as I held up the mini butane torch he'd purchased.

"I got two refill cartridges to go with it."

"Awesome. But, shit, it's gonna smell so fucking bad in here."

"Want me to prop the door open?" Preacher asked with a grin.

"Nah. We'll wait and see how many it takes, and if the smell gets too bad, we'll open the door and take a break while the room airs out."

The guys chatted about mundane things while I used the duck tape to secure his hands to a short piece of pipe that Stamp had brought. As I worked, I made sure to wind the duck tape between each finger, leaving the fingers and thumbs sticking up rather than having them grip the pipe.

"I watched this movie while I was in prison," I told the man conversationally. "You knew I'd been in prison, right? Murder was what they put me in for, but that was ages ago, and they were only able to prove one of them was me. They thought they'd get me for all four, but the evidence was shaky on those other three. Anyway, while I was in prison, I watched this movie, and this scene in it really interested me."

"I remember watching a movie where the good guy who was sort of a bad guy with good intentions started things out just like you're doing, but it was with a steering wheel, wasn't it?" Stamp asked in that same conversational tone as if we were discussing the weather rather than how to torture a person.

"Denzel," Chef's deep voice rumbled. "He's the man."

"Exactly, and he plays deadly crazy really well," I agreed as I finished with the tape and started to take the large tin snips out of their packaging. I glanced up and saw the man's eyes widen as I flexed the tin snips to see what they could do. "These will go through bone pretty easily, I think. He used a knife in the movie, but I'm tired, and I've got plans later, so I don't want to fuck around."

I set the tin snips down on the table in front of the man and picked up the torch. I fiddled with it until I had the flame set just how I wanted it. I turned back to the man and saw that he was sweating profusely now. I realized that it could be because it was hard to breathe through his broken nose or because he'd seen the same movie.

I guessed, considering his eyes were staring at the

tools I'd laid out in front of him, that it was the movie reference.

"Here's one more chance to talk. I won't have you spitting at me again, or when we're finished, I see how well those fucking tin snips work on your tongue."

The man's eyes cut to mine, and he nodded in understanding.

Before I could say anything else, Stamp reached for the tin snips and snapped them together a few times before he said, "These seem like a useful tool. I'd never really considered them before. I wonder if the guys back home know about these."

"Doesn't the mafia just shoot people?" Kitty asked.

"Well, mostly, but there are occasions when they need answers and have to find inventive ways to get them."

"Back to today's subject," I said as I yanked the rag out of the man's mouth. "Why did you target my girlfriend?"

The man bit his lip and shook his head as he glanced from the tool Stamp was holding and then up at my eyes. I watched him make the wrong decision right before I heard him say, "Because I wanted to make her *my* girlfriend."

I sighed and picked the rag up. As I stuffed it back into his mouth, I said, "Wrong answer, bud. Way wrong answer."

Stamp handed the tin snips to me, and I easily cut off the man's index finger at the second knuckle. When he threw his head back to yell, I yanked the towel out of his mouth and dropped his finger into it. Chef held his jaw closed and his head still as the man tried to fight the inevitable.

"I just came up with that part all on my own," I told him with a dark laugh. "Saves us having to pick up the pieces later."

"That is so fucking gross, man," Santa moaned from across the room. "That's on a whole other level of disgusting."

"I think it's sweet," Hook disagreed as he grinned. "It's fucked up, but it's a nice gesture that he's cleaning up as he goes."

I picked up the torch and sloppily cauterized the man's wound while Chef held his head still and his mouth shut. He swallowed and gagged a few times before Chef pried his jaw open and checked inside his mouth.

"You puke, and I'll spoon-feed every fucking drop back into you," Chef warned.

I sighed dramatically and said, "Let's try this again, shall we?"

Three fingers and one unconscious asshole later, I decided it was time to call in Sin and his men. This was more than just some man targeting Jennifer. This was connected to the problems Tenillo was having with drugs, and it was so much bigger than any of us had realized.

"This is a nice setup," Executioner, one of the men from the AIMC, said as he looked around the well house. "I like it."

"Thanks. We just came across it today, as a matter of fact," I admitted. "It's working well for us."

"You are fucking kidding me! That was a great movie!" Wrecker said as he looked at the man in the chair, his injuries, and the tools in front of him.

"I saw it on cable when I was in prison."

"No offense, man, but they really should pay more attention to what they let the guys in there watch," Saint said gravely. "It's working out in this situation but some things . . ."

"I know, right? I got addicted to Breaking Bad while I was inside," Kitty interrupted. "I missed a few episodes for one reason or another, so that was the first thing I binge-watched when I got out."

"Have you ever watched Justified?" Wrecker asked him as if we were sitting on a patio somewhere drinking beers and shooting the shit.

"Gentlemen," Sin said in a low voice. "Let's catch up on our watchlists later, and remind me to tell you guys about Ozark. Anyway, what do we have here?"

"This is Marcos Dirtbag Santiva. He pestered my girlfriend a few times before he broke into her house today. We were dealing with that, getting to the whys and what fors when he started telling us about how they transport and deal drugs out of a few of the food trucks that roam around town. That's what he wanted to talk to my girl about to begin with but then she argued with him and made a police report. We didn't have any leads, but he showed up inside her fucking house this afternoon, and she had to defend herself."

"Oh, that was a horrible idea," Executioner said with fire in his eyes. "Is she okay?"

"She's bruised up. He hit her *and* her friend more than once," I growled. "But she beat his ass like he owed her money, and she and her girlfriend tied him up and locked him in the walk-in until Hook and I got here."

"She whipped his ass?" Sin asked.

"Fuck yeah. She did all of that," I told him as I motioned toward the dickbag's face. "We haven't touched him other than to hold hands while we talked. All of this is her handiwork, and I'd guess from the way he's wheezing that she broke a few ribs."

"Damn. Does Jenn have a sister?" Wrecker asked. "She looks like that *and* can fight like a cage fighter? You better treat her like a queen."

"I have a feeling that if he doesn't, he'll end up looking like this guy," Santa quipped, causing the men in the room to laugh.

Marcos was sitting very still with his chin resting on his chest as we laughed at him. All the fight had gone out of him after he swallowed finger number three and started singing, answering every question we asked quickly and precisely.

"I asked you gentlemen here because I've gotten a bunch of information from him so far, but I thought you might know something I don't or be able to come at it from a different angle."

"It's so nice of you to share your toys," Executioner

said with a sinister laugh.

"Did he tell you if there's just one man in charge of the whole operation, or if there are separate factions at play?" Sin asked.

"Well?" I barked as I nudged Marcos's shoulder. "Answer the man's question, puto."

"I don't know," Marcos whined. "I report to Balderas. The only other one I know above him is a white guy with slicked-back hair. I've never talked to him, just seen him."

"Does your boss or his boss, what the fuck ever, run the extortions along with the drugs?" Wrecker asked.

"I don't know."

"What's the deal with the women that keep disappearing?" Sin asked.

I watched Marcos's eyes dart around before he answered, "I don't know."

"I think you do know," I said softly, close to his ear. "As it stands, you could still function with the number of fingers you've got. You want to lose a few more?"

"You're not going to let me out of here anyway," Marcos growled, finding his second wind.

"You're right. You put your hands on my woman and hurt her. For that alone, I'll see you dead. However, you've got information in that noggin of yours that I want, and I'm going to keep fucking with you until I get it. At my count, you've got seven more fingers and 10 toes left before I start going for your teeth. Hook, how many teeth does a grown man have?"

"32 if he's got his wisdom teeth and hasn't had any pulled," Hook answered.

"Well, then," I nudged Marcos with my shoulder. "Let's do the math. 17 digits plus 32 teeth, add two eyeballs, divide two testicles, minus one severed dick equals you should *answer the fucking question.*"

"Fuck you!" Marcos growled. Hook stuffed the towel into his mouth as Stamp lit the torch. I snipped off the middle finger on his left hand, and when Hook pulled his head back, I dropped it into his mouth. While Hook forced him to swallow it, I cauterized his wound, and we started over.

"That is so fucked up," Executioner whispered. "So unbelievably fucked up."

"I know, right?" Preacher cackled.

Hook opened Marcos's mouth and checked it before he let his head drop forward. Marcos took a deep, pain-filled breath and started talking.

"Hey, sweetheart," I murmured into Jenn's ear as I brushed her hair back from her face. "Come on upstairs, and let's get you in bed."

"Paula's in the . . ."

"Hook's taking her home, babe," I told Jenn as I helped her stand up next to the couch. "We took care of the animals and locked up the barn. The boys are already upstairs in their beds, and now it's time to get you upstairs in our bed."

"Did you take the trash out?" Jennifer mumbled as she walked toward the staircase.

"I did."

"Good. I don't want it to blow back into the yard and bother me again."

"It won't, babe."

"Thank you."

I watched my girl's ass as she walked up the stairs in front of me, all the while wondering what to say to that. She'd just thanked me for killing a man and disposing of his body.

As if she'd read my mind, she said, "I know that's weird, and you probably won't ever look at me the same again, but I don't want to always look over my shoulder and worry, you know?"

"You don't have to worry, sweetheart, and I'm not going to look at you funny because of it."

"Are you sure?"

"I promise," I assured her. If anything, the fact that she was perfectly okay with tonight's events, even though she didn't know specifics and only knew the outcome, was perfection in my book. I was not the type of man to let things slide. Being a police officer, that would have to happen occasionally when I handed things over to the court system. However, when I put my badge on the dresser and changed into my cut, I could fix things in a way that meant certain problems wouldn't resurface

I knew that was what she meant by having to look over her shoulder. When I took off my badge this evening, I made sure that wouldn't be an issue, at least with that scumbag.

"Boss . . ." Jennifer started to say something else, but I stopped her when I took her into my arms.

"If you need to talk about what happened, I'm here for you, but right now, I'm tired. I want to take a shower with my lady, crawl between her legs, and forget everything but how she tastes and feels underneath me. Can we do all that and talk tomorrow?"

"I want to do all that, and I don't want to talk about what happened today ever again."

"I am okay with that too. So will you shower with me?"

"Of course I will," Jennifer whispered as she tiptoed up to kiss me. "Did you get the sandwiches I sent down with Kitty?"

"We did. Thank you for dinner, sweetheart," I told her with a big smile. It had shocked the shit out of all of us when Kitty came back from checking in with the girls carrying a huge basket full of sandwiches, chips, and brownies along with a cooler full of bottled water.

"You're welcome. I can't leave my man hungry, now can I?"

"Oh, honey, I'm ravenous right now, but it's you I'm

gonna eat this time."

Jennifer just laughed and dragged me toward the bathroom.

16

JENNIFER

I heard a long, low howl and then a hiss right before Moe yelped and his nails clattered across the tile downstairs.

"I keep telling you, pal - don't fuck with the cats, or their claws will come out. When that happens, they *will* fuck you up," Boss's gravelly voice had a stern tone as it wafted up to the bedroom, but I heard Moe's collar jingling, so I knew Boss was soothing his hurt feelings. "They get you every time, but like any other dog, you never learn and keep chasing the wrong kind of pussy."

I smothered a laugh at Boss's life lesson and snuggled farther down under the covers. As I stretched my body out, I turned my head and came face to face with Elvira, my new archenemy. She was glaring at me, if skunks could glare, and I truly believed they could because she did it every single time we were in the same room.

"Good morning," I whispered and watched her blink a few times before she turned around and aimed her ass at my face. Thank God she didn't have her scent glands anymore, but I couldn't help but chuckle when she tried to use them. The skunk hopped off the bed and sauntered to the door, her tail swaying saucily as if she'd marked me with her stink, and her job here was done. "You're such a bitch, Elvira."

At the bedroom door, she turned around and shot

another skunk glare my way before she darted across the sitting area to go to our man. After just a minute, I heard Boss cooing at her and knew she was in his arms where I wanted to be.

In the week since Boss had moved in with me, the animals had been getting to know each other better, just like Boss and I. The transition wasn't seamless, but it hadn't been unpleasant either.

Boss had his quirks just like I did, but I hadn't noticed them when he stayed the night. The day after he and the animals had moved in, they'd started to show. I glanced over at his nightstand and stared at one of those quirks for a second before I smiled.

Somehow he had all of his important possessions organized on the top of that nightstand as if he didn't have an entire house to spread out and enjoy. The five books he'd brought with him were standing up meticulously aligned in a perfect row. Between each book or stuck in the books' pages were Boss's important papers and a few photographs.

When I'd asked him about his row of 'treasures' he'd shrugged. Later, he admitted that for a decade, everything he owned had to be confined to one small shelf, and it was a habit he couldn't seem to break.

The fact that I stashed things all over the place and then forgot where I put them irritated Boss to no end. I was constantly losing my reading glasses and the keys to my truck and trailer. Boss had ordered a chip on Amazon and connected it to my keys so that either of us could touch an app on our phone, and the keys would start chirping until we found them.

As far as my readers went, Boss started collecting them in a large plastic container that he stashed under the bar. I'd always just stopped at the nearest convenience store or pharmacy and grabbed a new pair when I couldn't find any others, so I had quite a collection. At last count, the container had 17 pairs of glasses, but I'd added a new pair yesterday on my way to the fairgrounds when I'd forgotten to bring one with me.

I'd promptly lost them somewhere in the trailer and had to squint at the card reader every time I rang up a customer.

Boss visited the trailer while he was on patrol with Wrecker, saw what was going on, and ran over to the pharmacy nearby to buy me another pair - this one with a hot pink ribbon attached so I could wear them around my neck.

I'd balked at the thought of wearing them like a necklace as if I were one of those old ladies that took forever to put her glasses on before she took even longer to write out a check in the grocery store line. I was *not* that old lady. However, since he'd bought them for me, I wore them the rest of the evening.

I hated to admit it, but I'd kept up with them all night and was probably going to invest in a prettier chain and wear my glasses around my neck every time I worked now.

I stretched one more time and then got up and walked into the bathroom. I took my time in the shower and braided my hair into two Dutch braids while it was still wet, hoping it was warm enough for us to take the bike to run our errands today. I walked out of the bathroom wearing my robe and was surprised to find Boss sitting up against the headboard shirtless in his pajama pants, reading his book.

"Good morning, handsome," I told him with a smile as I walked around the bed to the closet.

"You're going to walk over there and get dressed before I even get a good morning kiss?"

"You were reading, and I didn't want to interrupt you," I told him as I turned back to walk up on his side of the bed. I leaned down for a quick kiss, but he had other ideas. His hand went to the back of my neck and held me there while his other hand reached out and untied my robe. He tweaked my nipple before his fingers trailed down between my legs and cupped my sex. I pulled my mouth away from his, just far enough to whisper, "Good morning to you too."

Boss's hands came up and pushed my robe down my arms. It fell down onto the floor at my feet just as he wrapped his arms around me and pulled me over him to the other side of the bed.

"Did you sleep well, baby?" Boss murmured as he kissed my neck. He rubbed his hand up and down my back for a few seconds before he cupped my ass and pulled me closer to his body.

"I did, but I have a feeling I'm going to need a nap when you get through with me."

"Oh, you're going to need another shower, too, sweetheart," Boss growled in my ear before he bit my shoulder.

"I thought we had stuff to do today," I argued.

"They moved Pop's release time to 3:00 this afternoon."

"We do have time then," I whispered as my lips found his neck.

"I've got plans for you this morning. You know that Amazon package that was delivered for me the other day?"

"Yeah," I mumbled as I scooted down to lick his nipple.

"It had goodies that I bought for a morning just like this." Boss twisted his body around and picked a box up off the floor. He settled it behind my back as I stared up at him. I heard his hand rustling around in the box as he lifted his head up to look over me and see inside. He pulled something out, and as his hand moved, I felt something trail over my skin as he brought his hand back between us. It was a slender remote control with a cord coming out of the bottom of it. As he lifted it higher in the air, I saw a small, purple egg at the end of the cord. "This is a remote control for you to keep handy while I fuck you."

"Oh," I whispered, interested now. I'd seen these in catalogs and online and wondered if I should buy one. Boss had beaten me to it.

He dropped it between us and then pulled something else out of the box. He dropped a bottle on the bed, and I glanced down and saw that it was lube just before he pulled something else out of the box. He held it up for me to look at, and I knew instantly that it was a butt plug. When I looked up into his eyes, he was smiling. "I washed everything while I was downstairs and got it all ready for us to play with this morning."

"Aren't you just a boy scout?" I murmured, marveling at the size of the plug and anxious to see how it felt inside me.

"You seem to like it when I play with your ass while I'm licking your pussy or fucking you from behind. I thought we'd take it a step or two further."

"I'm down for that," I whispered as Boss's hand trailed over my hip and then dipped down to cup my sex. I lifted my leg and put it over his hip to give him access, and he took it, pushing the palm of his hand against my clit as he stroked his fingers back and forth in my heat.

"You're already wet and ready for me," Boss murmured before he gave me a long, slow kiss. His fingers delved inside of me, and I had to pull away and suck in a deep breath. Boss's hands were almost as magical as his mouth, and I was already tense, ready for my first orgasm of the day with just his simple touch.

Boss pushed me to my back and crawled over me before he lifted himself up on his arms and slid down my body, touching me from nipples to hips with his bare chest until he settled down between my legs and licked my clit with one quick swipe. I gasped at the touch and heard him chuckle before he used both hands to push my thighs farther apart and got down to business.

I was coming down from my orgasm when I heard a click and felt Boss's thumb push against my ass. He was slowly lapping at my pussy now as I came down, giving me a minute to calm before he touched my sensitive clit again. I felt him start to push his thumb inside me and then realized it was the plug instead when he pulled it out and then pushed it in farther. It didn't hurt, but it was a foreign feeling, so I tensed at the intrusion.

Boss felt that and used his mouth to take my mind off of what he was doing by flattening his tongue and pushing against my clit as he slowly moved his head back and forth. I pulled at his hair with my hands, trying to draw him even closer to me and get him to move faster, but he wasn't having it. He kept a steady rhythm against me and sucked my clit in between his teeth and hummed as he pushed the plug all the way inside.

It was almost too much sensation at one time, and I screamed as I came again, writhing under his mouth as he tapped against the plug.

"Ohmygod, ohmygod," I chanted as I came down slowly, panting and whimpering as Boss kept tapping and slowly licked me.

"Hold it inside and ride me, sweetheart," Boss told me as he crawled up my body and laid down on the bed beside me. I gave him a second to pull the pajama pants off and toss them aside. Once he was naked, I started to lift my leg over his hips, and he stopped me with his hands and said, "Turn around. Reverse it so I can play with you at the same time."

I moved on the bed to face his feet and squeezed the toy inside me tight to hold it there while I adjusted myself over him. He held his cock up, and I sunk down on it slowly until he filled me completely. I rested on his body for a second as I got used to the new sensation of the plug inside me along with his cock. Boss took that time to use his hands and massage my ass cheeks like he enjoyed doing and then he started in with that dirty talk that drove me wild.

"Love your ass, Jenn," Boss whispered as he squeezed my cheeks with his big hands. "I love to watch your ass move as I fuck you from behind, and today, I'm gonna play with it while you ride me."

"Yeah," I whispered as I leaned forward and rested my hands on his thighs and lifted my hips until I almost lost him and then slowly lowered myself down again. I heard Boss hiss and knew he felt the same bliss I did at the movement, so I did it again and again, slowly moving up and down as he watched where we were connected. I felt him touch the plug and gasped when he twisted it and tugged on it gently before he pushed it back in. I couldn't help but start to move faster, enjoying the full feeling as I fucked him while his hands roamed all over me. I'd found the perfect rhythm, and I knew this because of the sounds Boss was making behind me and the tension in his thighs where I held myself up. I wasn't close to another orgasm yet, and that was okay. I'd had my time, and now it was his.

Boss had other ideas. I heard a buzzing sound right before his hand came around my hip and he cupped my sex with his palm. The egg touched my clit, and I screamed at the sensation, grinding myself against his hand as I swirled my hips around with his cock deep inside me. Boss used his other hand to pull the plug almost all the way out and then push it back in, fucking me with it at the same time he held the toy against me.

It was too much at once, and I sat straight up and screamed as I came, my body clutching at his so hard I heard him moan. He held onto me and kept the toy there while he pushed the plug in and out of my ass. One orgasm rolled right into another one until I could barely breathe. I heard Boss let out a growl, and the vibrator dropped away right before he clutched my hips with his hands and lifted me up, then brought me down roughly on top of him. I felt Boss curl up behind me and then he wrapped his arms around me as he came with a loud roar.

Boss held me still as his cock twitched inside me and my body clutched at his while my orgasm waned. Both of us were panting, trying to catch our breath, and I leaned my head back to rest on his shoulder while he held me tight.

"I've never felt anything that intense," I whispered between breaths. "That was . . . fuck a duck, that was awesome."

Boss chuckled, and it made him move inside me, causing me to gasp. He took his arms away and put one palm on my back as he pushed me forward so that I was propped up with my hands on his thighs again. He slowly pulled the plug out of my ass and then smacked my cheek with his free hand, "Roll off, baby, and I'll clean us up."

I fell to the side and collapsed on the bed. I felt like I'd melted, and I wasn't sure I would ever recover. I was breathing steadily by the time Boss came back with a wet washrag, and I let him lift my leg and clean his seed before he put it back down gently. He laughed softly when I moaned and flopped to my other side and curled up, clutching his pillow in my arms.

I yawned loudly and let my eyes drift shut just as the bed dipped, and he fit himself behind me.

"You can't go to sleep, honey. We've got shit to do

today."

"Mmhmm."

I heard a vehicle coming toward the house, and Boss said, "That's Stamp and his assistant, babe. He's here for the kitchen."

I mumbled, "It's ready for him. I cleaned yesterday."

"Your kitchen is always clean, baby," Boss told me with a laugh. "What the hell did you have to do to get ready?"

"I dusted the signs," I admitted. "I wanted them to look good in the video."

I collected tin signs from estate sales, auctions, and antique stores. There were quite a few of my favorites hanging around the kitchen and dining area. Some of them had funny sayings and others were advertisements from products that didn't exist anymore. Stamp had taken pictures of them last week and sent them to his producers to make sure he could have them as the backdrop for his videos. Once he had the all-clear, he and I had planned for him to come in today and film. He was going to shoot three videos and it would take him all day to do it, so Boss and I made plans with Paula and a few of the guys to have lunch and get Pop settled in the facility Cap found.

On Monday night, just three days after the attack in my kitchen, I cooked dinner for Boss and his brothers so they could have a meeting in the dining room. I thought I would have to make myself scarce when they started talking about club business, but that wasn't the case at all.

Instead, they talked about the different nursing homes

and assisted living centers they'd each toured, pulling out pieces of paper with notes they'd taken, brochures and packets they'd been given, along with printouts of information they'd found online.

For two hours, the men had talked, giving the merits and drawbacks of each place until they'd taken a vote on the top two over dessert. Cap's choice was the winner, and the next day all nine of them had met at the facility to take a tour and get to know the staff. I was sure they intimidated them, either unconsciously or on purpose, in the hopes that Pop would be their number one resident for the foreseeable future.

The home they'd decided on cost thousands of dollars a month more than Pop's insurance was willing to cover, so Preacher had created a spreadsheet listing the expenses and what they'd need to contribute so that Pop's stay was paid.

I'd sat in awe of how invested each man was in Pop's recovery, his health, and his comfort. For such large, gruff men with criminal and sometimes violent histories, the fact that they were putting their heads together to take care of the man who'd given each of them a new start brought tears to my eyes. I'd expressed that to the men while they sat there, and none of them understood just how special it was that they were taking such an interest.

To them, this was what needed to be done for their mentor, so they did it without a second thought.

To me, it showed the unity of the group and the true brotherhood they shared because Pop had brought them all together. When I'd mentioned it to Boss after everyone left, he explained that each of them had seen or heard of men they served time with falling back into the old lifestyles that took them to prison in the first place.

Boss and his brothers in the club knew that they could have been men like that, lost with no one to depend on, no job or income, and no safe place to call home. Without Pop's help, any one of the men, including Boss, might be back in prison because they just didn't know how to function outside in the world after so much time inside.

I hadn't been involved in the research or the vote on where Pop was going, but I'd do my part to make the transition smooth and keep Pop, Boss, and the MC in the good graces of the staff there.

I'd baked treats to deliver today while we got Pop settled, and I planned to make sure there was a tray of something special delivered to the staff every week for as long as Pop was a resident there. I'd already talked to the director of the facility and let her know that anyone who came to my trailer with their work ID wouldn't spend a dime. I also made arrangements to bring the trailer out on special days with a sugar-free selection of goodies for the residents who wanted something sweet.

When Boss found out my plans, he'd pulled me close and hugged me so tight that I could barely breathe and then walked out onto the porch to be alone for a few minutes. I'd left him there, knowing he was working through the emotions of having Pop out of the hospital and on the road to recovery. When he'd come back in, he'd thanked me for thinking of his mentor and told me just how special I was in his eyes for the effort I planned to put forth on Pop's behalf.

For more of those soft smiles, sweet kisses, and the

gentle lovemaking I got that night, I'd bake treats for anyone and give all of them away free. My night was that good, and it took me until noon the next day to crawl out of my orgasm coma and join the real world.

Like right now, as Boss hurried downstairs to open the door for Stamp and his crew, I was expected to get up out of bed and be a normal, fully functioning woman even though my bones were jelly, my muscles were pudding, and my mind was running on one cylinder.

Every time I was naked with Boss, he fucked me stupid, and I enjoyed every second of it.

"Get up, Jenn!" Boss called from downstairs. "Stamp's got questions."

I groaned and sat up in bed, then walked naked to my closet, not caring that if the men downstairs were looking up into my room, they might see my bare breasts. I didn't give a shit. They could look all they wanted. My breasts, my body, my mind, and my heart belonged to Boss.

BOSS

"Lorene, Julia's still at her baby's doctor appointment. Can you bring me the file I requested from the health department? I saw it on her desk earlier."

"Sure, Chief," Lorene told me, but her voice sounded strained. "I'll bring it back in just a second."

I hung up the phone without saying another word and opened the blinking messenger screen on my laptop. I had a message from Preacher telling me he was on his way to the office with something urgent. He'd sent it 15 minutes ago, so he should be here anytime now.

I'd made a list of men who were welcome in my office any time I was there. Preacher, along with my club brothers and any man wearing an Ares Infidels MC cut, was on it. Of course, department employees could access my office at any time unless I was gone and had it locked.

And by locked, I meant with the coded keypad I'd installed myself that allowed *no one* to come into my office while I was gone unless they kicked the door down or broke the window and crawled in through the hole.

Preacher had found the video evidence of Julia planting the eagle in my office, but we weren't sure if she picked the lock herself or if someone who never got into camera range had done it for her. Either way, I'd kept Julia close since then, but had never given her access to my office unless I was in it.

Since that day, she'd accidentally left her phone in my office three separate times. Strangely enough, I'd seen Julia with her phone, and the case on it looked nothing like the case on the phone she kept mindlessly leaving behind.

Finally, not even giving a shit that doing so would tip Julia off that I was on to her, I'd taken the phone she left into the breakroom and ran it through the dishwasher along with my lunch plate and my coffee mug. After an hour or so, I'd called Julia's desk and asked her to get my mug out of the dishwasher and bring me a fresh cup of coffee.

She'd brought my coffee, which I didn't dare take a sip of, and never said a word about the ruined phone she'd found inside the machine. Since then, she'd rarely come farther into my office than the doorway, and she'd definitely never left any electronics near my desk.

I'd noticed last Monday, after the crazy weekend we'd had at our house, Julia had been off somehow. Her eyes were constantly red as if she'd been crying, and she was jumpy and moody with everyone in the office, including me.

I surmised she was having problems at home. When she'd sent a text this morning letting me know her little one had a doctor appointment, I assumed that might have been the cause for her behavior last week. I remembered times when my daughter had been ill or had an ear infection. Neither my wife nor I got any sleep as we walked the floor with our baby girl, wishing we could take away whatever was wrong with her so she could sleep peacefully in her own bed.

I'm sure I'd shown up to my job jumpy with red eyes

more than once when she was small.

Lorene appeared in my doorway holding a thick file folder. I looked up at her and started to say thank you when she walked in and slowly shut the door behind her.

"What's going on, Lorene?"

"Where did you say Julia went this morning?"

"Her son had a doctor appointment. I'm not sure if he's sick or if it was a check-up, but she'll probably be in after lunch. Why do you ask?"

Lorene sat in the chair and stared down at the floor for a second before she finally lifted her eyes to mine. "I don't like to be a rat, Chief, and I take pride in the fact that I keep my head down, get my work done, and mind my business."

"Okay," I drawled, unsure where she was going with this but understanding I was probably about to get pulled into some office drama.

"Julia's been different for a while, and we just chalked it up to what was going on at home, but . . ."

"Different how?" I interrupted. "She was upset last week, I noticed."

"Yeah, last week she was so skittish, and I heard her crying in her office more than once. But, before that, she had steadily gotten meaner. Not all the time, but she'd get jittery and be mean as a snake until she left for an appointment or went to lunch. Then she'd come back and be her mellow self again until the next time. I guessed it was the stress of the divorce, but it was just so extreme."

"She's getting a divorce?"

"Well, yeah. That's why I thought it was so weird when you said she was at an appointment with her son. I realized you don't really know any of us, so you might not be aware of some things you really need to know."

"Like what?"

"Julia's 'little one' is actually five, and she's not allowed to see him anymore. They're in the middle of a divorce, but Child Protective Services got involved after something happened at her house. Her husband got an order through Judge Martinez that says she can't have contact with any of her kids."

"How long has she been married?"

"Well, her kids are 12, 8, and 5 now, so I'd say at least 12 years. She was married when she started working here 10 years ago."

I took a deep breath and blew it out through my nose. Those quick fucks in the parking lot and bar bathroom were done with a married woman. No wonder she never pressed me for my number or a follow-up.

"A lot of things have happened since she started working here, but she was close to the old chief, so she never lost her job. I know that she's in charge of HR or at least has access to their files, so after you called me a few minutes ago, I went into the file room and looked at Julia's folder. There's no record of anything that's gone on in 10 years. No record at all."

"Okay. List the shit out for me then," I said softly as I

leaned forward. "Julia was close with the former chief?"

"Yeah, they'd sit in here for hours talking quietly, and she'd run errands for him all the time. Some of us thought they might be having an affair, but we were never sure. Like I said, I keep my head down as much as I can."

"What else?"

"You thought she had a baby?"

"My first day in the office, she told me she'd just returned from maternity leave and had been out for a few months, so she was getting readjusted." Lorene's eyes got wide, and her mouth dropped open. "Her kid's five, so that was a lie. Where was she?"

"Rehab."

"That happens," I admitted. "Although I'm not fond of the fact that she thought she needed to lie about it, I can't fault her for getting help."

"She's been five or six times over the years, and whatever happened with her kids that got the state involved had to do with her addiction. She lost the right to see her kids and went off the deep end. She disappeared, but the chief and Detective Clinton found her and took her to rehab. She came back the week before you took office."

"Clinton, huh? She's tight with him?"

"Yessir." Lorene snorted and rolled her eyes. "They're thick as thieves and have been forever, but that's not who she's been dating recently. Clinton would be a step up from that scumbag."

"Who has she been dating?"

There was a knock on the door, and Lorene got up to open it. Preacher was standing there looking harried as usual and had some papers in his hand.

"Hey, Preach. Have a seat for a minute. Lorene, just pretend he's not here. You can trust him. Now, tell me about the man Julia's dating. What's his name?"

"Marcos," Preacher hissed as he tossed the sheets of paper onto my desk.

Lorene shivered and said, "He's so creepy. I hate it when he comes in here."

I felt my eyes go wide as I looked from Lorene to Preacher. That would explain at least part of why Julia was planting shit in my office. That would also explain her behavior last week. Her loving boyfriend had disappeared without a trace, and she was worried about him.

And now, looking back, I could attribute Julia's moodiness, red eyes, and jittery behavior to something other than lack of sleep staying up with a new baby. My office manager was fighting drug addiction, and the scumbag boyfriend who fed her habit had disappeared without a trace.

She'd need to get a new scumbag boyfriend to feed her habit. I knew for a fact that Marcos was no longer available.

"Lorene, let's you and me shelve this for today. However, since I feel like I can trust you, I'm going to have you do a couple of things for me. Grab some copy paper boxes and pack up all of Julia's shit, and set it to the side. In a few minutes, my friend here will unhook her computer and take the tower and any other electronics with him. I'm going to have another friend or two up here soon, and they're going to shut themselves in her office for a while and then come in here and talk to me. While that happens, I want you to draw up the paperwork terminating Julia effective immediately. I'll sign off on that and send out an email to HR and IT ordering them to revoke any access she has to files and such along with freezing her badge privilege." I was watching Lorene's face as I gave her instructions, and I saw her eyes get wide. "As of right now, you're going to keep on with your original duties until we find a replacement for your spot, but you're also going to start acting as my office manager. I need someone I can trust in that position who has a backbone and isn't afraid to come to me with problems. I can trust you, can't I, Lorene?"

"Yes, Chief. You can trust me."

"And the other ladies in the office? Is there anything about them that I need to know? Scumbag boyfriends, odd behavior, secret lives?"

"No, sir. The other girls are a lot like me. But since you mentioned that you appreciated how I speak my mind, I'd like to ask you a direct question based on what I'm sensing is going on around here."

"Go ahead."

Lorene looked from me to Preacher and then back at me, holding my eyes as she asked, "Are you really trying to figure out who's crooked and get rid of them? Because if that's the case like I think it is, then me and the other girls really need to sit down and tell you a few things we've picked up on over the years."

"Fuck," I hissed. "Yeah. That's what I'm doing, and the men I've cleared to visit me are helping me in that process. I'd appreciate it if you kept that to yourself and didn't share it with the other ladies in the office just yet, but rest assured, that's what is happening. Your help will be very much appreciated."

"Keep it close for now because if you really have seen some things that pinged on your radar, then you know it's not all that safe to stand up and shout. You get me?" Preacher asked as he leaned forward and caught Lorene's eyes.

"Yes." Lorene nodded. "I get you."

"Go pack her shit, hon. I'll get with you and the other ladies soon. We'll have dinner at my place one night where we can all talk freely, okay?"

"Okay, Chief," Lorene agreed as she stood up. She nodded at Preacher and then walked out of my office and pulled the door shut behind her.

"What she said about the other ladies in the office is true. I can't find a fucking thing on any of them, and they've got enough debt that there's no way they've had an influx of cash recently. On the other hand, Julia is living outside her means in a high-dollar apartment that's leased by some car dealer here in town. The car she's driving came from him, too, so maybe she's just got Marcos on the side or vice versa. No telling, but that girl is shady, and she's been all over your shit since the day you started here."

"Yep."

"Where is she now?'

"Called in and said her baby had a doctor appointment. That's what brought Lorene in here. Her 'baby' is five years old, and Julia's lost rights and custody to all three of her children because of her drug use. Clinton, the detective that Sin spotted as crooked, the one who's been in charge of the missing women's cases, and the former chief are buddies with Julia and have covered her ass as far as rehab and the company she keeps. She's knee-deep in whatever shitstorm is going on around here."

"You're calling Sin and his men to look through her office?"

"I am. At the rate we're going, I'm going to need to put his whole damn crew on the payroll."

JENNIFER

"Hey, I'm glad you made it!" I told Paula as she sat down across from me at the table. "I thought you were gonna stand me up."

"I got a late start," Paula said with a blush.

"Are you blushing?"

"No!"

"You are!"

"No, I'm not. Schoolgirls blush. I'm a grown-ass woman."

"Then you're having an allergic reaction to something because your face is all flushed, and so's your neck. What's going on, friend of mine?"

"I got a sunburn."

"It's February, and it's raining outside, Paula. Try again."

"Bad shellfish I bought from a vending machine?"

I laughed so loud that the woman at the table a few feet away flinched and stared at me in shock.

"Spill it, woman!"

"I had a gentleman caller last night, and he didn't leave my house until a few minutes ago."

"Hook kept you tied to the bed and made you late, didn't he?"

"I wasn't tied up, but I was underneath him and screaming his name, so, yeah, Hook made me late."

"I thought something was going on when you bailed on coffee the other day."

"Okay, that day, I really *was* tied up," Paula admitted. Then she whispered, "And it was fucking awesome."

I laughed again as my friend's face turned red.

"Good for you. Is this a *thing* thing or a temporary thing?"

Paula lifted her shoulders and let them fall before she said, "I guess we'll see?"

"I guess we will."

"I will say that when we first met, I was not looking my best, and he didn't seem to mind. Now when I put forth some effort, he'll be suitably amazed at my beauty," Paula said as she reached up and touched her face. Both of us were almost healed, and the bruising that was left could easily be covered with makeup, although Paula still had a cast on her arm.

"I can't believe your fucking hand was broken, and you didn't even realize it."

"There were other issues that seemed more pressing at the time."

"Isn't that the truth?" I muttered as I looked down at my menu.

"You have got to be kidding me," Paula hissed before she picked her phone up and started sending a text message.

"What?"

"Nothing yet. Might be a red alert, might be nothing."

"Have you been drinking?"

"What? No! It's not even noon yet."

"What's the red . . ."

"Red alert! Incoming! Incoming!"

"Jennifer." I heard Ethan's hiss as I felt someone walk up beside me.

"This is a nightmare. I'm asleep in bed, and I'm going

to wake up any minute now."

"Don't be stupid, Jennifer. I've sent you multiple emails and text messages kindly asking for a meeting. As usual, you've been too lazy to check them."

"Oh, he did *not* just start off by insulting you!" Paula was glaring at Ethan and then she looked over at me.

"Leave me alone, Ethan," I said in a calm tone of voice. "If you don't, bad things will happen to you. I don't know why you're even *in* Tenillo. It's been more than a week since I chased your skinny ass down my driveway. If that wasn't enough to tell you that I don't want to see you, then let me make it absolutely, no doubt about it, *clear as a motherfucking bell*, that I don't *ever* want to see you or speak to you again."

"That was very clear. Concise, to the point, and perfectly enunciated. Five stars, would definitely recommend, clear."

Ethan glared at Paula, and she stuck her tongue out at him and then put her fist in the air and pretended to turn a crank with her other hand, slowly raising her middle finger to flip him off.

I burst out laughing and heard three very large men laughing behind me accompanied by a low growl that could only be Boss.

"I told you that it would not end well for you, Ethan," I whispered as I turned around slowly to greet the men that had just arrived. Boss was wearing his uniform shirt, faded jeans with his badge clipped to the belt over his left pocket, and I knew there was a gun in a holster on his lower back. He was sexy as all hell, and even though I'd had two orgasms this morning at his hands, I could feel another begging to be released. Boss, on the other hand, was not thinking of naked fun times. His glare was murderous, his hands were fisted at his sides, and he looked ready to kill. To lighten the mood somewhat, I smiled brightly at him and said, "Hi, honey! Do you guys want to join us for lunch?"

"Guess what?" Wrecker said with a grin of his own. Ethan glanced at Boss and then looked back at Wrecker, waiting on his next words. He lifted a hand in front of his chest and pointed a finger gun at Boss. "That's my superior, so you can go ahead and make that complaint about me now."

Preacher and Paula both laughed outright. I saw Hook smile before he bit his lip and looked down at the floor.

"I have no business with you gentlemen. I'd like to talk to Jennifer alone for a moment. I'd appreciate it if you'd move along so we can have a private conversation."

I glanced up at Ethan and then back over to Boss who was snarling. I had to wonder if Ethan's balls had finally dropped, or if he really had bumped his head after all.

"Let me go ahead and put this out there since my buddy can't seem to unlock his jaw right now," Hook interrupted, and I could tell he was holding back a laugh. "You're gonna need to tell us you've already booked a flight back to Doucheville, or my pal, Boss, is just gonna go ahead and pick you up and throw you there."

"It would save money on flying, and you wouldn't have to bother with TSA," Preacher added. "Although the landing might fuck you up."

Wrecker snorted and put his hand over his mouth to

hide his smile. I glanced over at Paula, and she was doing the same thing.

"Boss, I don't want you to get into any trouble here," I whispered as I glanced around the restaurant. "There are people all over, and they haven't started paying attention yet, but if the guys start screaming *'finish him!'* and then you rip his spine out of his body, they're going to notice."

Wrecker snorted again, and Hook outright laughed.

Boss's eyes shot to me, and I saw one side of his lips quirk up before he pulled them both between his teeth and looked down at his boots.

"Ethan, let me just tell you that this is *not* going to end well for you. I'm never going to give you another chance. I don't care if my mother *is* on your side. You can keep her, as far as I'm concerned. Every time you say my name, it makes me cringe. The thought of having to fucking look at you one more time in my life makes me want to poke my own eyeballs out with a fork. I'm never going to give you a dime, and I'm not going to give you back the company. I also think it's fucking hilarious that Homewrecker Barbie cheated on you. And, to add to that, I hope green goo starts coming out of your dickhole because of it. Please, for the love of your health and my sanity, leave me the fuck alone."

"Jennifer . . . "

I interrupted him by turning to Paula and telling her through clenched teeth, "I'll give you $10,000 if you punch him in the dick right the fuck now."

Without even blinking, Paula pulled back her casted arm and punched Ethan in the crotch. He let out a high-pitched squeal that sounded like someone letting the air out of a balloon. He fell in slow motion to his knees and then to his side on the restaurant floor while holding his hands over his crotch.

"Fuck, that hurt!" Paula gasped as she tried to shake out her already broken hand.

Wrecker, Hook, and Preacher laughed so hard that people had started to look at us. The woman who I'd scared earlier with my outburst of laughter glanced down at Ethan and then up at Paula with wide eyes. Paula, always quick with a retort, told her, "He called me a fat ass!"

"Asshole," the woman swore as she glared down at Ethan and went right back to staring at her phone.

"Let's get you out of here before you get sick on the floor," Preacher said as he leaned down and pulled Ethan to his feet. Ethan's face was pale, and he kept gagging as he held his crotch, but he stood on his own and let Preacher lead him to the door of the restaurant.

"Well, I'm going to join him and make sure Sir Crunchy Hair of Doucheville understands he has a limited time on this earth if he doesn't leave town. Ladies, it's always a pleasure," Wrecker said as he nodded at Paula and I.

I watched Wrecker turn around and hurry toward Preacher who was bearing most of Ethan's weight now.

Boss pulled out the chair beside mine and sat down before he hooked his hand around the back of my neck and pulled me toward him for a searing kiss. When he was done, I breathlessly whispered, "Hi, honey."

"Hey, babe," Boss growled before he kissed me again.

When Boss and I were done, I looked up and found that Hook was seated next to Paula. Their chairs were barely an inch apart, and his arm was hooked over the back of her seat while he fiddled with her hair. Paula's grin went from ear to ear, and so did Hook's. They were absolutely adorable.

"Were you guys already coming here for lunch?"

"Paula knew I was headed to see Boss, so she texted me when she caught sight of your ex," Hook explained. "It's less than a block away, so we just walked over."

"Well, okay then," I said with a long sigh. "Paula, would you like cash or a check for that crotch shot?"

"You don't have to give me money, Jenn. It was absolutely my pleasure."

"It's technically his money since I got everything in the divorce, so really, *he'd* be paying you to punch him in the junk."

"In that case, I'd like cash, please."

BOSS

"We have to assume that everything that's been said in your office went from Julia to whoever rules her little corner of the world. We didn't find a single recording device in her office, so I assume that she was the end of the line as far as that went," Sin told us after we explained what I'd found out about Julia earlier.

Sin, Wrecker, and Saint had met me at home this evening, and we were camped out on the back patio near the firepit with Hook and Cap while Jenn and Paula were in the kitchen.

"Marcos and his higher power, I suppose. Preacher took the computer and laptop out of Julia's office and picked through them to see what he could get on her. I swear, if my IT department finds out about all the electronics I'm handing out to the general public, I'm going to end up back in prison."

"Ah, fuck 'em. Preacher is also looking into the car dealer whose name is on Julia's lease and trying to find any leads on Marcos's lifestyle," Hook explained.

"I've gone through the list of trucks that have food service licenses through the city. We'll check with Jenn to see if there's some sort of calendar or social media group the owners follow to see where they need to be and when. When we figure that part out, we can split the list to start making random visits. I figure we'll leave Boss and Wrecker out of that part. They can coordinate with us by phone, and we'll all be the boots on the ground."

"Good plan," Sin agreed. "While we're talking to each truck owner, we can also ask if they've been approached about protection money, who they pay, and when. Stuff like that."

"Gentlemen, I'd like to thank you and your crew for helping us with this. I know you've got a vested interest because of the geezers and because this is your town, too, but I'd like you to know that me and my crew appreciate your help. We want to find out who shot Pop more than anything, but we also want to nip all this other shit in the bud while we do it."

"We want to find out who shot Pop. That could have easily been Harvey or Jack or any one of the old geezers who can't sit still when they see shit that's not right," Saint pointed out.

"And now, if you look at things in the right light, we're setting the town up to be clean and straight for when we're the old geezers, I guess." Hook shook his head and laughed softly. "Fuck, I don't know about you guys, but some mornings I feel like I'm older than I really am when I hear my joints creak as I stand up in the morning. Then I look in the mirror and wonder who the fuck that old guy is staring back at me."

"You've got a few years on us, but I get what you mean. All of my brothers tore themselves up in the service somehow, so we all do that creaking thing, for sure. As for looking in the mirror and wondering about the fucking old guy, I don't have that problem because I'm one handsome motherfucker, and I will be even when I'm as old as you guys," Sin teased.

"Shit," Captain scoffed. "I've got years on you boys, and I'm still one the ladies chase after. I'll make sure and leave you some leftovers since Boss and Hook seem to be off the market."

"Back to what I was saying before. I cleared it with the missus earlier, and we'd like to host your club here at the house next week for dinner and some beers. We've all been on edge the last month and haven't been able to sit down with both groups and get to know each other. I know that we've got some great minds and some amazing skill sets between us. I think if we compare notes, we can find out what our strengths are and play them up."

"Thanks for the invite, Boss. Just let us know when, and I'll make sure my men are here."

I nodded at Sin and started to say something else when Jenn stuck her head out the door and told me I had a phone call inside.

"We're going to get out of your hair, Boss," Sin said as he and his men stood up. "You've probably got dinner waiting on you, and we've got places to be."

I stuck my hand out and shook their hands before I walked into the house to get the phone.

"Who called the house phone looking for me?" I asked Jenn as I walked past.

"Who the hell has a landline anymore?" I heard Paula ask from her seat at the bar.

"Boss, it's Lorene. From work," I heard a voice on the line say.

I smiled because I thought it was funny she might somehow think I'd forgotten who she was after our conversation this morning. "What can I do for you, Lorene?"

"Myrna called me a few minutes ago and said Julia showed up at the office and tried to scan her badge. When she figured out it didn't work, she took off like a shot. Myrna didn't talk to her, and as far as she knows, no one else did either, but I just thought you might want to know."

"Thanks, Lorene. I do want to know about things like

that and reiterate to the others in the office and the rest of the staff that Julia is not to be allowed behind the glass again for any reason unless she's escorted by the deputy chief or me. Understood?"

"Yessir."

"If anyone else tries to bring her in, hit the locks and call me. There's no reason for her to be in there anymore."

"I'll make sure they know that. And again, I'm sorry to bother you at home."

"Anytime, Lorene, and program my cell into your phone. You can call me or text me anytime with anything. I promise I'm not gonna snap at you or get mad."

"Okay." I wasn't sure she believed me. "I'll do that. You have a good night."

"Night," I told her before I hung up.

"I found a few vagrants on the driveway when I was walking Sin and the boys out front," I heard Hook call out as he walked through the front door. Preacher, Bug, Chef, and Stamp were behind him, and I heard Kitty and Santa's voices come in from the porch.

"What the hell?" I asked as I leaned down to pick up Elvira. I held her to my chest and watched her glare at Sammy and David for a second before she nuzzled her face up under my neck. Ed Earl started squawking as soon as he saw Chef, and the guys all laughed when Chef hurried around the table to get away from the big bird.

"Did your other friends leave?" Jenn asked as she

smiled at the men who had each dropped a kiss on her cheek as they passed her to get beer out of the kitchen. "I have plenty of food ready. I called all the boys to come eat, by the way. I knew you wouldn't mind. Chef, there's a six-pack of that beer you mentioned out in the walk-in if you want to get it."

"You want one, Cool Cat?"

"I'd love one, Chef. Thank you." Jenn smiled up at the big man when he leaned down and kissed her cheek. "You're the sweetest."

Chef's deep laugh rang out as he walked toward the other kitchen. I had to bite back a laugh of my own at the thought of anyone describing Chef as sweet.

Stamp was right at Jenn's side, pulling on one of her frilly aprons and nudging her over so he could help get the food on the table. Hook was standing behind Paula's chair, whispering something in her ear that made her blush. At the same time, Santa, Kitty, and Bug all sat down at the table and started talking about their new office space and their caseload. Captain walked through the kitchen and snagged the beer Preacher had just opened and put it to his mouth for a sip as he read something on his phone.

Jenn was right in the center of it all, in her element, feeding the masses with a smile and a kind word for each of the men. She'd never had kids of her own, which was a crying shame. She didn't realize it, but she was a mother to each of the men in this room, even if they were older than her. She showed them kindness and respect that they weren't used to, and some had never experienced at all.

If I had created a list of everything I required in an old lady, it would read like I was describing Jenn. I couldn't have it any better, and I knew it.

I stopped in my tracks for a second and felt a pang in my chest. I must have squeezed Elvira a little too tightly because she made a garbled noise and jumped out of my arms. I put my hand on my chest and stood there watching my girl interact with my family while I analyzed that feeling.

I was in love with Jennifer McCool. Undeniably, head over heels in love.

I'd felt like this before with my wife and again when my daughter was born. I never thought I'd find it again, especially after all my years behind bars followed by my years trying to get back into the real world.

"You okay?" Cap asked as he suddenly blocked my line of sight to Jenn. "You don't look so good, Boss."

"I'm just thinking," I told him as I rubbed my chest.

"Are you having a heart attack?" Cap glanced from my face down to my hand and then back up worriedly. "You okay?"

I laughed softly as I tilted my head to look around him and see what Jenn was laughing about now while I said, "It's not a heart attack. I just had to stop and think for a minute."

"Cupid just shot you in the ass."

"I believe he did, brother. I do believe he did."

JENNIFER

"You can't tell me that you believe without a shadow of a doubt that you're just Italian. Nothing else of any nationality other than pure Italian." I scoffed at Stamp and put my hand up when he started to argue. "Don't give me that mafia bullshit. I'm saying that in your lineage, there are no other ethnicities other than Italian. All those countries over there so close together and you're saying your family just stuck to the hills and married their own."

"Not like that," Stamp argued. "But I'm all Italian like Chef is totally African American."

"I call bullshit on that too," Jennifer blurted before she glanced over at Chef with a wince. "Sorry to drag you into this, Chef, but I'm making a point. Are your ancestors *only* from Africa, or are there some other things mixed in?"

"Fuck, I don't know. My family's from Dallas, Texas. My grandparents were from Galveston, and as far as I know, so were their parents. If anything, I'm just Texan to go with the African part."

"Oh, fuck this," Jenn grumbled as she picked up her phone. "I'm buying all of us DNA kits from Amazon, and I'm going to prove you wrong, Stamp."

"I'm not giving the government my DNA!" Preacher was incensed, and he sat forward and pointed at Jenn. "I'm not doing it, and no smiles from you are gonna make me, either."

"Come on, Preacher. Do it for me?" Jenn leaned forward in my lap and rested her arm on the table before she reached across to snag Preacher's hand. "Please."

"No! The government's not getting my DNA!"

"You do realize they got it while you were in prison, right?" Captain pointed out. "Might as well take the test to prove Stamp wrong with his elitist Italian bullshit since the government is already using your DNA to make super soldiers or some shit."

"Super soldiers from Preacher DNA?" Bug whispered as he glanced around the table. "Really?"

"Doubtful, bud," Santa told him. "Those would be the most fucking paranoid army men ever created."

"I am not paranoid; I'm a realist, asshole," Preacher snapped, and the argument was on.

Jenn leaned back and rested against my chest as she fiddled with her phone and then showed me the screen that said the DNA kits would be delivered in less than two weeks.

"You know they're going to argue about this shit until you force them all to spit in that little vial, right?"

"I know." Jenn grinned. "It's kind of fun to stir shit up with them, though."

"I know that's right. Pop loves to do that when we're all together. He gets them all riled up and arguing and then sits back and smokes his cigar while he watches the show."

"Are your friends coming over for the cookout next week?"

"They are. Thank you for doing that for us, baby. Thank you for all of this."

"All of this? What do you mean?"

"Inviting the guys over, making them feel at home, making *me* feel at home - all of it."

"This is your home, Boss, for as long as you want it to be."

"In that case, it's forever."

"Really?" Jenn whispered as she leaned closer for a kiss. "I like the thought of forever with you."

"Good. It's settled then."

"It's settled. Me and you. Forever."

JENNIFER

"The next time he comes over here with his charming smile and bulging muscles, I'm going to tell him to kiss every single spot of cellulite on my ass and to take his fucking animals and go," I grumbled as I settled down on my knees beside the fence. Earlier, Lee Majors had kicked a hole in the fence when Ouiser, one of the goats, jumped on his back. Ouiser was startled because Kenickie, one of the miniature pigs, spooked her when Ed Earl chased him out of the barn. "When I lived in Seattle, I didn't even own a fucking fish. I may have been miserable, but I wasn't covered in shit half the time."

Rizzo, the other mini pig, rooted around by my pocket where I usually kept the treats, and I absentmindedly scratched her head for a second as I looked around to see what else needed to be repaired. I was out here with a hammer and a plastic bowl full of nails. I might as well spot check the area while I was already covered in hay, dirt, and slobber from my myriad of farm animals.

My phone rang, and I pulled it out of my pocket as I sat back on my ass and let Rizzo and Kenickie settle down beside my outstretched legs.

"Hey, sweetheart," I answered when I saw it was Boss.

"Babe, I just left Pop's appointment, and the doc cleared him to come to the house and visit for a few hours.

You down for that soon?"

"Yes! We'll have the guys over, and I'll make a spread. I'll even let Stamp help this time."

"He'll like that. How about an early dinner late Saturday afternoon so we can get him back by six o'clock for his meds?"

"That sounds great. Stamp is on his way over to film for a while. While he's here, we'll work out a menu that Pop can eat on his new diet. We'll eat some yummy bad stuff after you take him back."

"I like how you think, sweetheart. I'm going to get out of here and go to the office. You take care of yourself."

"I'll be fine as long as I stay away from Elvira. I think she tried to push me down the stairs earlier."

"No, she didn't. Elvira loves you as much as I do, baby. She just has an odd way of showing it. I'll call you later."

"Okay. Later," I whispered as Boss hung up.

I let my hand fall down to my lap and stared off into space for a second. That one sentence could lead down two completely different avenues. One could be that it was just a figure of speech, and the other could be that Boss really does love me; he just wasn't willing to admit it yet.

"I'll take the second, thanks," I whispered to myself as I stood and dusted off my hands. I thought about it as I put my tools in the barn and secured everything so I could walk back up to the house. "I do love him. I do. Holy shit. I love him."

Considering that just two months ago, I was content to be that crazy lady who lives outside of town with her own personal petting zoo, this entire situation was nuts. Now I was waking up with a hot man in my bed, tripping over his pet skunk, and planning meals for his club family like I was Mrs. Cleaver, and we were having Beaver's scout group over for milk and cookies.

I had to say, I loved my new life. Even with the crazy extortionist drug dealer who just happened to get dead and might possibly be buried somewhere on my property. And besides the fact that 99% of the people I associated with every day were ex-cons and most of them had killed people.

I loved it. All of it. Because those things came with Boss, and I loved him.

And I was okay with that.

I was distracted as I walked across the yard to the side door to avoid being mauled by Ed Earl and the boys by going through the sunroom. I didn't realize I wasn't alone until I walked around the corner of the house. When Boss's secretary appeared in my line of vision, it gave me a jolt, but I covered it with a smile.

"Julia! What are you doing here?"

"I came to see those animals you told me about," Julia said with a smile that didn't quite reach her eyes.

"I didn't hear your car drive up, or I'd have greeted you on the porch. How long have you been here?"

"Just a few minutes. Not long."

I studied Julia's face and noticed the drastic change in her features since I'd last seen her. Her skin was sallow, and she'd lost weight. Her eyes were unnaturally bright as they looked everywhere but me, and they sported some serious dark circles underneath .

I'd seen people who were high before, but not many. I'd watched enough Criminal Minds episodes to know she was either fucked up on drugs or unhinged somehow. Maybe both.

"I just got off the phone with Boss, and he didn't tell me you were coming."

"Oh, he didn't know. It was spur of the moment. I was in the area. Can you show me your barn? Is that where you keep the animals?"

"Yeah," I said slowly, drawing the words out as I waited for her to step past me and head out into the yard. "Some of them live inside, but I've got quite a few that live in the barn at night and play in their yard during the day."

"Do the chief and his friends ever go out to the barn with people?"

"What? No. Why do you ask?"

"My friend. He, um, was going to come out here to visit, and I wondered if he saw the barn."

"Who's your friend? Sin?"

I couldn't imagine that she and Sin had much in common. From what little I'd gathered about Julia, she was a married woman with a small child at home. I didn't think she was referring to any of Boss's brothers either since I'd never heard them mention her, and all of them had come to town after Boss had already taken office.

"No, I don't know anyone named Sin. It was another friend."

I opened the barn door and followed Julia inside but left it propped open instead of closing it behind me. All of the animals were in the outdoor pen, so none of them could escape through the open barn door. For some reason, my gut told me to leave myself an easy out.

I was getting that vibe. Julia's jittery nervous energy was rubbing off on me, and I felt unsettled and on edge.

"This is where the miniature donkey sleeps. His name is Lee Majors. My friend Paula made nameplates for each of the animals. Aren't they cute?"

"You were supposed to leave, you know?" Julia whispered from beside me. When I looked over, she was staring into Lee's stall with a blank expression.

"I was? When?"

"When I saw your face on the missing person flyer, I called the number. I talked to a man that said he was your husband, and he wanted you back."

"You're the one who called Ethan?" I barked, pissed off that she'd brought that asshole to my sanctuary. "Why the fuck would you do that?"

"You were supposed to leave so that I could get Boss

back. I had him before, you know? But that was different. I was supposed to make him trust me, but you got in the way."

I stepped back away from Julia and reached into my pocket for my phone. Still off in her own little world, she didn't see my hand move. I looked down long enough to hit the recent call list and dial Boss. I knew that Julia would lose it if she saw me calling him, so I slipped my phone into my hoodie pocket and prayed that he could hear us talking.

"Julia, you're acting strangely, and I'm not sure I'm okay with you being in here," I told her in a loud voice - too loud for the situation.

Julia whirled around and pointed her finger at me before she screamed, "Marcos was going to have me sleep with Boss to get him on our side, but you were in the fucking way! He wanted to get rid of you, but you wouldn't listen. I know he came to talk to you, and now he's gone! Gone!"

"What the fuck?"

"When he tried to talk to you in the trailer, you *wouldn't listen!*" Julia shrieked as she stomped closer to me. Her hands were in her hoodie pocket, and when she pulled them out, I saw that she had a knife.

"What's the knife for, Julia?"

"Where is he? What did you do with him? I know he was out here! I dropped him off. I was supposed to wait for him, but he never came out! I waited and waited, but he never came back to the car!"

"You brought that motherfucker to my *house*?" I yelled, pissed now and not giving a shit that Julia was armed, and I wasn't. Instead of backing away like I should have, I stepped closer to her. "Do you know what he was going to do to me?"

"He was going to kill you so Boss would be heartbroken. He was going to kill you just like Boss's wife died, then Boss would be grieving, and I could make him feel better. Marcos wanted me to get Boss in line so we could be happy!"

"You are a few pecans short of a fruitcake if you think your man killing a woman so he could whore you out to her man is okay. What the fuck is wrong with you?"

"I am not a whore!"

"Well, you were gonna be if that fucker had his way, weren't you?"

Julia screamed and swiped the knife at my middle, but I jumped back. She wasn't steady on her feet and spun with her swing. I took that opportunity to rush her and slam her into the wooden frame of Lee's stall. I pushed against her to hold her there but couldn't' get traction because of the hay on the ground. I decided that my best course of action would be to run, so I pulled Julia away from the wall and slammed her into it before I ran toward the open barn door.

I'd only taken a few steps when she jumped on my back, and I lost my balance, taking us both down to the floor. We rolled twice before Julia ended up on top of me. I saw her arm bringing the knife down toward my chest, so with my right arm, I did a palm strike against her face. The hit knocked her to the side while at the same time, I pushed up with my legs to unseat her.

I pulled my arm back to punch her but lost power when she sliced at my other arm, cutting me from elbow to wrist. I landed the punch, but it was just hard enough to stun her. I pulled my injured arm into my chest and hit Julia again and again, praying that she'd drop the knife to cover her face.

I'd hit her at least five times when I saw her arm arc up and then felt a burning pain in my hip.

The adrenaline took over, and I forgot about the injury to my arm. I grabbed the hair on the top of Julia's head to jerk her up so I could punch her again. After the third hit, Julia's nose shattered, and my hand exploded with pain. Instead of hitting her again, I slammed her head back into the concrete floor.

She was writhing underneath me, fueled by insanity and drugs, and I wasn't sure I'd be able to fight her much longer. I pulled her up even farther and used all of my weight to slam her head back down. I heard a hollow thump, and Julia stilled underneath me.

"Ohfuck ohfuck ohfuck," I chanted as I watched her face for a second, waiting for her eyes to blink. They never did. She was staring up at me sightlessly as blood pooled around her head, running down the sloped floor toward the drain a few feet away.

My arm was numb now, but my side was burning like fire. I looked down and realized that the sleeve of my sweatshirt was soaked with my blood. It was dripping off my fingertips onto the concrete, mixing with Julia's as it flowed toward the drain. I clutched my arm close to my chest and pressed it in with my other arm to put pressure on the wound as I tried to stand up.

After three attempts, I made it to my feet and staggered out of the barn door into the yard. I was dizzy now and knew I needed to call for help. I used my good arm to reach into my hoodie to search for my phone. When I had it in my hand, I held it up close to my face so I could see the screen as it swam in front of my eyes.

My ears were ringing, and there was a loud roaring sound, so I shook my head to clear it. My phone still showed a call in progress, so I put it up to my ear.

"Boss?"

"Jenn! Are you okay? I'm coming, sweetheart. I'm almost home."

"I killed her."

"It's okay, baby. It's gonna be okay."

"She's dead, and I'm bleeding," I whispered as I lost my footing and fell down to one knee. "I can't walk. Boss, it's dark. I'm outside, but I can't see."

"Oh fuck, Jenn." I could hear the anguish in Boss's voice, and it made me sad.

"It's okay, Boss. You'll take care of everything, right? You'll take care of me because you love me."

"I do love you, Jenn. I fucking love you so much. Hold on, baby, I'm almost there."

"I love you too." I whimpered as I sat down on my ass right in the middle of my yard. "Will you take care of my house and my babies, Boss? Don't get rid of them, okay? Love on them for me."

"You are not going to die, Jenn! Help is coming. I'm almost there."

"Okay. I'll wait for you," I mumbled as I fell back onto the grass. I could see the clouds, but there was a dark haze around them, and they started to spin. The roaring in my ears got louder until it was deafening. The last thing I heard was a man's anguished voice as he called my name. And then my world went black.

BOSS

When Wrecker turned the corner at the end of our road, I could see Stamp on his knees in the middle of the backyard. I'd been on the phone with Jenn until seconds before we made that turn, but she'd faded out right before I heard Stamp yelling her name.

Wrecker turned into the driveway, and we fishtailed up the gravel and around the side of the house. He parked off to the side so the ambulance behind us could get all the way back into the yard where Jenn was laying. Before the car stopped, I was out and running to Jenn.

I hit my knees beside her and didn't know what to do, where to touch her, or how to help at all. Stamp had her arm between his palms and was pressing it, but I could see blood seeping out between his fingers.

"Jenn, baby," I whispered as I leaned down and touched her face. "Jenn! Wake up!"

The paramedic moved me aside as they assessed her.

The one on Stamp's side took her arm and held it up as the one beside me reached over Jenn and wrapped it in a tight bandage. In less than a minute, they had her on a gurney, pushing her into the back of the ambulance.

"Go with her," Wrecker said as he pushed me that way. "I'll take care of things here. Go."

I jumped into the ambulance and sat off to the side just like I had with Pop, praying the entire time that the machines the paramedic hooked to her chest didn't start beeping erratically like they had with him.

"You can talk to her, sir," the paramedic ordered. "Let her know you're here."

I leaned over and spoke close to Jenn's ear as I brushed her hair away from her forehead. There was blood on her face, but I could tell it wasn't hers. As I talked to her, I tried to rub it away with my thumb. I didn't want any of the stink of what was going on to ever touch her again. I needed to get it off her.

"It's okay, baby," I whispered in her ear. "I love you, too, you know. I wanted to tell you earlier, but I didn't know how. I figured it out the other night, but I thought you'd think I was fucking crazy. I promise if you wake up that I'll tell you every day—all the time. I'll say it so much that you'll get sick of hearing it. I just need you to wake up, sweetheart. Wake up for me, Jenn."

The vehicle shifted to a stop, and the paramedic who'd been monitoring Jenn burst into action right before the doors opened. Three people were waiting on the ground, and they pulled the gurney out and took off with Jenn as I tried to follow right behind them.

"You need to stay in the hall, sir," a nurse ordered as she pushed at my chest. "Let us take care of her now. We can't do that with you in our way."

I let the nurse push me back, and the doors shut in my face. I walked backward a few steps until my back hit a wall and then I slid down to the floor. Jenn was in there because of me. Just like my wife and daughter, Jenn was paying for something I'd done, something I'd stirred up.

I'd lost them years ago, and it damn near killed me. If I lost Jenn now, I knew I'd never survive it.

"Boss," I heard Stamp call from a few feet away. "Come on, man. Let's get cleaned up and then we'll wait together."

"It's my fault."

"No, it's not. That woman attacked Jenn. I saw her there. I saw the knife."

"Julia was there because of me. Because of me being a cop."

"She was there because she was a fucking psycho with a goddamn knife, Boss. You didn't give her the knife, you didn't push her down the driveway, you didn't force her to fight with Cool Cat. This is not on you, man."

"I heard her say it. I heard her tell Jenn she was supposed to go away so Julia could get in with me and direct me away from the shit we're looking into. It's my fault."

"Come on. Let's get cleaned up, and we'll talk about

it. You're not thinking straight, and you won't be until Jenn tells you to shut up herself."

I reached up and took Stamp's hand and let him pull me to my feet. As I let it go, I realized it was covered in Jenn's blood. His shirt and pants were soaked. There was so much blood that I didn't know how she could survive it.

I rushed over to the nurse behind the triage desk, and she looked up at me with a small smile. "Sir, I need you to . . ."

"The woman in there, my woman, she needs blood, right? If you don't have enough, I've got people who can donate. I have lots of men who can come right now."

"We can always use blood donations, sir."

"No, her. I want to help her. Find out what she needs, and I'll get it."

"That's not how . . ."

"Find out what she needs, and I'll get it!" I roared at the woman, and she jumped out of her chair.

She looked over at another nurse, and I saw the woman pick up the phone before she said, "I'm calling the police. I need you to leave."

"I *am* the fucking police! Find out what she needs so I can help her!" I yelled again, but my voice broke as I pleaded, "Please, just let me do something to help her. Please."

"Boss, come on, man. You're not helping her this way. Let's get cleaned up," Stamp whispered as he pulled me away from the desk.

I still held the woman's eyes, and I begged, "Please find out how I can help her."

"I'll check. Go wash up, and I'll find you as soon as I know what the team needs," the first nurse told me before she rushed away toward the room where they had Jenn.

The second nurse had already put the phone back in its cradle. She walked over to us and put her hand on my arm before she said, "Come with me, and I'll find the two of you some scrubs so you can get cleaned up. Alice will know where to look for us. We'll be right back there."

I let the woman pull me toward a room off to the side that looked like a break room. She directed Stamp to the shower and gave him a bag for his clothes. He stripped right there in front of her and stuffed his clothes into the bag before he walked into the small shower and pulled the curtain. I pulled my hoodie off, and the woman's eyes got wide when she saw my uniform shirt with the embroidered chief badge.

"You're the new chief of police?"

I sighed. "I am. Sorry, I yelled at you and the other nurse. I just wasn't thinking straight."

"The woman they brought in? She's your . . ."

"She's mine. She was attacked in our barn while I was at work. I told her I'd fix the chicken coop when I got home tonight, but she's stubborn and wanted to do it herself. She was attacked out there in the barn. I was on the phone and heard it. I'm sorry, I'm rambling. She does that, not me, you know? When she's upset, she rambles on and on. It's cute."

"I bet," the nurse agreed as she smiled softly up at me.

"Is that shirt soiled too?"

"No, I don't think so," I told her as I ran my hand over it. "Just the hoodie."

"Use the sink to wash up, and I'll go find your friend some scrubs to wear, okay?"

"Thanks. I'm really sorry I yelled. I won't let it happen again."

"Sometimes, a person like you can't contain your emotions when you run up against something you can't fix. That's your way. My husband is like that."

"He is?"

"He's a police officer too. Well, he *was* a police officer. The former chief suspended him, so he left. Now he works for my father-in-law's plumbing company."

"Why did he suspend him?"

"They had a disagreement about an arrest my husband made. The chief dropped the charges and let the man go free, and my husband was angry. He knew the guy was guilty, and he had more than enough evidence to convict him, but the chief let him go."

"Tell your husband to get in touch with me or the new deputy chief. I'd like to talk to him about what happened. Will you do that?"

"I'll send him a text right now. Did you know the chief that was here before you?"

"I met him once and have been trying to clean up his

fucking messes since my first day on duty."

"I'll tell my husband that too. He'll be glad to hear it. I'll be right back."

I scrubbed my hands and arms until they were clean, and I heard Stamp in the shower splashing water as he tried to get the blood off his body too. The nurse came back in with scrubs just as Stamp stepped out of the shower with a towel around his hips.

"What's your name, doll?" Stamp asked as he took the clothes from her hand.

"My name's Chastity. The other nurse is Alice. She's making a phone call to the blood bank right now to see what they have for his wife."

"Thanks," I told her as she turned around to give Stamp some privacy. He tugged on the pants and stepped into his boots before he pulled the shirt over his head. Once we were finished, we followed Chastity into the hall.

"Your wife is O positive. We have some on hand, but it might not be enough. If you're serious . . ." Alice, the first nurse, stopped talking when Stamp interrupted her.

"I'll call our guys and let Sin know too. Where should they go to donate?" Alice started walking back toward the desk, and Stamp followed her to get the information for the guys. I stood looking at the doors they'd rushed Jenn through, wondering what was happening.

As if I'd wished for it, a doctor walked through the doors and stopped directly in front of me.

"She's lost a lot of blood and needs to go into surgery. I understand you might have some people who can donate?"

"I do. They're coming now. Can I donate?"

"What's your blood type?"

"O negative."

"Go with the nurse, and she'll get you started. We're prepping her for surgery now, and we'll take her up in just a minute."

"Can I see her?"

"You can see her, or you can go to the lab and get started so that we can get her sewn up," the doctor said bluntly. "It's up to you."

"Where's the lab?"

JENNIFER

"That tickles!" I laughed as I tried not to squirm away from Boss's hands.

"Woman, am I going to have to tie you up again?"

"Maybe."

"Be still, or I'm never going to get through with this foot," Boss ordered as he looked back down at my toes.

I was propped up against the headboard with both of my arms on pillows beside me.

My left arm was full of stitches and had a splint along with a brace to keep my fingers immobile so the swelling around my nerves and tendons would go down. The specialist was optimistic that I would regain my range of motion and feeling in my hand if I let it heal and followed through with physical therapy. My right arm had a dark purple cast that went from the tips of my fingers almost all the way up to my elbow. When I'd hit Julia and felt shooting pain, it was because I'd broken three knuckles, several bones in my hand, and sprained my wrist.

I had stitches in my hip, too, but compared to my arms, that wound was nothing. The knife had gone through the fat on my hip, and it was just a minor annoyance compared to my other injuries.

I'd been home for three days, and today was the first time Boss had left me alone so he could go to work. He'd been at my bedside for a week while I was in the hospital and waited on me hand and foot for the first two days I was home.

Last night, I'd finally convinced him to go back to work. He'd gone, albeit reluctantly, leaving me with Paula and Preacher after he'd given them 30 minutes of instruction regarding my care. He'd somehow forgotten that I could actually talk to let them know what I needed myself. I let him do it anyway because it gave him some semblance of control in this crazy situation.

He'd been gone for four hours when he reappeared for lunch and let me know he was home for the day.

Right now, he was stretched across the foot of the bed, painting my toenails to match my cast, and he was doing a damn good job. He was meticulous about the task, moving slowly to make sure he got the nail and not the skin around it, but the way he was holding my foot was tickling the ever-loving shit out of me.

"You're killing me, Boss."

"Be still. I've only got two toes left. The clear coat is next. Should I do two coats of clear too? The video didn't say."

"You watched a video on how to paint my toenails?"

"I did. For future reference, when you Google something like this, make sure you are *very* specific. Some of the fetish shit that popped in my search results is going to be really hard to explain to the IT guys if they ever ask."

"That's sweet. You looked up how to do it just for

me."

"Originally, I searched 'how to pamper your girlfriend while she's incapacitated from a stabbing', but that got me some other really weird shit. Since that didn't work, I asked Lorene and the other ladies for some ideas. They said to paint your toenails, brush your hair, massage your legs, and buy you shiny things."

"Are you gonna do all of those?"

"Yep. Got it covered."

"Oh, really? You're going to brush my hair? Paula washed it for me this morning, so I finally feel human again. I had her braid it so that it's out of my way. I thought about having her cut it since I . . ."

Boss's head snapped up. "Please don't cut it. I'll take care of it for you."

"Okay," I agreed through my laughter at his reaction. "I get a massage too?"

"Whenever you want."

"So, let me get this straight. I've got a personal chef downstairs cooking us dinner while he does another video shoot, Preacher is going to teach me how to play chess when he gets here for dinner, Hook and Paula are taking care of my animals, and your friend Brea is going to start running my truck for me. And you are now my hair stylist, personal masseuse, and toenail painter."

"Yep."

"That's awesome. I should get sliced up in fights with

292

psychos and almost die more often." Boss glared at me. "Too soon?"

"There will *never* be a time when it's okay to joke about that."

Trying to change the subject, I asked, "So all that's left is something shiny."

"I already took care of that."

"What is it? Did you buy me a shiny sling for my arm? I want some bling for it. Maybe some rhinestones and shit. I bet Paula can find some for me at the craft store. No, I'll wait until I can go with her. I really need to get up and do something."

"No."

"He said I can start moving around more."

"No. No craft store. You can shop on Amazon."

"You're going to have to let me get out of bed someday, Boss."

"You're still weak as a kitten, Jenn. You almost fell on the stairs."

"Then help me downstairs, and let me go to the craft store. I want something shiny."

"How fucked up are you right now?"

"Not too fucked up. I've been taking my pills as prescribed, and Paula brought me some edibles."

Boss slowly lifted his gaze until he was staring at me

blankly.

"I only ate a tiny corner of one! Jeez, you act like you're a cop or something."

"Will you remember this conversation tomorrow?"

"Definitely. It's almost time for another pill, and the edible wore off an hour ago."

"Do you want the shiny thing now, or do you want to wait until you feel better?"

"You already got me something shiny? I thought I had to buy shit on Amazon."

Boss sighed and stared at my face for a second before he glanced at each of my hands. Finally, he shifted on the bed and reached into his pocket.

"I was going to wait because it's not going to work great with the whole cast and splint and your fingers being swollen, but you want the shiny thing, and I want to make you happy, so I'll do it right now."

"Do what?"

"Will you marry me, Jenn?" Boss asked as he held the ring up so I could see it.

"Oh shit!" I whispered, my heart in my throat. The girl who used to look in the mirror and tell herself 'this is as good as it gets' was wrong. This. This was as good as it gets. "Yes. I'll marry you!"

I had tears streaming down my face, and I couldn't reach up to wipe them off, but I didn't care. I watched as Boss looked from one hand to the other again before glancing down at my foot. He slipped the diamond ring on my second toe.

"I love you, babe."

"I love you too."

BOSS

"Now before any of you get a beer or eat any food, we're going to take a test," Jenn announced as the guys started walking into the house.

"I have test anxiety," Bug told her. "I'm not taking any kind of test, Cool Cat."

"All you have to do is spit!"

"That's what she said!" Chef, Santa, and Cap yelled in unison. As the laughter trailed off, Jenn used her purple cast to slide the stack of boxes across the bar toward the men.

"I had Paula put your names on the boxes so we won't get them confused. I know it's weird and all to spit in a vial, but I'm going to do it, too, if someone will hold the thing for me. Then, in a few weeks, we can prove to Stamp that he's just as much of a mutt as the rest of us and that Chef isn't just Texan."

"Really?" Preacher whined. "We're back to this? I told you . . ."

"*They've already got your fucking DNA on file!*" Captain yelled. "Spit in the motherfucking vial, and I'll close it up for you. I'll even mail the goddamn thing. Jesus. It's like pulling teeth."

"Someone's cranky today." Chef attempted to whisper, but his voice boomed even when he was trying to be quiet.

Captain glared at Chef before he started passing the tests out. After a few tense seconds, everyone laughed as Stamp read the directions out loud in his best Goodfellas voice.

"Then yous gotta snap the fuckin' cap closed and put it in the fuckin' box to give to Mr. Postman," Stamp read as the guys started spitting into their plastic vials in between their laughter and sarcastic comments.

"This is science shit. Shouldn't Chef be in charge of it?" Kitty asked.

Hook laughed before he argued, "I've got a degree in veterinary medicine. Maybe I should be in charge of it since you're all filthy fucking animals anyway."

I held my hand out with Jenn's vial as I held my own in front of my face. She glanced down at the vial and then back at me before she smiled wickedly. "I've told you before that a lady never spits. She swallows."

"And that right there is what got you the *big*, shiny ring."

"Fuck, how much do I have to put in there? I've got bread in the oven!" Stamp complained.

"I feel dehydrated," Santa chimed in.

"I told you that I've got test anxiety! My mouth is as dry as a popcorn fart," Bug told the group, and that led to more laughter and even more jokes.

I leaned toward Jenn and whispered in her ear, "Are you sure you're ready to sign up for this, babe?"

"More than ready. I'd marry you tomorrow if I could."

"You'll have these fools around for the duration."

"As long as I have you, they're just icing on the cake."

——————————— THE END ———————————

COMING SOON

The Time Served MC is part of the Tenillo Guardians series together with the Ares Infidels MC written by Ciara St. James. Each series will stand alone, but Cee and Ciara have written their books in a way that will give the reader a perspective from each club as they work together.

The first book in the Ares Infidels MC series entitled Sin's Enticement will be released by Ciara St. James on May 1, 2021, and it will follow the timeline of Cee's book that you just finished.

After years of serving his country, Sin reclaims his life and forms the Ares Infidels MC with like-minded military brothers. They decide his hometown of Tenillo, Texas is the perfect place to build their futures by forming a club where they get to make the rules and give out orders, rather than obeying and complying with the constraints and regulations of their individual military branches.

Sin and his brothers feel like life is going great until a conversation with the new chief of police and Time Served MC president, Boss, opens their eyes to a seedy underbelly of

Tenillo. They discover their town is in crisis - a crisis they are determined to conquer. The Ares Infidels join forces with Boss and his club to take out the trash and ensure their community is safe and protected.

However, Sin is blindsided almost immediately by the beautiful Lyric. She's a high school teacher fearing for the safety of her students, and she's looking for someone to help her.

After just one meeting with Sin, Lyric proved to be an enticement that he was helpless to resist. She became his entire universe in an instant.

As Sin works to convince her to give this former Navy SEAL turned biker a chance, more crimes and shady dealings come to light. Tenillo is in dire straits. The problems they uncover are more serious than they ever imagined.

Sin's men and his allies land in danger time and time again. And each time, Lyric seems to be at the center of it all. Sin, the Ares Infidels, and the Time Served guys battle to defend their town, their loved ones, and their futures.

Sin and Lyric's tale may end in happily ever after for them, but the trials and tribulations are far from over for these two clubs or Tenillo. They will pull together to rescue a town from the forces working to destroy it from within, and they'll bring the fury of the Ares Infidels down on anyone who gets in their way.

You can find information about Ciara St. James and

her books on www.ciarastjames.com.

About the Author

Cee Bowerman is proud, lifelong resident of Texas. She is married to her own long-haired, tattooed biker and is the proud mom to three mostly adult kids - a daughter and two sons. She believes in love, second chances, rescue dogs, and happily ever after.

Cee received her first romance novel along with a bag of other books from her granny when she was recovering from surgery at 15. She has been hooked on reading romances ever since. For years, she had a dream of writing her own series of stories, but motherhood and all the other grown up responsibilities kept getting in the way. Luckily, with the support of her family and the encouragement of her son, she purchased a computer and let her dreams become a reality.

Made in the USA
Monee, IL
30 October 2023